the
OPENING

a novel

Tim McWhorter

The Opening
ISBN: 978-1-958370-24-7 (paperback)
ISBN: 978-1-958370-23-0 (eBook)

Published by Manta Press, Ltd.
Pickerington, OH 43147

Cover Design by Tim McWhorter
Author Photo by Julie A. McWhorter

Second Edition

This book is a work of fiction. Names, characters, places and events
portrayed are either the product of the author's imagination or are
used fictitiously. Any resemblance to actual persons, living or dead,
events or locales is entirely coincidental.

Printed in the United States of America

PROLOGUE

A crowd had gathered.

Some were tourists in town for only a week, soaking up as much sand and surf as they could before returning to the concrete jungle for another year. Residents of Angler Bay filled in the gaps. Familiar and pained faces stared up at him—eager to do something—poised to stop what could never be undone. If not, the next few moments were certain to be horrific. Moments they would never forget, the images burnt into their brains. Maybe it was the acrid fumes keeping their feet rooted in place. Fear of getting caught in the fray. He only hoped they kept their distance.

"Don't do it, Floyd!" one of them shouted.

"It's not worth it!" cried another.

He heard the pleas and ignored them.

He raised the red gas can above his head and drained every drop before tossing it aside. The container clanged end over end down the concrete steps, coming to a stop on the sidewalk.

He coughed as fuel streamed down his face. It stung his eyes. The fumes constricted his throat. He choked on the lack of fresh air. His lungs burned. Breathing became a struggle as he reached into his pocket for the second half of the equation.

He pulled out the lighter, a scuffed black Zippo he'd had since Korea.

"Somebody get help!"

"Somebody call Helen!"

He held the lighter down and away from his body. He didn't want to see it. Doing so might bring back memories, obstacles he'd overcome in the past. The dented and paint-chipped lid, having once saved him from the point of a bayonet, might cause him to second guess.

The pleas kept coming.

"Somebody, please! Do something!"

He turned his back to the crowd and looked upon the doors of The Chamberlain Theater. *His* theater. A steel chain snaked through the long, gothic-styled handles. The two ends converged at a padlock and sealed the entrance. Taped to the glass, a sheet of white paper. The bank's letterhead, as much as the chains, barred him from entering the premises. He'd owned the theater for over forty years. A lifetime. He remembered the day they installed the heavy, custom-built wood doors leading to the auditorium. The morning the marquee sign arrived, polished and majestic, strapped to the back of a flatbed truck. From that day forward, The Chamberlain Theater was no longer an afterthought, sought only when rain had washed out the summer sun and surf. It became the anchor of the town center.

At least the bank couldn't have those memories. He'd be taking them to hell with him.

Gasoline dripped from his nose, his chin. It pooled at his feet.

Pleasant memories became harder to come by as time had worn on. Thanks in part to an economy in the toilet and bills that never stopped coming, even after the customers had. He'd spent countless afternoons in his office, brainstorming ways to bring in more business. He'd failed at every turn. And when the bank's patience had reached an end, they'd foreclosed and taken the only thing he'd ever had in the world. The bastards in their ostentatious suits may as well have filled the gas can and placed it in his hands.

He wiped his face with his shoulder and coughed into it.

An hour ago, he'd kissed his wife's cheek while she slept

beneath the roof he could no longer provide. He was too proud, too ashamed to see his failure reflected in her root beer-barreled eyes. He'd fed the cat, scratched behind her ears the way she liked, then quietly closed the door behind him.

Losing the theater wasn't the only reason he stood outside its walls, soaked to the bone with gasoline. There was that other thing. Good or bad, he'd done what he'd done. Would most certainly do it again. If he could, he'd drag the entire building down to hell with him. Then they would never discover its secrets. Nobody would find out what he'd done. The mistakes he'd made.

He raised the lighter to his chin.

The chorus of pleas swelled, the crowd sensing the end was near. His name filled the crisp morning air. And as a lone brave soul, unable to stand idle any longer, charged up the steps, Floyd Cropper took one last stagnant breath.

He closed his eyes.

It's my turn now...

He spun the flint.

Act One

ONE

Nick popped a blue Xanax and let it dissolve on his tongue.

It was opening night at The Chamberlain Theater. Finally. The smell of fresh buttered popcorn hung in the air. Money was being exchanged for tickets. And moviegoers were filtering into its remodeled lobby in numbers like the theater hadn't seen in years.

In his father's words, Nick should be as happy as a tornado in a trailer park.

Yet, his father was no longer around, and the tornado of which he so often spoke currently spun its way through Nick's stomach. The curtain wasn't due to raise for another hour, and already, his undershirt clung to him like a clammy second skin. The night was almost too important. The stage, too big. His mind looped through the list of businesses he'd built, then watched fail. The whimsical do-it-yourself frozen yogurt shop he'd called "Fro-Yo-Self." The video store / pizza shop where patrons could order a pizza, then search for a DVD while they waited. Seems he was always chasing new takes on old ideas. Would this 4D movie theater be the one to elevate him above the title of failed entrepreneur? Or, because it was the biggest, costliest venture yet, would The Chamberlain Theater serve as the crown jewel atop an already hulking coronet of failures?

Nick popped another Xanax for good measure.

He took a deep breath and tried to quell the tornado. At least he'd made the right choice with the music he piped into the lobby. Epic film scores not only seemed fitting, but they always calmed his mood. The growing crowd was in good spirits, everyone talking and laughing. There were no fires to put out. All were things going in his favor.

So far, so good.

Deep breaths.

And don't look in Amber's direction, Nick told himself. All his progress toward putting himself at ease might disappear. The box office had only been open fifteen minutes, and already she'd needed help with the register twice, despite claiming extensive experience with that particular model in her interview. *She'll get it*, he assured himself. She had to, and not simply because he dreaded the hiring process. Replacing Amber at this point would be difficult. Like any community, Angler Bay was full of teens in need of a seasonal job, but it seemed few of them wanted to work at The Chamberlain. The fact he'd only received a handful of applications told him most were steering clear of the place. With a building this old, rumors of hauntings were inevitable. The previous owner torching himself on the front steps only added more fuel to an already growing fire. No pun intended.

Nick sucked it up and glanced Amber's way. When their eyes met, he gave her a thumbs up, hoping to get one in return. When he did, the tension in his shoulders eased a bit more.

"Looking good, Nick."

Nick's heart dropped into his queasy stomach.

Shit. So much for good energy.

The voice had come from behind him, but Nick knew to whom it belonged. If there had been any question at all, the meaty hand clamped onto his shoulder was a dead giveaway.

Nick turned, ducked out of the grasp, and reached to shake the man's large hand. "Mayor Blackwood."

The mayor of Angler Bay wasn't particularly tall, but at six-foot two, he towered over Nick. The man also had a good hundred pounds on him. Whoever said no man was an island unto himself had never met Jonas Blackwood. The guy was his own damn continent, with an ego to match. His hand devoured Nick's the way a great white devours a baby seal.

"Glad you could make it." Sweat trickled down the back of Nick's neck as he watched the mayor take in the new lobby: the fresh crimson paint on the walls; the shiny mirrored glass of the new concession counter; the gold floor-length drapes creating the illusion of window coverings, even though they cloaked nothing but drywall behind them.

"Ain't no way I'd miss opening night." The mayor had a wicked twinkle in his glassy eyes. His cheeks were red. His sloppy smile spoke of merriment and Tanqueray. He'd most likely come from a four-course dinner he was so famous around town for: a steak and three gin and tonics. "Hell, I feel like she's as much my baby as yours."

And there it was.

Nick bristled before mustering a semi-cordial smile. "Well, it was your hands that pulled the strings, Mayor. Wouldn't be much of an opening night without all your help."

Ever since he purchased The Chamberlain, the mayor hadn't let him forget it was his doing that made it happen. It was the mayor who pressured the bank to hold the theater's previous owner to terms, to stop allowing him more time on his payments. It was the mayor who wanted to see the theater make money for the town, and not the other way around. Nick sometimes wondered if he'd always feel indebted to the guy, no matter how long he owned the theater. Only upside was it provided another shoulder for the guilt about the way it had all gone down.

Poor old bastard.

Nick shrugged it off. He wasn't letting the mayor, nor the ghost of the theater's previous owner, get under his skin tonight. Not on opening night. He had enough on his plate. And it wasn't like he was responsible for the livelihood of the town's four thousand residents. That was the mayor's cross to bear.

"Well, shit. I appreciate that, Nick." With a wink and a grin, revealing teeth that were no stranger to fine cigars, the mayor took his leave. He sauntered over to the concessions counter and began taking stock of the offerings.

Nick wiped his hand on his pants leg, all too happy to be rid of the mayor. The guy could eat his weight in popcorn and candy for all Nick cared. As long as it kept him out of his hair.

Fanning air into his collar, he scanned the room's growing population.

From across the lobby, he once again checked Amber's status. The line at the ticket counter had all but disappeared. When the young woman smiled and gave another thumbs up, he weaved his way through the crowd.

"Hey, Mr. Fallon!" Amber chirped when he approached. "What's up?"

Nick pulled a crumpled paper towel from his pocket and wiped sweat from his forehead. "Manny come through, yet?"

The engineer had worked for Nick since the day he'd closed on The Chamberlain. Not only was Manny the first employee he'd brought onboard, but Manny had helped oversee the engineering involved in transforming the old, lackluster theater into a high-tech movie house. He was smart, knew his way around electronics, and was one of the few people Nick had counted on throughout the theater's makeover. Manny had never failed to show up for work, had never let him down, unlike most of the contractors he'd hired. So, the fact he hadn't seen him yet that evening was one of the things contributing to Nick's opening night anxiety.

"Nope." Amber scanned the lobby. "No, sir, I haven't."

Nick checked his watch for the third time in what could have only been ten minutes. "Well, if you see him before I do, please tell him I'm looking for him."

"Will do." Amber smiled and feigned a salute. Then her smile disappeared. "Oh. Speaking of looking for someone, that reporter came in a few minutes ago. You know, from *The Standard*?"

The perspiration under Nick's collar turned cold.

Nori Park gently closed the heavy wooden door behind her.

Being an investigative reporter in a town where little needed investigating, she found excitement in her job where she could. Tonight, that meant being the first to check out the new theater with the troubled past, which was about as interesting as things got in the sleepy coastal town of Angler Bay.

After college, she'd shot for the big city. Like most in her field, the prospects of pulling back the curtain on political corruption, corporate espionage, and organized crime stoked her ambition. Ultimately, she'd fallen short, landing at a small-town newspaper along the North Carolina coast. Despite the lack of any real excitement to report, the trade-off wasn't without its benefits: down time at the beach. She'd even taken a handful of surfing lessons last summer. Angler Bay wasn't a terrible place for a kid from the gritty streets of Seoul, South Korea, to end up.

The auditorium greeted her with the combined scents of fresh paint, newly stretched vinyl, and the slightest hint of old smoke hovering above it all. Other than the smoke, everything smelled new, looked new. Everything had a shine. She'd been to the old theater once before, a disastrous first date three years back. The Chamberlain had been run down, but still possessed a quaintness and character despite its peeling paint and soda-stained carpeting. A historic place where one could almost feel its history. It was said Eisenhower had once attended a function at The Chamberlain, had sat in that very room.

But never in seats like these, she observed.

Nori ran her hand along one of the slick seat backs. These seats were plush, clean, and word had it, high-tech. They were nothing like the creaky, velvet-covered antiques she remembered being so uncomfortable.

She grabbed an end seat in the back row and tried it out. The cushion gave, cradling her butt. She leaned back, her head against the cushioned rest. The back seemed a little too upright, and the armrests a little thin. Otherwise, the new seats would make for a fairly enjoyable movie-watching experience.

Don't get too comfortable, she told herself. *You're here to work, remember?*

Nori rose to her feet. After pulling an iPad from her bag, she slung the satchel over her shoulder. She started down the sloping center aisle toward the giant silver screen down front, taking inventory of her surroundings. Row after row of the red and black seats spread out in curved lines. Overhead, various black boxes hung from the ceiling. They weren't speakers. Those were easy to spot, hanging along the front and edges of the large room. The black boxes had pipes and thin tubes running between them. She raised the iPad and snapped a few photos.

"Interesting."

TWO

"Seriously?" Nick lacked the skill needed to keep disappointment from his voice. "Amber, I asked you to let me know *the moment* she arrived."

Amber met his chagrin with a pained expression.

He instantly felt bad. The tension in his set jaw lifted. He took a deep breath.

"Okay, so. She got here a few minutes ago?" he continued. "Can you define *a few minutes*?"

"I don't know," she shrugged. "Ten? Maybe twenty?"

Nick took a deep breath. *Fuckin' hell!* He urged the Xanax to quit screwing around and kick in already.

"Any idea where she might be now?" He looked around the lobby, fearing the worst. Had the reporter grown tired of waiting for him and left? He'd lose a golden opportunity if she had. He was counting on the publicity an article in the local newspaper would generate. He searched the growing throng of gatherers. He didn't see the reporter anywhere. And there were few places she could hide.

A dull ache sprouted behind his eyes.

"Maybe," Amber said, eyes glued to the floor, "she's checking out the auditorium?"

Shit.

Nick spun on his heels. *Shit! Shit! Shit!* He considered

reminding Amber of his number one rule for the evening: no one was to enter the auditorium before it was time. But it was too late for reminders.

With the wooden doors closed behind him, the auditorium's calm silenced the chaos of the lobby.

Nick allowed himself a moment. He closed his eyes, willing away the headache scratching and clawing its way to life behind them. He took a deep breath, counted to five, and let it out. Opening his eyes, he took a few steps down the sloping center aisle.

At first glance, he saw no signs of Ms. Nori Park. For the reporter to help spread the word about the new and improved Chamberlain Theater, a good impression on his part was a must. Not being available to greet her upon arrival was not a step in that direction.

He scanned the rows of newly installed red vinyl seats, an exciting and integral addition to the auditorium's landscape. Their ability to rock, toss, and cajole the moviegoer at precise moments was a crucial component of the 4D experience. He could hardly wait for someone to try them. Someone other than himself, Manny, and the crew that installed them.

It didn't appear that someone would be Ms. Park. As far as Nick could tell, she wasn't seated among them. The aisles leading down to the front of the auditorium were just as empty. Perhaps the reporter hadn't come this way after all.

He took a painstakingly deep breath and let it out.

It was only the weight of his opening night responsibilies that kept Nick from grabbing one of the seats, kicking back, and drowning himself in a sea of memories. It was times like this, when he was alone in the auditorium, he missed his parents most. His father, especially. He couldn't begin to count how many Sunday afternoons he and his father had spent enveloped in the magical world of a darkened movie theater, popcorn in one hand, soda in the other. Some dads were football guys. Some lived to share their love of music. His was a certified, true blue movie buff. If he were honest, when the opportunity to own his own movie theater arose, the prospect appealed as much to the son in him as the entrepreneur. He only wished his father was around to see it. The 4D experience would have knocked his multi-colored socks off.

Nick chuckled and looked to the ceiling rafters. "Miss ya, Pop."

He was about to walk back up the aisle and return to the lobby when a last glance around stopped him. A flash of movement down front caused him to take a double take. Were his eyes screwing with him? Was that? He chuckled. It was. In the front row, an ass in black slacks rose into the air. He started making his way down the center aisle.

When he reached the bottom and came upon the rest of what he assumed was the reporter, Nick cleared his throat. "Miss Park?"

A head popped up where the ass had been. The owner of both bolted upright, her long russet ponytail swinging through the air. The woman displayed all the grace of a child-thief caught stealing cigarettes from her mother's purse.

"Mr. uh, Fallon. Hi." She reached out her hand, then just as quickly, pulled it back, as if the action was out of sequence. With an awkward grin, she bent and retrieved her satchel from beside her feet. Only when the canvas bag was slung over her shoulder did she once again offer her hand.

"We finally meet." Nick took her hand and gently shook it. "But, please, call me Nick."

The reporter smiled, nodded.

"Okay, Nick," she said, already enjoying an expeditious recovery. "But only if you call me Nori. Miss Park is a reminder I am still unmarried; thus my mother is still without grandchildren.

It's hard enough keeping her voice out of my head. I sometimes worry it's stuck there."

Nick smiled. "Understood."

First impressions being what they were, the supposedly tough reporter seemed nothing like the mayor had described. His nickname of "ball-buster" didn't fit the bill. In fact, she seemed rather nice. Her smile appeared genuine, lending a look of pleasant courteousness to her handsome face. A face some might even consider 'alluring'--

Whoa, Nick urged. *Slow down, cowboy.*

Taking a step back, he erased all intimate thoughts from his mind. Having not had a date in over a year didn't help. First things first, though. He spread his arms wide.

"So, what do you think of the new and improved Chamberlain Theater? I see you're familiarizing yourself with our state-of-the-art, fully interactive seats."

"Oh." Nori tugged at her ear. "Yeah, sorry."

Nick smiled on the inside. Tugging her ear was something his grandmother used to do. And just like that, he decided he liked this Nori Park.

"Not at all," he said. "Please, have a look around."

Even as he suggested it, Nick realized there wasn't much to see. Unless you dug deep under its slick façade, The Chamberlain looked much like any other movie theater. Except for the seats. To the untrained eye, they appeared bulkier and sat higher than standard seats.

"Are you familiar with 4D cinema?"

Nori shook her head, glancing around the expansive room. "I have to be honest, Mr.... um, sorry, Nick. I'd never heard of 4D before this. Around here, very few 3D movies have come our way, let alone 4D."

"Well, here at The Chamberlain, we're gonna skip right past 3D and go straight to four. Do not pass go, do not collect two hundred dollars." He smiled, paused an adequate amount of time for the reference to sink in. When the silence became awkward, he patted the top of the nearest seat. "So… uh… please, make yourself comfortable."

Nori accepted the invitation, taking the seat she'd been looking under the hood of earlier. Satchel in her lap, she clasped her hands over it and leaned back. She wore the crooked grin of someone mildly excited, yet unsure of what they were getting themselves into.

"Now," Nick said, once she appeared settled, "I can't actually start the film, but I can give you a small sample of how it all works. The kind of experience our moviegoers are in for."

"Sounds great."

He offered an abbreviated bow.

"If you'll excuse me."

He made his way up the aisle and through the doors to the hallway, questioning himself the entire way. Was he being charming enough? Too charming? Was he coming across as too eager for a good review? He didn't know, and ultimately, he couldn't worry about it.

Where was Manny?

Nick could only hope the reason he hadn't seen his engineer was because he was in the control room, running through last-minute preparations.

As soon as Nick entered the control room, Manny met him with a toothy thumbs up.

"Way to go, Nick! She's way more attractive than the ladies you normally date. If you dated, I mean. I can imagine."

Nick shook his head, downplaying any suggestion of interest in the reporter. Sure, Nori was attractive. And admittedly, his relationship status teetered on the verge of nonexistent. However, his interactions with the reporter would be strictly business. Had to be. No way would he muddy the waters and risk a critical review based on how noisily he ate chicken wings instead of how he operated his theater.

"It's not what you think, Manny," he said. "And where—"

"Yeah, but it's not *not* what I think, right?" Manny tilted his head forward, eyeing Nick over the top of his black hipster frames. His over-exaggerated wink and mischievous smile told Nick his engineer was overthinking it. Manny was a brilliant engineer. Not to mention one hell of a poker player. But Nick sometimes found him a little too carefree with his thoughts. The tendency to over share was a Millennial trademark. He blamed social media.

"Miss Park is here on behalf of the media—"

"Nori," Manny interrupted. "She asked you to call her Nori."

"Right," he said. "Nori's here on be—" *Wait a second.* Nick's expression contorted into a full-face furrow. "How did you know? Were you eavesdropping on us?"

Manny shrugged.

Nick shook his head, but there wasn't much admonishment behind it. He tried to be upset with Manny for listening in on his private conversation with Nori. *Should* be upset. Whether it was the excitement of opening night, or the headache sucking all his energy, he wasn't feeling it.

"Anyway," he said, recalling where his original thoughts were heading, "I want to show *Nori* a little of what we have to offer. Can you give her a taste?"

"Love to."

Manny pushed his glasses further up the bridge of his nose. He turned toward a touchscreen the size of an iPad and tilted it toward him. The screen glowed a light blue. A large red and white Raxon Technologies logo hovered in the middle. Square icons, the size of postage stamps, lined the bottom of the screen. According to

Manny, the system was straightforward. Nick wouldn't know. He had yet to learn it. That was what he paid Manny for.

"What do you wanna throw at her first?" his engineer asked. "A little wind? Rain? A blast of stink?"

Nick rubbed his temples with his thumbs as he considered all available options. "How about we start with the seats?"

Manny's smile turned upside down.

"For starters," Nick encouraged.

Pouting like a child a fraction of his age, Manny turned to the screen. He intertwined his fingers and turned them inside out. He cracked his knuckles the way a classical pianist might when sitting down at the ebonies and ivories. After studying the screen for a moment, he said, "Let's give her posterior a little jolt, shall we?"

As Nick stepped around the control panel and peered through the tiny window that overlooked the auditorium, two things happened: first, he heard Manny tap the screen; and the top of Nori's head popped up above the seat back. Her shriek of surprise exploded through the control room. Startled, Nick shrunk away from the explosion of sound. It was as if the reporter was there beside him, instead of a hundred feet away on the other side of an insulated wall.

He turned to his engineer. "Seriously, dude. Turn off the house mics."

Manny offered a wry smile as he complied.

With another tap on the screen, all the seats in the theater reclined backward. Instinctively, Nori's hands shot out and grabbed the armrests, as Nick knew they would. The sensation of falling always produced the same predictable reaction. It was as inevitable as tears at a funeral. He smiled. He couldn't wait to watch an entire theater full of moviegoers have the same unilateral reaction.

He checked his watch. Forty minutes till showtime.

"What next?" Manny asked, a childlike eagerness in his voice.

"Can I at least hit her with the mist?"

Nick gave it some thought. As eager as he was to show off the theater's bag of tricks, he also felt the need to make Nori wait. He preferred she experience all the new Chamberlain had to offer along with the rest of the town.

"Sorry. I know what I said, but I think that's enough." He patted his engineer on the shoulder and turned to leave. "The first rule of entertainment, Manny. Always leave the audience wanting more."

THREE

When Nick met Nori outside the theater doors, the reporter had to work to conceal her smile.

"Interesting seats, Nick. But I hope there's more to this 4D experience than the shaking and soft-core groping of moviegoers." As she spoke, her fingers danced across the screen of her iPad. "So? Is there more?"

Nick clasped his hands behind his back. "Well, of course there is, Ms. Park—"

"Nori."

He nodded his apology. "Of course, there is, Nori. But wouldn't it be more fun to experience all The Chamberlain's secrets along with everyone else?" He looked once again at his watch. "Which won't be long now."

The reporter stopped tapping. "I still have a few questions if you have time."

Nick sighed. If only she was the only one vying for his attention at the moment. Besides everything else he had going on, his headache demanded equal representation. Not to mention the haze creeping into the edges of his vision. He simply didn't have time. They would all have to wait.

"As you can imagine, Nori, tonight's a busy night." He paused, allowing the furor growing in the lobby to emphasize his point. "But if you'd like to walk with me…"

"Sure," she said, pointing to the auditorium doors, "but real quick, did you notice it kinda smelled like smoke in there?"

Nick nodded. He'd expected this. The auditorium had a faint smoky smell from time to time. Like burnt wood or paper. From what or where, no one knew. His contractor had cleared the auditorium of painters the first time he'd detected it. Nick called in not one, not two, but three electricians to check the wiring. Every search came up empty. As unsettling as the smell of smoke could be, especially in an enclosed space like a theater, it had been determined there was no danger. Nothing was burning, nothing was on fire. Where it originated, what brought it out, these were questions that remained answered. Apparently, there wasn't anything that could be done about The Chamberlain's unusual smell of smoke.

Except hope it went away at some point.

"It comes and goes. As of right now, no one has been able to determine why. But I assure you, the building has undergone several thorough investigations, and The Chamberlain Theater has earned a seal of approval. It is completely safe." He turned to the lobby and directed Nori toward it with a raised hand. "Shall we?"

The atmosphere in the lobby had intensified while he'd been away. The number of dressed-up townsfolk congregating in the lobby, complimentary glasses of champagne in hand, had doubled. A modest line had reformed outside. And what had started as an indistinct murmur among the crowd had grown to a tempest, drowning out the music being piped in.

Despite his condition, Nick flushed with satisfaction and the sense that everything was going well.

Nori cleared her throat.

"Can you tell me about the films you'll be showing here at The Chamberlain?"

Nick exchanged a smile and nod with a passing well-wisher and the elegant woman accompanying him. The man looked familiar, but he couldn't place him. He could have been from the bank. The mayor had introduced him to so many suits over the past year, they were like minnows in a seine net. He had a hard time telling one from the other.

"Initially, I'm offering three films, all developed specifically to run in accordance with our 4D capabilities." Nick continued to nod and dole out smiles as he snaked his way through the crowd, Nori in tow. "One is a family-oriented film that takes the audience on an adventure around the globe, exploring the wonders of nature. The audience will feel the stifling heat of the desert, as well as the chill of the arctic. When we reach the rainforests, well, let's just say the dampness you'll feel on your skin won't be sweat."

"The black boxes!" Nori interrupted. "The ones hanging from the ceiling."

Nick spun on his heels and pointed at the reporter. "Exactly! It's a stunning ride, and the kids will eat it up. Perfect summer matinee fare." He turned and continued making his way through the crowd. "The other two films, well, they're more adult oriented. Specifically, the one we'll be showing tonight. It's a murder mystery with a lot of tension and more than a few scares." As he spoke, a cloud floated through his vision. He stopped for a moment and rubbed his eyes. Perhaps he'd spun around too quickly a moment ago. Or had taken one too many pills. He shook it off. "Um… do you scare easily, Nori?"

"Afraid not," she chuckled. "My father is a big horror buff with questionable parenting skills. He recruited me as his watch buddy at an early age. So, if you hope to scare me tonight, Nick, you have your work cut out for you."

He smiled, though it was growing increasingly painful to do so.

"Challenge accepted."

"Nick!"

From across the room, one of his employees waved his hand,

attempting to gain his attention. With an apology, he excused himself and made his way to the concession counter.

"Can't find the straws anywhere, Boss." John-David emphasized his plight with empty hands raised in the air.

In addition to the complimentary champagne, The Chamberlain was offering a full complement of movie theater concessions for opening night. That included a soda machine offering as many flavor combinations as one's imagination could conjure. There were the basics: Coke, Diet Coke, Sprite. And then there were combinations only a demented mind would conjure up: grape cream soda, orange root beer, pomegranate ginger ale. You name it, the machine could make it. All of which would be easier to drink with straws.

Nick fished in his pocket and pulled out a cluster of keys. He thumbed through the keyring in search of one silver key in particular, struggling to focus. He blinked his eyes twice, squeezed them shut a second time before reopening them. Once he found the right key, he isolated it, and handed the keyring to John-David.

"Check the storage room," Nick said, fighting back a grimace. "I know I ordered them."

With a respectful smile, the young man with alternating strips of black and purple hair took the keys and made his way through the crowd.

Nick scanned the counter. "How's everything else look, Zach?"

"Good, Nick." The other young man working the concession counter was John-David's twin brother, identical minus the purple streaks in his black hair. For which Nick was thankful. It was the only way he could tell them apart. Zach was putting the finishing touches on a pyramid display, alternating boxes of Raisinets, Sno-Caps, and Goobers. "Everything's pretty much set up. But no one's really buying anything."

"That's alright," Nick said, glancing around. "We're just glad they're here."

He checked his watch again. It was becoming a habit, and not a good one. Showtime couldn't come soon enough. He rapped his knuckles on the glass countertop. With one more quick inspection of the concession counter—napkins in the dispenser? Check. Fresh popcorn popping? Check. Sweat breaking out on his forehead? Check—Nick turned, bumping into Nori.

"Those two look familiar." Her head was down, fingertips once again doing a number on her iPad. "They wouldn't happen to be…"

"Zachary and John-David Blackwood," Nick said. She didn't have to finish her thought. He knew where it was heading. He nodded, though not enthusiastically. "The mayor's nephews."

Nori's head popped up. "Yes!" Her eyes were wide, alert with the scent of a scoop. "But I thought they were both in jail…"

And here it comes.

His stomach tightened. He'd heard the rumors, the talk concerning the mayor's delinquent, yet hard working nephews. Heard how the police in Angler Bay tended to look the other way because of their last name. It was a small town, after all. Nick also knew questions regarding their hiring were bound to come up once people learned of their employment at the theater. He'd armed himself with the best answers he could come up with. Only now didn't feel like the right time to mount a defense.

He'd hoped to at least get through opening night first.

"Work release," he said, and hoped to leave it at that.

Nori's eyes narrowed. She studied his face. Her eager fingers hovered above the iPad's screen like circling vultures over a carcass.

"And did hiring them have anything to do with returning a favor or…?"

"Um…"

Luckily for Nick, a large contingent of Angler Bay's city council entered the lobby together. Feigning distraction, he ignored Nori's inquiry. There was too much riding on the evening—and her review—to get caught up in controversy.

Not to mention the fact his vision was coming and going in waves of pixilated clouds. His skull was about to crack and split open from the pressure mounting behind his eyes.

"Ladies and gentlemen." Nick busied himself, shaking every hand he could find, kissing every cheek thrust his way. "Welcome to the historic Chamberlain Theater. Or, should I say, the new and improved Chamberlain Theater."

Heads turned this way and that. Everyone craned their necks to take in the lobby's new décor. Smiles broadened across the faces of some. Several remained pensive, appearing wary of being there. He saw it in their eyes: the theater's recent history running through their minds like a scrapbook full of newspaper articles. When he'd first embarked on this venture, he knew history was a hurdle he would have to overcome. Self-immolation of a beloved member of the community wasn't something a small town soon forgets.

Nick raised both his hands and his voice as he addressed the room.

"For those of you who have been here before, I'm sure you'll notice the many updates we've made. Including a new concession counter with more drink options than you could dream up." Nods of approval accompanied most of the gazes. The more they glanced around, the more the apprehensive among the group seemed to warm to the idea of being there. "But I assure you, the updates don't stop here in the lobby. I think you'll find much to like in the auditorium where we made the most significant changes. Not to mention, spent the most money."

Nick waited for the small laughter to die before he continued. "We'll start seating in about twenty minutes, so feel free to look around. And please, help yourself to some champagne."

After a few more congratulatory handshakes, Nick found himself without an audience, though not alone. He was surprised, and maybe a little disappointed, the reporter insisted on sticking around. He had hoped to lose her and her probing questions somewhere along the way, then catch back up with her after the movie when she'd undoubtedly have more immediate things to ask about. Apparently, she would not be easily dismissed. He filed that information away for future reference.

"So, would now be a good time to answer some questions, Mr.· Fallon?"

His heart sank like a stone.

Aw, shit.

The reporter had fallen back on addressing him as 'Mr. Fallon' instead of Nick. And it didn't sound like a misstep on her part. A bad sign for sure. Was it because he hadn't been forthcoming regarding her question about the Blackwood twins? Had he done something else? Something he wasn't even aware of? He didn't know, and the category 5 hurricane brewing in his head wasn't about to let up long enough for him to find out.

"I'm sorry, Ms. Park, but I have some last-minute business to attend to before we open the doors to the auditorium." *Ms. Park. Shit.* Their relationship was apparently back on formal ground. He reminded himself to tread lightly. A positive review, while still within reach, may well be teetering on the precipice. "Any chance we could resume this interview a bit later? After the show, perhaps?"

He didn't wait for a response. The coward in him couldn't get away fast enough. He weaved his way through the crowd, heading toward his office down the hall. Once he felt he was out of Nori's field of vision, he altered course. His office promised last minute interruptions, and therefore, wouldn't provide the solitude he sought. He needed to be alone for a few minutes before the movie began. Circling back around, he made his way toward the auditorium doors. A quiet theater all to himself was the best place he could imagine riding out the next twenty minutes.

And this fucking headache.

FOUR

When the house lights went down at 8:00 pm, The Chamberlain Theater was only a few seats shy of capacity. Considering Nick's lean marketing budget was word-of-mouth dependent, he couldn't be more pleased. A sellout would have been optimal. Not to mention how good it would have looked for the piece Nori Park was writing. But a near sellout was a victory. Who cared if he'd comped half of the evening's tickets? Given the theater's recent history, most townsfolk were reluctant to even step foot on the premises. He wasn't about to disparage those who had braved their fears, lured in by free admission or not.

When the lights faded, so did the chatter. A hushed anticipation befell the auditorium. Darkness reigned. Those who hadn't yet put on their black-framed 3D glasses did so now.

From his end seat in the back row, the butterflies nesting in Nick's stomach took flight. He imagined it was how a painter or sculptor felt when they were about to reveal their work to the world. The only difference was, except for writing a bunch of checks, he'd had little to do with making The Chamberlain the state-of-the-art masterpiece it was. He'd never so much as gotten his hands dirty.

This fact hardly tempered his excitement.

What did quell his excitement, however, was realizing the lights had been down for a full two minutes, and the movie had yet to begin.

Two became two and a half.

Nick wasn't the only one to notice. Around the room, murmurs and idle chatter crept back into the fray. The noise level rose. A soft din soon replaced pin-drop silence as everyone grew uncomfortable sitting in the dark. The only light in the room was the glowing red exit sign down front, casting an eerily crimson glow over its corner of the auditorium.

Subtle waves of nausea rippled through his stomach.

Two and a half minutes turned into three, three into four. And as darkness continued to embrace the room, whispered musings turned to heightened grumbles. A shout from down front. Using not so flowery language, the patron urged the movie to start. Another voice seconded the motion. The cursing seemed a little out of character given the nature of the event, and Nick blamed the free-flowing champagne. In hindsight, it might have been a bad idea if credits didn't start rolling soon.

He'd gone thirty-two years having never picked up a musical instrument, but Nick now played the kick drum with his foot. He looked at his watch. The tiny hands proved elusive in the dark. He was about to get up and see what the hell was taking Manny so long when a beam of light pierced the pitch.

The large screen down front lit up in a brilliant white. A buzz tickled the air. Seconds later, the screen once again went black before ferrying in the opening credits. Names and responsibilities crawled across the screen in misty white lettering. From somewhere off screen, the breathy panting of a young woman seeped into the auditorium. Strategically placed speakers soon filled the room with an almost tangible adrenaline.

While the rest of the audience tensed with apprehension, Nick relaxed. He smiled and settled deeper into his seat. A year in the making, and the new Chamberlain's first official showing was underway…

The credits end and the screen cuts to a starry night. A light fog lingers around the edges. The camera pans down and a stretch of woods comes into view. A muddy path weaves its way through moonlit trees and brush. The source of the panting bursts onto the path from behind a clump of shrubs. A young woman, clad in a white tank and cut-off jean shorts. Her traversing of the path resembles more of a series of stumbles than a run. Her torn tank top flutters from one shoulder, and her long, dark hair is matted. Streaks of mud and dead leaves cling to her bare legs.

She appears alone.

The woods are thick with the unknown.

When the woman casts a glance behind her, her eyes widen. Her pace quickens and her breaths come more rapidly. Steam and fearful whimpers escape her trembling lips. She slips. She falls. When she hits the ground, the seats in the theater tremble. Murmurs bubble up from the audience. Sprawled out, the woman turns and looks behind her. For the first time, the catalyst of her fear is revealed.

A towering man, his face lost in the shadow of a grey hoodie.

The woman's scream echoes through the trees, reverberating through the auditorium.

She crawls on her hands and knees. Tears streaming down her face, her pursuer closes the distance. From behind, he lifts his soiled boot to the woman's backside. He shoves her face first into the mud. She sprawls. He pins her down, a knee straddled to each side.

The woman whimpers, too out of breath to scream, too weak from exhaustion to fight.

The camera cuts away. Silhouetted against a crescent moon, a long, carving knife rises into the night sky. It hovers long enough for the audience to gasp and the desperate woman to mutter a single phrase...

"Please, no..."

The knife arcs downward.
The screen goes black.

A sudden poke in the back elicits screams from the audience. The simulation of being stabbed is subtle and perfectly timed. It is all part of the 4D seat experience.

The screen explodes with light as the sound of tires on gravel roars from the surrounding speakers. A jeep full of teenagers, top down, driving dangerously fast up a wooded mountain road. Their music is upbeat and loud. So are their spirits. An empty beer can soars out the back.

Inside the theater, screams of shock devolved into nervous laughter and chatter. The audience let out a collective sigh of relief. And Nick couldn't help but smile, thinking how quickly word of The Chamberlain Theater was going to spread.

The first sign something was wrong came moments later.

On the screen, two of the teens stood inside a cabin, gearing up to head out into the stormy night. A third teen had gone out to the Jeep for a cell phone charger and never returned. The teens opened the cabin door. A fierce wind whipped at their jackets.

At the same time, a blast of wind swept through the auditorium. Six concealed and powerful fans transformed the room into a storm-riddled forest.

Murmurs followed.

Nick smiled. *Here we go.*

Aware of what was coming, he braced for it. The audience, however, was unprepared. When the teens stepped out into the rain, a fine mist fell from the auditorium's rafters. Brief and light, it wasn't enough to get the audience more than the slightest bit damp.

Within seconds, however, the first scream erupted.

Others soon followed.

The mist continued to fall.

The wind continued to whip.

A foul odor permeated the room, bringing Nick upright in his seat. Soon, a thin film covered the lenses of his 3D glasses, tinting the movie screen and everything else in the room a deep red.

He tore the glasses from his face. Something was seriously wrong. The watery mist should have been clear. What spewed from the overhead misters was anything but. A red liquid covered everything around him.

He tasted copper on his lips.

Shouts and screams soon formed a chorus. The overwhelming stench overtook the auditorium. The red mist continued to rain down.

"The fuck?" someone shouted.

"My God!" cried another.

By the time Nick realized the misting pumps had sprayed blood onto the audience instead of simple H20, everyone else had realized it, too.

Cries of disbelief joined the mist in filling the air. Some cried out in anger, others in terror. All were born of shock. People rose from their seats, their once-pristine suits and dresses awash in red.

Chaos was erupting, faster than Nick could react. He too found himself on his feet, and just as quickly, the center of attention.

He raised his hands to the crowd gathering around him.

"Everyone, please, remain calm."

Not a soul listened. Initial shock subsided, replaced with panic.

"I assure you," he shouted, shuffling backward toward the door, "it's just a malfunction of some sort. Maybe a prank. But I promise you there is no danger. Everyone please remain calm. I repeat, there is no danger!"

He wiped blood from his forehead, preventing it from seeping into his eyes.

Shielding her head with her satchel, Nori Park joined him at the back of the room. A hundred of her closest friends trailed closely behind. "If this is a prank, Nick, or some sort of publicity stunt, I'm going on record to say it's pretty screwed up."

Row after row of blood-drenched theatergoers spilled into the center aisle. In a scene straight from a George Romero movie, they eked their way toward Nick and the exit doors, all cloaked in blood, all slipping and sliding through its muck. A grotesque mob had assembled before his eyes, growing angrier and more panicked by the second. Any chance of quelling the situation before it spiraled out of control was slipping away.

"Please, let us out!"

Other voices echoed the sentiment, though not all were as polite. The sounds of people spitting the metallic-tasting blood from their mouths could be heard throughout the auditorium. Somewhere down front, some poor soul retched violently. Soon another followed. The sound turned Nick's stomach. He could only pray the retching didn't set off a chain reaction.

He turned and grabbed the door handle. The plan was to get everyone out, take stock of the malfunction afterward. The door, however, wasn't on board.

It wouldn't open.

Wouldn't even budge. Grabbing hold of both handles and giving them a tug didn't improve the situation. The other door was also locked. Spitting both blood and expletives, Nick jerked the handles back and forth. He shook the doors. The fact they wouldn't open both bewildered and frightened him. *How? Who? Why?*

"Manny!" He looked to the projection window. Where was his engineer? The streak of faint blue light remained connected to the screen down front. The beam spotlighted falling red flecks. "Manny! Unlock the doors!"

Gasps all around.

"The doors are locked?" The frantic voice came from behind him. "You locked us in? What the--"

Nick spun, faced the crowd.

"No! no!" he shouted. "They're not supposed to be locked." His heart raced. His mind reeled with potential scenarios as to why the doors might be locked. None of them were good. None were logical. "I don't know *who* locked them," he admitted. "Or, why."

He dug into his pocket for his set of keys. His pocket was empty. He checked other pockets. The only thing he found was an empty baggy that used to contain four oval-shaped blue pills. And then he remembered: he'd given his keys to John-David. He'd been so eager to sidestep Ms. Park minutes later, he'd sidestepped John-David as well and had forgotten all about his keys.

Blood continued to rain from the ceiling.

The movie continued to play. On screen, the two teens trudged along a muddy path, clutching jackets tight around their collars, shouting their friend's name over the din of falling rain. The screen flashed a brilliant white. Lightning lit the stormy night.

In the auditorium, a flash from an overhead strobe coincided perfectly. Thunder crashed through the speakers, further fraying his nerves. He turned back to the control room window.

"Manny!"

Still no response. Nick wiped metallic, red rain from his eyes. Tried to, at least. The blood only smeared, leaving behind a slick residue.

Where the hell was his engineer? How could Manny not see what was going on in the auditorium? Not hear the screams? And who the fuck had locked the doors?

Nick's attention drifted back to the screen where the teenagers' story continued to play out. Realizing what was to come caused a sick ball of lead to form in the pit of his stomach.

FIVE

"Let me through, God dammit!"

Nick's heart took a nose-dive. The voice was unmistakable and the last thing he needed at the moment.

"Let me through!"

The first commotion gave birth to a second, internal commotion. A parting of the crowd made its way up the center aisle, heading straight for him. Even while dealing with their own distress, people couldn't get out of the man's way fast enough. It was as if the headless horseman was plowing his way through the sea of people. As the commotion inched its way closer, Nick took a deep breath, readying himself for the confrontation boring down on him.

"Let me through!"

The crowd before him split in half, spitting the mayor out at his feet.

"Damn it, Fallon!" roared Blackwood. "What's the meaning of this?"

Another disoriented flash of light. Everyone, Nick included, braced themselves for what would follow. He covered his ears. Those paying attention, mirrored the move. For those too slow to act, the exploding thunder sheered the air, piercing eardrums.

The room shook from the massive display of power. Fissures crawled up the walls. The floor rose, tremoring violently. Legs buckled and people fell. Above the crowd, rows of suspended lights swayed back and forth.

Eyes turned skyward.

Nick held his breath.

The lights held their place.

Once the moment had passed, and the thunder had faded, the audience pounced with an aggression not seen to that point. A great throng of people rushed forward, pinning the mayor against Nick and Nick against the doors. Panic was the new order of business. The crowd threatened to overtake him, their alarm growing into something with teeth. The Chamberlain's 4D experience had gone bad, and its patrons had had enough. Opening night was officially over.

"Everyone, please!" Nick screeched, fighting to breathe. The speed with which the mob's anger intensified startled him. Matters were spiraling out of control. He'd been too caught off guard, too ill-equipped to stop it.

"Please stay calm!" he shouted, working to free his arms. An elbow dug deep into his sternum. He tried to slink away from it, but there was nowhere to go. His back was already against the door. "Has anyone tried the emergency exit down front?"

Not a single voice responded. Screams and animalistic cries were the film's new soundtrack. The noise level in the room was deafening, and his shouts barely rose above it. He struggled to breathe, crushed by the weight of hysteria. He clawed his way onto his toes and checked the progress at the emergency exit. People were gathering down front. Gathering, but not exiting. The door remained closed. He could only assume someone had tried to open it by now. Tried and failed.

"Fallon, I swear!" The mayor grabbed him by the lapels of his sport coat and lifted him, his back sliding up the door. "Let me out of this fucking theater!"

Grasping the mayor's thick arms, Nick tried wrenching the

man's powerful hands free. His attempt was feeble, his grip weak. The man's skin was too slick with gore.

"Mayor!" he shouted, adrenalin fueling his courage. "If I could, I would! Now let me go!"

The mayor's eyes brimmed with brutality. His nostrils flared. His lips straight-lined. Nick sensed it was everything the man could do to keep from snapping his skinny neck. He readied his fists in response, prepared to fight his way free. Then, just as suddenly as he'd grabbed him up, the mayor let go of his jacket, dropping him back onto his feet.

Without explanation, the mayor spun and erupted. A madman set loose. In brutal fashion, he shoved people to the side, clearing out space all around him. Had someone pushed him from behind? Was the guy claustrophobic? Had the stress of seeing the town's salvation bathed in blood sent him over the edge? Nick didn't know, and he didn't care. He was thankful for the space and the distraction. He had room to breathe.

As he sucked in some welcomed air, a presence crept up beside him. Fists poised and ready to swing if need be, he turned to it. Nori Park greeted him with eyes wide. He sent some of his tension away with an exhaustive exhale. As much as he'd tried to avoid her, the reporter was a sight for desperate eyes. When her hand snaked around his arm and found his, his heart swelled. He knew the gesture, knew the empathetic motive behind it. It was more for his benefit than any security she sought.

And it was a godsend.

"Deep breaths," she said. Nori's soothing brown eyes bore into Nick's. Her gaze held his captive. "These people need you to stay calm."

He nodded, not ready to give up the connection. He took a deep breath as instructed. The benefits were immediate. His pulse slowed. His breathing steadied. The anvil of bedlam surrounding him dropped from his shoulders. When he could finally tear his eyes from Nori's, he closed them for a beat.

Deep breaths.

Reopening his eyes, he looked out over the mass of people with more calm and clarity than before.

Patrons still gathered at the emergency exit. Others continued to push and shove their way up the aisle toward him and the doors. Caught between the two blocked exits, a huddled mass had filtered into the middle of the room and now stood there, unsure of their best option. As if there was one.

Crimson rain continued to fall.

Given no other direction, the film played on.

A high-pitched scream erupted from the speakers. The screen drew the room's attention in time to see a table lamp crash down upon the head of one of the teens.

In the auditorium, things went from bad to worse.

The entire overhead lighting system came to life. Riggings began swaying back and forth. It was as if a giant hand worked the bars like the strings of a marionette. One after another, bolts sheered. And one after another, riggings careened downward. Patrons scrambled, attempting to escape the falling debris. There was nowhere to go. The screams melded into one mass of static white noise.

Helpless, Nick could only look on as a man shoved his wife out of the path of an untethered rigging. The long steel bar swung downward. It just missed the woman, but caught the man, swiping him across the face. The metal took skin, muscle, and bone as souvenirs. The man collapsed in a heap. The white noise drowned his wife's anguish.

Nick clutched his stomach, hoping to keep his dinner down.

All throughout the room, light riggings swung and light riggings fell. The handful of patrons who looked up were punished for their decision. Wails of despair filled the air as fractured metal and shattered glass ruined eyes and changed lives. The auditorium bloomed with an unworldly pandemonium. The ability to discern the blood coming from the misters from the blood of the innocent had been stripped away. There was no escaping the red liquid. Those who tried slipped and fell, joining the bodies of the dead that littered the concrete floor.

Nick gasped as the crowd parted before him.

Toby Gesture, Angler Bay's School Superintendent, rushed up the center aisle, charging at Nick with a three-foot section of light fixture raised high above his head. Nick ducked away as the man in what may have once been a grey suit passed him by. The man hadn't been headhunting him, after all. Toby swung the piece of steel downward like an axe, crashing the metal bar against one of the wooden doors. The strike created a loud report, but if it made even a scratch, it wasn't visible in the dim light. A second strike proved as fruitless; the heavy, wooden doors too formidable. Toby's efforts were admirable but did nothing to release the crowd from its prison.

As the last of the riggings served another fatal blow, a woman slipped through the crowd and approached. Red goo plastered her hair to the side of her face. Her ripped dress barely hung on. Muscle and tissue showed through a deep gash that had opened from her shoulder to her collarbone. If blood loss wasn't an issue for her yet, it soon would be. Despite her condition and the surrounding chaos, the woman appeared calmer than anyone in her position should. A sad smile tugged at the corners of her mouth.

Nick wasn't a doctor, but he didn't have to be to diagnose the woman's condition: she was in shock.

"Excuse me, sir." Her voice remained as temperate as if she were asking a server about the day's specials. "I… I would like to leave now. Is there any way out of the theater besides these doors and the emergency exit down front? Any other exits at all?"

He mustered only a blank stare. The irony of her mentioning the emergency exit wasn't lost on him. The Chamberlain's emergency exit wasn't allowing people to exit during an emergency. He looked around, tried to process through the chaos. Tried to come up with an answer for a woman who probably needed it more than most. There simply wasn't one. The Chamberlain was, and always had been, a movie theater. It wasn't like a performing arts theater. There were no gangways or catwalks overhead. No backstage areas or hallways. Just one large room with three doors and a—

Nick's eyes lit up.

He craned his neck, turning his attention from the injured woman to the pane of glass through which the film continued to play. His gears started to grind. Hope pried its way into his chest. For the first time since the misters started spewing blood, he was developing a plan. An honest to goodness, 'holy shit, let's do this' plan.

The window to the control room was the size of a small microwave and at least fifteen feet off the ground. Difficult to reach, but still a way out. If they could somehow get someone up to it, albeit a small someone, they could break the glass and crawl through. Then the person could exit the control room and unlock the auditorium doors from the outside. What they might find inside the tiny control room was anyone's guess. He had a doomsday imagination, and it had already conjured visions of Manny sprawled on the floor in a pool of his own blood. What other explanation could there be for his engineer's absence? It was the only excuse Nick would accept at this point.

He searched the crowd and found Nori comforting a nearby couple. He sized her up. She defined petite. Narrow shoulders, slender waist, and if she stood even five two, he would be surprised. She would fit through the window. If only there was a way to get her up to it.

When Nick met Nori's gaze over the crowd, he wasted no time beckoning the reporter over.

"Nick, we need to get these people out of here," Nori said, after pushing her way through the crowd. "Tell me you have a plan."

"I have a plan." Nick bit his lower lip. "But you might not like it."

SIX

"What are we waiting for?"

Once Nick had detailed his plan, more specifically, her role in it, Nori hadn't hesitated, hadn't questioned if there were other options. She hadn't even glanced up at the window to see what she was up against. She simply took a deep breath and nodded. "Let's do it."

He returned the nod and addressed the crowd.

"Everyone! Can I have your attention?" Nick found he didn't need to shout as loud as before. No need to kill his throat. The screams had died down. Only sorrowful sobs could be heard while the film enjoyed a quiet moment. He made his way through the crowd, sidestepping bodies and puddles of blood. He did his best to ignore both, but he'd have better luck ignoring trees in a forest. "We have a plan, but we're gonna need help."

He grabbed a couple of large men by the arms.

"Okay, fellas. It's like this."

Nick laid out his plan while the men exchanged glances. When he was done, they took a moment to pass judgment on his idea, even though he hadn't asked their opinion. The men eventually nodded and began removing their blood-slicked jackets.

A long, black lighting rig stretched across four rows of nearby seats. One large metal post ran the length of the fixture, while smaller bars shot out to the sides every so often, effectively creating a reverse ladder, its rungs on the outside.

"Excuse us. Coming through."

Two of the men helped Nick transport the section of rigging to the back of the theater. They wedged one end of the long pole under the back of a seat and rested the other end against the wall. The top of the rig fell short of the window by a few feet but would have to do. It only needed to get her close.

"Is it gonna hold?" Nori asked.

Nick looked the structure up and down, taking an unqualified measure of its strength.

"Should. We'll hold it. Make sure it doesn't go anywhere. Oh, and…"

He made his way to the doors and searched the floor for the piece of metal with which Toby had attacked them. Scooping up the steel bar, Nick returned to the ladder.

"When you get up there," he said, wielding the piece of metal, "I'll toss this up to you. Just make sure you clear out all the glass around the frame so you don't get shredded."

Nori looked up at the window, her bottom lip tucked between her teeth. What was going through her mind? As the architect of the plan, Nick knew he had the easy job. He was also sure Nori knew it as well.

"Ready?"

It was like she flipped a switch. When Nori turned back to him, any hint of trepidation had left her expression. A calm determination had taken over. She took a deep breath.

"This is all gonna make for one hell of a story."

And she was right. Opening night at The Chamberlain Theater had turned into one hell of a story. The publicity would be even bigger than he had hoped. Unfortunately, it wouldn't be the type of publicity he was looking for. He'd heard the phrase, *"there's no such thing as bad publicity"* a million times. It was business mantra 101. But, gazing out over bodies, parts, and the throng of blood-soaked and desperate people looking to him for deliverance, he couldn't envision how anyone could put a positive spin on any of it.

The first cross bar hit Nori about mid-thigh. It was too high for her to reach on her own, so Nick helped her get a leg up with his interlocked fingers. The crossbar gave a little under her weight. He held his breath. Doubt entered the picture, and he started second-guessing himself. Who the hell was he to determine whether the bars would hold her? Who the hell was he to be looked upon as an authority on anything?

Nori tested her weight on the first bar. When the piece of steel proved worthy, she climbed up onto the second one. The other cross bars were spaced more favorably, and she took them one at a time with relative assurance as Nick and another man held the fixture firmly against the wall.

The loud revving of an engine filled the auditorium.

Heart in his throat, Nick turned to the screen.

The teenagers' jeep careened down a jagged embankment, straight toward a flooded creek bed. Simulating the bumpy ride, the plush theater seats rumbled, shook, and pitched from side to side. If anyone had been seated in the plush new seats, they would have felt like they were in a jeep careening down an embankment instead of a movie theater. Since everyone was either on their feet or on the floor, it proved a wasted display of the theater's power.

"Nick!"

The shout rocketed his attention back to Nori.

She had reached the halfway point and now clutched the steel pole against her chest. The rocking of the seat had caused the makeshift ladder to shift. It was no longer wedged beneath the seat. It was no longer stable. Making matters worse, Nori's weight made it top heavy. The pole lurched. It threatened to topple.

"Shit!"

Nick wrapped his arms around the steel bar and put all his

weight against it. The man who had been helping had disappeared, assumedly in a panic. Nick cursed him under his breath, saving some admonishment for himself. After all, he'd proven just as unreliable. He'd allowed himself to be distracted by the wonder of two hundred and fifty blood-drenched theater seats, all rocking about, all adding to the chaos. In doing so, he'd let go of the ladder. Just like he'd promised not to.

It was a misstep. One made worse since the seats hadn't stopped rocking. They should have. On the screen, the jeep had flipped and lay submerged in the creek bed. The only wheel rising above the surface spun freely. Still, the theater seats jerked about, causing the entire auditorium to tremble.

If he didn't know better, he'd say The Chamberlain itself was trying to shake the ladder out from under Nori.

"Keep going!" he shouted. The steel beam tried its best to wrench itself free. His palms seared with a burning sensation. The pain sharpened as the metal's edges sliced through his hands and forearms. He fought for control. He couldn't let go, despite the pain. Not again. He wasn't about to fail Nori a second time. "I got it!"

Blood trickled down his wrists and arms.

After exchanging gazes and a nod of encouragement, Nori once again started to climb. This time, she didn't stop until she'd reached the last cross beam. Nick relaxed by a shade. His initial assessment had been wrong. Not only was she high enough to reach the window, but if she raised up on the balls of her feet, she could peer into the control room.

Nori looked down. In her first sign of nerves, she hesitated. She locked her arms around the steel pole and rested her forehead against the wall below the window.

"Come on, Nori," Nick whispered under his breath. Was it the height? It appeared so, but he couldn't tell for sure. "You got this. You can do it, Nori!"

He released one hand from the ladder and bent to retrieve Toby's steel bar. Taking it in his grasp, he rose, ready to toss it to her whenever she was ready for it. His heart beat fast enough for the both of them.

After another moment's hesitation and a deep breath, Nori rose on the balls of her feet and peered through the pane of glass.

The window exploded.

The blast sent piercing shards of glass outward. Tiny crystals arced through the air and rained down on everything below. The makeshift ladder blew backward, taking Nori with it. Steel ripped itself from his grip. The long metal bar resembled a tree falling in the woods. It toppled, crashing down upon the backs of seats. Metal sliced through vinyl, tore away foam. When it met the seat's steel frame skeleton, the rigging stopped abruptly, shedding a lifeless Nori like a baby bird. The dark void between the rows eagerly swallowed her up.

Nick's heart stopped.

The explosion in the control room ignited a chain reaction. A second explosion ripped the auditorium doors off their hinges. The two heavy slabs of oak sailed through the air like missiles, mowing down anyone unfortunate enough to be in their path. Thankfully, most didn't see it coming. The swift action spared their corpses the painful knowledge of how they'd died.

Those left alive gasped with relief, and soon rushed the open doorway and spilled out into the lobby.

Nick did the opposite. He worked against the grain, parting his way through the oncoming melee. Nori had fallen hard. He feared the worst. The concrete floor, as is its nature, would have provided little cushion. And the blast…

"Nori!"

He searched among the seats, unsure which row had claimed her. One pathway after another revealed nothing but visceral debris—bodies, both intact and not—painted in slick crimson. Nori was nowhere among them. There was no sign of her anywhere. Had she somehow slipped past him? Escaped with the crowd without him noticing? Was she even capable of doing so after such a horrific fall?

Nick realized he was the last one remaining in the auditorium. He'd spent so long enveloped in chaos, the sudden silence proved haunting. Everywhere he looked, irony littered the auditorium. He shared the room with many of Angler Bay's most esteemed citizens, and yet not a one had breath enough to make a sound.

With his strength and search exhausted, Nick made his way up the blood and glass-strewn aisle toward the awaiting doorway and the lobby beyond.

SEVEN

Stepping through the doorway was like stepping back in time.

The lobby swarmed with people. Nick recognized many, having been trapped with them while the world he knew turned to shit. Only something was amiss. Nobody looked the worse for wear. Nobody looked as if they had been through the same harrowing ordeal as he had. Smiles graced faces. Glasses of champagne were in varying states of being emptied. Suits and dresses, stained with blood only moments ago, were crisp, clean, and elegant as the moment they left the hanger. And all throughout the room, a sense of festive anticipation filled the air.

It was opening night as intended.

Bewildered, Nick took a step back.

"Hey, boss!" Manny jogged down the steps from the control room, approaching from the side. "Don'tcha think it's about time—" His question and stride were both cut short.

From somewhere in the festive room, a sharp gasp kicked off the vibe's downward spiral. Laughter slowly died. A hush rode a wave through the lobby. All eyes turned toward Nick; all grew wide when they saw him. Champagne flutes fell away from lips. Hands rushed to cover mouths. Some arrived in time to quell oncoming gasps. Some didn't.

Even Nori, who'd been talking to the mayor's nephews, iPad in hand, stopped mid-question when she saw him. The sour expression on her face melted into one of concern.

Meanwhile, his mouth could have caught flies. The strength in his legs weakened. His mind raced.

What...

He turned back to the auditorium, the scene of the worst carnage he'd ever witnessed, then gasped. He took a step back. His psyche suffered another blow.

The auditorium was free of blood, no longer bathed in it. The seats, their vinyl already a nice Imperial red, showed no other shades of the color. No bodies littered the aisle way. No body *parts*. Even the light fixtures, which had caused irreparable damage to life and limb only minutes earlier, hung suspended from the ceiling where they belonged. The only evidence of the destruction he'd witnessed was the glistening of broken glass inside the doorway.

Nick turned back to the gawking crowd, caught somewhere between the past and present, reality and anti-anxiety-fueled hallucination. Pain lashed both his arms. Looking down answered one question but created others. Rivulets of blood trailed down each arm. The slick red substance coated his hands and fingers, dripping onto the freshly polished floor, forming two small puddles. Within seconds, they had converged into one large pool that surrounded the soles of his black dress oxfords.

It was that image that sent startled patrons shuffling toward the lobby's exit. And it was at that moment that Nick's future, and that of The Chamberlain Theater, changed forever.

The scene inside the theater's lobby resembled the end of an action movie. Die Hard, or one of Liam Neeson's many films where a loved one is wronged, and vengeance must be dealt. Red and blue lights swirled on the street. They shimmered through the theater's glass front, reflected on its interior walls. Angler Bay PD milled about, the detectives taking statements from anyone brave enough to stick around. Medics in dark blue windbreakers saw to Nick as he sat perched atop a concession case full of untouched buttered popcorn and uncorked bottles of champagne.

The credits were rolling on a shit show, and he'd found himself the unfortunate star.

The cuts on his arms had been bandaged and forgotten. It was the bump on the back of his head that gave the medics the most concern. Fainting on a tile floor, as it turned out, was a dangerous endeavor. Not to mention, a painful one. Everyone urged him to seek further medical treatment at the hospital. He shook them off, assuring everyone he was fine. The headache and wooziness weren't ailments a couple of Advil and a glass of bourbon couldn't cure.

They found blood on one of the four-foot wall sconces mounted inside the auditorium's doors. Glass littered the floor. By the looks of things, Nick had somehow wrapped his arms around the decorative light and held on for dear life. Why or for what purpose, nobody knew. And he couldn't explain. Or didn't want to. That's the thing about suffering hallucinations from taking too many pills. Doctors are wary to prescribe more. Still, he'd promised to check in with his physician the following day.

Eventually, the last of the well-dressed crowd dispersed. While some headed home, eager to slip out of uncomfortable neckties and girdles, others left for after-parties Nick was no longer invited to. There were no festivities in store for him that night. Not anymore. In the matter of an hour, he'd gone from town savior to the most talked about man in Angler Bay. And not in a good way.

As the last of the patrons filed out, their pitiful expressions told him they would not be returning. The town had given him one chance, and he'd shit the proverbial bed. One opinion above all was silently shared: perhaps The Chamberlain should have remained closed. Nobody mentioned the theater's previous owner by name. Nobody had to.

When even the police and medics had vacated the premises, the only soul left hanging around was the mayor. If Nick thought Blackwood had lagged from a lack of concern for his medical condition, the man proved him wrong. With a hand on his shoulder, the mayor looked Nick in the eye and asked when the theater would be up and running.

Nick could only shake his head in wonder as he walked toward his office down the hall, leaving the mayor alone in the lobby.

Was the guy for real?

He wasn't sure. But then, the mayor's motives weren't the only things Nick was having difficulty in deciding what was and was not real.

Act Two

EIGHT

They'd been at it for over an hour when the owner of the gourmet food shop with the supposedly haunted basement excused herself to check the status of a catering order. As she ascended the steps leading up from the cold, dank basement, the husband-and-wife paranormal team known as F.A.U.S.T. exchanged a look.

"Anything?" Börne asked.

Claudia exhaled. "Sorry, *meine Liebe*. I'm not feeling anything down here." Closing her eyes, she again rested her hand on the masonry wall in question. Black, child-sized handprints blanketed the old bricks, their origin unknown, their age as much of a mystery. After a moment, she looked back at her husband and shook her head. "Nothing."

Börne nodded and kicked at a nearby cardboard box filled with what appeared to be Christmas decorations. *Scheisse!* And to think, this one had had potential. Strange handprints *and* strange sounds? He should be used to it by now. More often than not, their investigations ended this way. In the ten years he and Claudia had been researching the paranormal, they had actually come across little substantial evidence. Nothing that 'proved' the existence of ghosts or spirits, even though he and his wife were both full-fledged believers. Claudia was very much in tune with the spiritual world, had been since long before they'd met. If there were spirits around, she'd connect with them. They were simply running into fewer and fewer spirits lately. And too many individuals who'd watched enough paranormal television shows to believe they had a haunting on their hands any time something out of the ordinary took place.

Most of them didn't.

Their careers had suffered for it. Their support had taken a hit. They'd refused to use the tricks other paranormal teams with less integrity used on their fake television shows. Which was a big reason F.A.U.S.T.'s cable show had been cancelled after two seasons. Viewers didn't want speculation, no matter how educated the guess. They tuned in to see results. Evidence. Proof. Their ratings slumped. So, when he and Claudia decided not to take the network up on their offer to 'conjure' a few spirits with the help of their production team, their plug was pulled. Now they produced their own videos and uploaded them to their YouTube channel, letting their handful of loyal fans decide for themselves which haunts may or may not be real.

Despite it all, Börne's hopes remained high at the start of every new job. He had to stay optimistic. Otherwise, what was the point?

Börne walked to the foot of the stairs and looked up. He could hear their host talking on the phone. By the sound of it, somebody was having a bad day.

"Could be awhile," he said, turning back to Claudia. "Wanna, you know…" He smiled and arched his eyebrows a couple times.

Claudia chuckled and surveyed the drab basement. "Not quite the setting girls fantasize about. Besides—"

The clomping of footsteps on the stairs cut her thoughts short. As the footsteps grew louder, Börne turned to Claudia with a shrug.

"Guess it's a good thing you turned me down."

The woman emerged at the foot of the steps.

"Why is it so damn hard for people to follow simple orders?" she asked. She used her thumbs to type something on her cell phone before sliding it into the front pocket of a pristine green apron. "So, you two. What do you have for me?"

Börne looked first to Claudia, gauging whether they were both on the same page. When his partner nodded, he turned back to the shop owner.

"Well, I'm sorry to say," he said, "we're not finding any evidence of the paranormal down here. Likely, it's a water pipe or your HVAC system making your noise. As for the handprints—"

"A water pipe?" The woman wore a scowl as she split her scorn between the two of them. "You think the noise we hear coming from down here is a damn water pipe?"

"I'm sorry," Claudia said, shrugging. "I'm not connecting with anything or anyone down here."

Börne began gathering and stowing the few pieces of equipment he had trucked down to the basement. Most of his equipment remained in the car out front. No use bringing it all down until they knew there was a need for it. And more because of their host's attitude than the fact they weren't having any luck summoning spirits, their work here was done.

As Claudia headed toward the stairs, the woman's irritation showed through, "Guess I'll try somebody else. Someone better."

"With all due respect, ma'am," Börne said, passing the woman on his way to the stairs, "there is no one better."

NINE

Nick stood on The Chamberlain's front steps scrolling through Google's list of local ghost hunters on his phone. While doing so, he also kept an eye on the young man twirling the colorful, arrow-shaped sign down on the sidewalk. The words 'now open' were emblazoned across the piece of cardboard. After the kid dropped the sign for the sixth time, Nick sighed out loud. Who had come up with such a ridiculous job anyway? Who had decided that twirling an advertisement was a skill worthy of getting paid money for? But the more he thought about it, the more he realized: if anyone was the boob in this scenario, it was him. He was the one shelling out almost ten bucks an hour for the kid's services.

He had to do something. It had been six weeks since the nightmarish opening night, and business at The Chamberlain was nearly nonexistent. Word around town was there was something either seriously wrong with the theater, or seriously wrong with its owner. Had the stress of remodeling and reopening the theater been too much for him? Had he flipped his wig that night and taken all those pills hoping to end it all? These were but a few of the theories going around.

Nick remembered little from opening night, so he didn't have a theory of his own.

The rumors spread like a virus, reaching all corners of the state, mutating as rumors often do. Occasionally one would make its way back to him while he sat in a bar or stood in line at the bank. He'd been pegged as everything from a haunted theater's unfortunate owner, to an out-of-control drug addict, to a deranged cult leader intent on recruiting the town's young for full moon sacrifices.

The less than flattering opening night review Miss Park had written for the newspaper hadn't helped matters.

And when strange occurrences started manifesting at the theater in the coming weeks—bursting light bulbs, unruly seats tossing patrons to the floor, the ever-present stench of stale smoke—the townsfolk flipped the script on his opening night episode. His hallucinations were simple hallucinations no more. They were now considered premonitions, a harbinger of things to come. The Chamberlain quickly earned the reputation of being cursed. When word hit the Internet, accounts of its phenomena began popping up on blogs and websites catering to fans of the paranormal. Only two groups of people were buying a ticket these days: paranormal enthusiasts, and vacationers unaware of the theater's growing reputation. Most nights, Nick showed films to mere handfuls of people. If he was lucky.

And if there was one thing he wasn't when it came to business, it was lucky.

He had to do something.

Despite their small numbers, enthusiasts in search of their own personal ghost story rarely walked away empty handed. It was as if the theater had taken on a personality all its own, and not one with a sunny disposition. Even those seeking phenomena sometimes got more than they bargained for. Bumps, bruises, minor cuts. The seats sometimes shook so hard, patrons would find themselves ass-up on the concrete floor. Exploding light bulbs rained slivers of glass that found their way into eyes, ears and hair. A handful of customers had required minor medical attention, causing Nick to spend many nights lying awake in bed, expecting to be sued or shut down. Neither had happened, and he continued to grapple with whether that was a godsend or curse.

He had to do something.

His search for "ghost hunters near me" had been a shot in the dark. More for a laugh than anything. He didn't actually expect any listings to come up. And while none of the entries looked professional or instilled much confidence, that he'd found enough to constitute an actual list surprised him. Though few were what he considered 'near him.'

The kid with the sign attempted to spin it behind his back and failed.

Nick continued to scroll, doing his best to ignore the debacle taking place on the sidewalk. He was about to retreat into the cool air of the theater when he recognized a familiar face heading his way. The large man sported a light grey suit, dark sunglasses, and used a folded newspaper to fan himself from the afternoon heat. As he approached The Chamberlain's steps, he took them two at a time.

A dark cloud passed in front of the sun, and Nick's mood soured. He tried to put on a happy face. He more than likely failed.

"Afternoon, Mayor."

"Nick." The mayor's face was glum.

"Too nice of a day to look so down, ain't it?"

On the sidewalk, the cardboard sign once again twirled through the air, bounced out of the kid's hands, then hit the ground. When the wind blew the sign tumbling into the gutter, Nick bit his bottom lip.

Fuck my life.

"Too nice of a day, huh?" Even as the mayor fanned himself, the sweat beads on his forehead multiplied. "Tell that to those blood-thirsty sonsabitches in city council. Nick, I'm telling ya, I just came from a meeting, and if we don't turn this damn theater around, we're both as good as the Titanic. S.U.N.K."

"And here I thought it was too hot for icebergs."

The mayor fake sniggered. "I ain't kidding around, Nick. You better embrace one fact: the whole reason you're still in business after your little fiasco is because I laid my ass on the line for you. You and this damned theater were supposed to save us, remember? Bring people from all over to Angler Bay. Remember?"

Nick remembered alright. Though by his recollection, all he'd wanted to do was own and operate a theater. Make his way in the world, blah, blah, blah. The whole 'saving the town' idea was the mayor's, and for Nick, well, that would be great if it happened. He liked Angler Bay, would love to be part of a revitalization. But, saving his business, his livelihood, his dream was his priority. And possibly, his last chance. Blackwood calling his ambition into question made the devil's sweat break out under his collar.

"Now, the way I see it," the mayor said, pointing the newspaper toward the theater, "you either start promoting the hell out of what's going on in there, start bringing in the freaks who are into that kinda shit, or clean up the mess and start running a viable movie theater where families can come and shell out their hard-earned vacation dollars without concern for their little shits' safety. Vis-à-vis, the original plan."

Nick held his tongue and counted to ten. What was the boiling point of blood, anyway? To say his relationship with the mayor had become strained over the past few weeks was like saying cats and dogs didn't always see eye to eye.

"You don't have to remind me of the importance here, Mayor." Nick envisioned himself punching Blackwood in the teeth, sending the guy somersaulting down the steps to the sidewalk. He smiled a little inside. "But there's more to what's going on in there than a 'mess' that can just be cleaned up."

The mayor snapped him in the chest with the folded-up newspaper.

"Look at the numbers, Nick." The mayor turned away and started down the steps. "A fuckin' mess is exactly what we've got here."

Nick smirked at the mayor's use of "we," like they were in it together or something. If that were the case, then why did he feel all the weight was on his shoulders? "Think I'm gonna call someone," he said. "There are these shows on TV—"

Blackwood stopped halfway down the steps. "Hey, you gotta make a call, then make a call. Make five of 'em. Make as many as it damn well takes."

"I need someone to come out and investigate," he said. "Figure out what's going on in there. According to the paranormal websites I've searched—"

"Ghostbusters?" The mayor full-on chuckled. "You shittin' me, Fallon? That's your plan?"

Nick looked away, his mood now beyond saving, despite the ideal weather.

"Hey," the mayor continued, turning away. "Do, what ya gotta do. I mean, shit. Who am I to judge? I'm only the dumb bastard who gifted you this golden goose."

As the man strolled down the steps toward the sidewalk, Nick hoped the sign would get away from the kid one more time and smack him upside the head. Maybe take out an eye.

He had no such luck.

As the credits rolled on the evening's final showing, Nick chucked a tub of buttered popcorn into the trashcan. He was glad he'd only made one tub's worth, which was pathetic in and of itself. But these were the tricks of the trade when running a theater that too often showed its films to a room full of empty seats. You make one tub of popcorn. If it sells, you make another. If it doesn't, you don't lose as much money. And on the off chance someone requested two tubs, well then, he would worry about that trifling dilemma if and when it happened.

Now that he was The Chamberlain's sole employee, all the tasks fell on his shoulders, even the mundane duties like cleaning out the popcorn popper. Nobody wanted to work at the theater. Help was hard enough to find before opening night. Since then, all the ads he'd placed had gone unanswered. Even Manny had taken his engineering talents elsewhere, citing his own lack of desire to do the mundane jobs.

But Nick wasn't naïve. There was more to his engineer leaving than a fear of a greasy popcorn popper.

When the auditorium doors opened, the evening's only four customers spilled out into the lobby. The teenagers, two young men dressed in black from head to toe, and their bleak-looking girlfriends, started making their way through the lobby. One of the young men wore a dark grey skullcap, despite the summer heat. All four flaunted black and grey ink everywhere skin showed, and none of them would make it through a metal detector without setting it off.

They were society's fringe, and Nick was grateful to have them.

"Hey, bra," said the skullcap, with three silver rings in his eyebrow and two in his lip. "We want our money back."

Nick cringed.

Here we go.

He was getting used to refund requests when those unaware of the theater's growing reputation were surprised by the occurrences. Most of the time, he'd put up a fight, try to convince the unhappy customers it was all part of the show. But there were some things, like an exploding exit sign sending plastic shrapnel into the audience, that couldn't be explained as such. He could only shrug his shoulders at that point. Easy come, easy go.

It didn't mean it wasn't getting old.

"Yeah, man." The other young lad was a good half a foot shorter than his girlfriend. It didn't stop him from walking with his arm cocked up, draped around her neck. It looked awkward. It looked ridiculous. He looked like he was hanging on for dear life. "Nothin' happened."

Nick choked on his own saliva. "Wait. Nothing happened?"

The two young men shook their heads in unison, as if they shared a brain. The young ladies never lifted their eyes from their cell phones, both clad in pink spider web cases. No irony there.

"So, no mist?" Nick asked. "No wind? What about the seats? Did they move around?"

"We got all that, man." The kid shrugged. "It was cute."

"So…" Nick cocked an eyebrow. *Wait, a second.* Did they really want their money back *because* nothing out of the ordinary happened? Not possible. "You're kidding me, right? You paid for a movie, and now you want a refund because a movie was all you got?"

"We didn't pay for the movie, yo." The taller kid spoke with his tattooed hands, emphasizing every other word with a gesture. "Could give two shits about the movie. We paid to see some sick shit go down. All we got was a butt massage and some wind in our hair—"

Nick nodded to skull cap. "And you felt left out, am I right?"

The young man ignored the cut and kept talking.

"We wanted to see some ghost-type shit. Like everyone is talkin' about online. And like he said, ain't nothin' happened."

"Yeah, man. Fuckin' lame."

Nick was no genius, didn't have to be to realize he wasn't winning over these two jerkoffs. He would have had better luck convincing Jason Voorhees to stop killing sexually active camp counselors. He'd refund their money alright. He simply couldn't believe it had come to this. How ridiculous the situation at the theater had gotten.

"Come on." Nick walked over to the ticket booth, followed close behind by the fearsome foursome. A minute later, he counted out their money and laid it on the counter. "There ya go. Thirty-two dollars. Can I assume the Twizzlers and Slushies were to your satisfaction? Or will you be needing a refund for those, too?"

"Nah, man," skullcap said, scooping up the cash. "They was alright."

He watched the four teens exit through the front door. As he followed, he couldn't help but chuckle through the awkwardness. Maybe he should close the theater and open up a candy shop. The sweet stuff was the only thing he was making a profit on. Nobody ever returned their box of Whoppers because they *didn't* find stale pieces inside.

As he turned the lock on the door, a young woman's ghostly face appeared in the glass. He jumped, nearly losing control of his bladder. *Holy shit!* Recovering, he couldn't help but chuckle again and shake his head. If he was easily frightened, then he was the wrong owner for The Chamberlain.

The girl rapped on the glass.

He turned the lock back and opened the door. "Change your mind about the Twizzlers?"

The young lady was cute. Her impish smile and diamond-studded dimples were both brighter when she wasn't staring down at her phone. Catching another glimpse of her date standing on the sidewalk, Nick determined she could do better.

"You know what would be cool, man?" she said before popping her gum. "If you called these guys."

The young lady opened her white denim vest, revealing a black t-shirt underneath. Emblazoned on the shirt was the image of a woman: pale-skinned, flowing auburn-red hair, dressed in a long black gown with a blood red parasol resting on her shoulder; and a man: equally pale, spikey blond hair, also dressed in black save for a white frilly shirt and a vest the color of a good cabernet. A grey and white wolf sat obediently at the man's feet. In the background sat a long, black hearse. It was night in the photo, and a larger than life-sized moon hung over their shoulders. The letters F.A.U.S.T. glowed beneath the scene in neon yellow letters.

"Faust." He remembered the name from his lit courses in college. Faust was a character in German folklore who sold his soul to the devil for knowledge. Cool story, but he didn't see the connection. "Why would I call them?"

"They investigate places like this," she said. "Haunted places." The raised eyebrows and the way her statement lifted at the end like a question told Nick she couldn't believe he hadn't heard of F.A.U.S.T. Like they were a household name or something.

"Ghost hunters?"

The girl now popped her gum even as she spoke. "They explore haunted places, film it, and post the videos online. Even had their own TV show. They're, like, famous, dude. Maybe they can make this ghost thing work for ya. Or get rid of it, if that's what you want."

Nick looked at the photo on her shirt again. "They look like ghosts themselves."

The girl let out a sigh and allowed her jacket to fall back over her shirt.

"Never know, might be good for publicity, nothin' else." The girl looked around the theater lobby, then back at him. "Looks like you could use some of that, old man."

With a boisterous pop of her gum and middle finger in his direction, she was gone.

Old man?

Locking the door behind her, Nick fought the urge to return the gesture.

TEN

Nick's kitchen doubled as a home office. With stacks of paper everywhere, the table saw more use as a desk than anything. Three of its four chairs gathered more dust than butts. He hadn't been in town long enough to make any real friends. At least that's what he told himself. He also used the excuse he'd been too busy with the new business. The excuses depended on the day and his mood. Only thing he knew for sure was, as things regressed at The Chamberlain, the likelihood of his making friends would more than likely remain on the same downward trajectory.

He downed the swill at the bottom of beer number five and set the bottle beside numbers one through four. He'd never been much of a beer drinker, but some unseen magnet in The Sand Dollar Carryout's neon sign had pulled his car into the lot on his way home that night. It had been a long day. And having recently sworn off prescription medicine—some might call it being scared straight— he had to fill the void with something. The humidity of the summer night had suggested a cold beer would go down nicely.

It hadn't been wrong.

Now, with his laptop open on the table, the name F.A.U.S.T. stared back at him.

Börne and Claudia Forrester. A husband-and-wife ghost hunting team who were, as described, relatively famous. At least in the world of paranormal research. He perused their website, finding YouTube video after YouTube video of the Finding Apparitions and Uninvited Spirits Team. More affectionately known as F.A.U.S.T. Each video had at least fifty-thousand views. He'd heard the term "internet star" before but hadn't known what it meant until now.

The website was simple. Photos of dusty old televisions, screens full of static. An antique doll slumped in a rocker, the passing of time and shadows gave the child's plaything a sinister aura in the black and white photos. Grainy images of old houses and what looked to be an abandoned hospital or insane asylum. He wasn't sure which and didn't really care. The building was creepy either way. And coming from a guy whose theater had become spirit central as of late, that was saying something. Crimson words scrolled across the screen, telling him to 'enter if he dared.' It was the only color on the page, unless shades of grey and black were considered 'colors.'

He yawned and twisted the top off the last remaining beer. He was beyond drunk. Another twelve ounces of pale ale in his belly ensured he'd have a hangover in the morning, but he felt obligated. It seemed wrong to drink its five buddies, but not beer number six. He flicked the metal cap across the table toward the others. He took a long drink, winced, then turned his attention back to the screen.

He blinked. He opened his eyes wide and pulled his lower lids down with his fingers, trying to make them focus. He blinked a couple more times.

The word 'ENTER' hovered in the middle of the screen, fading in and out like a ghost. Was it him, or were the letters blurry as all hell? He maneuvered the arrow to the center of the screen and waited for the prompt to fade back in. It took its sweet time while his head swam through pale ale waves. He could feel himself fading in and out. Growing impatient, he repeatedly clicked the mouse until the word reappeared behind it.

"Gotcha!" he exclaimed when it finally appeared.

The screen went dark.

When it came back on seconds later, an image of a beautiful woman with sultry, long red hair graced the screen. Her eyes blazed a wild green as they peered deep into Nick's soul. Beside her, a toe-headed man leaned against a hearse. Both dressed all in black, both resembled fabled creatures of the night.

It took him a few seconds to put two and two together: it was the same couple as on the young lady's t-shirt.

The couple known as F.A.U.S.T.

After clicking through a few more gritty videos showing Börne and Claudia Forrester creeping around old decrepit buildings, usually at night and sometimes in night vision green, Nick had seen enough. If anyone could help with the disturbances at The Chamberlain, it was these two. Plus, he needed to get to bed. Morning was guaranteed to be a ball buster, and the longer he put off sleep, the worse it would be. He'd blame The Sand Dollar and its damn neon sign.

Before shutting down his computer, however, he scrolled the mouse to the top of the screen, took a deep breath, and clicked on the link that said 'CONTACT.'

Börne Forrester set down his black bag filled with video equipment and stretched his back out. It had been a long night of climbing rickety stairs, lugging equipment, and capturing nothing of real importance to show for it. The old Porter farmhouse had been a bust. And damned if it hadn't started out so promising. The property's backstory checked all the right boxes: a multi-generational homestead; folks described as quiet who kept to themselves; rumors of incest and marital rape dating back to the turn of the century; the death of a young girl at the hands of her schizophrenic stepmother. The decrepit, old building had all the makings of a classic haunting.

Yet, once again, they'd captured nothing. Not on film and not on audio.

Tapping the space bar on his keyboard, he woke the computer. The motor started to hum. While he waited for the screen to come alive, he dropped into the wheeled chair in front of what amounted to his desk. The office was makeshift, set up in an alcove of their dining room with a short counter that could be used for little else. It was an odd architectural aspect of their Chicago home, something not found in the houses back home in Germany, but it served a purpose. Answering fan mail and editing countless hours of video footage required little space.

Claudia sauntered into the room and ran a hand over his shoulder, up his neck and through his blond hair. An open bottle of wine sat breathing on the table. She set a pair of crystal and pewter wine glasses beside the bottle. Pulling out one of the dinette chairs, she dropped into it. She let out a sigh of relief when she drew the silver zipper down the length of her calf. Her new pair of spike stiletto stretch boots with the 7" heel were sexy as heck, and played a huge role in her personae, but comfortable they were not. She kicked her bare feet up onto the chair beside her. She crossed one bare ankle over the other and flexed her toes.

"Well, that was more fun than anyone should ever have." Sarcasm stained her words as she reached for the tall, green bottle. Tilting it sideways, she poured the ruby-red *Spätburgunder* into one glass. She didn't stop until the glass was full, well past the standard level. "Not sure this bottle's enough to drown out this evening, but it's a start." She slid the glass of wine across the table toward Börne, then went about pouring a glass of her own.

He scrolled through two days-worth of new emails, none of which piqued his interest. At least none that couldn't wait until morning. He spun his chair away from the desk and took up the glass of wine.

"To what are we drinking?" he asked, kneading his wife's foot with his free hand.

Claudia ran her fingertip around the rim of the glass.

"How about the simple fact this evening is over."

Börne's lips curled into a wicked smile. He let go of her foot and slid his hand up her leg. "Who said it was over?"

She leaned down, looked at him from behind hooded eyes, and placed her lips within reach.

"Prost," she whispered.

Börne closed the distance and gifted his wife a kiss. Pulling away, he clinked his glass with hers.

"Prost."

He had just sat back and taken a sip of wine when the computer binged. A new email. His attention shifted across the room to the monitor.

"Leave it," she said.

He took another sip before setting down his glass and shrugging.

"Force of habit," he said, then rolled his chair back to the desk. After clicking on the subject line, he began perusing the latest email.

"Worth interrupting the moment for?" Claudia asked, unbuttoning the top two buttons on her dress. Tipping her head back, she reduced the amount of wine in her glass by a third.

"Maybe." When he finished reading the email, he scrolled back up and read it again. "Interesting, at least."

Claudia dipped her nose into her glass, savored the hint of cherry. "You going to share?"

Börne spun around so he faced her. "How would you feel about a trip to the beach?"

Claudia laughed. She held dear her alabaster skin. Protected it. Her image was nothing without it.

"Do I look like someone who enjoys spending time at the beach?"

"Okay, then," he said, his smile returning. "How about a dark and creepy movie theater?"

ELEVEN

Thirty-three.

That was how many tickets Nick sold over the next week. Not even a fourth of the theater had they all shown up at once. And the smart money would bet even those numbers wouldn't continue.

Part of the reason they were so high was because of the busload of cosplayers from a horror convention being held in nearby Wilmington. They all piled in on a Friday evening, all dressed in horror getup. It was his first experience with cosplay, and he'd been impressed. Every subgenre of horror had been represented. There was a Jason, a Freddy, all manners of aliens and demons, and not one, but two seductive vampiresses. Flesh-eating zombies made appearances in one version or another, some more realistic than others. One unfortunate soul even left a severed arm behind in the men's restroom. Nick kept the prop under the concession counter, but doubted anyone would be returning for it.

So Tuesday, when two cosplayers knocked on The Chamberlain's glass door an hour before the first scheduled showing, he wondered if the convention was still going on.

"Sorry," Nick said, poking his head out the door. "The first show isn't until one. Doors don't open 'til 12:30." He looked the pair up and down, then gave them a thumbs up. "Great costumes, though."

The woman looked at the man. The man looked at her. They both looked back at Nick.

"We are looking for Nick Fallon." The man's accent was heavy, thick with European influence. Austrian, maybe German. He tilted his head forward. He slid his dark, red-lensed sunglasses down the slope of his nose to reveal icy blue eyes. "Would you know where we could find him?"

It was Nick's turn to look from one to the other. There was something familiar about the twosome. The woman's flowing red hair. Her skin, pale as a cloud. Both clad in black from head to toe despite the summer heat. He knew them from somewhere, he just couldn't settle on where. Then it hit him, and he shook his head. How drunk had he been that night?

"Wait. F.A.U.S.T., right?" He pointed at the twosome, literally wagged his finger at them. He caught himself and self-consciously pulled his hand back and slid it into his front pocket. "Sorry. But you are, right? You're the ghost hunters."

The man and woman exchanged another glance, this time with visible scowls, as if something in his declaration had caused them pain.

"We are F.A.U.S.T., yes." The woman nodded. "I am Claudia Forrester, and this is my husband, Börne." Her voice was sultry, an octave deeper than most. "But, ghost hunters, we are not. We are paranormal investigators. Ghost hunters are frat boys who measure their testosterone levels by stumbling around abandoned warehouses, using cell phone cameras to *capture* things they want you to believe they see and hear. I'm afraid we don't do anything of the sort. May we come in any way?"

Nick stood, mouth agape, blocking the doorway. It was as if he'd never been taught simple manners. His mother, *God rest her soul*, would be ashamed.

"Shit. Absolutely." He stepped aside, holding the door so the two could enter. Once they had passed through the doorway, he glanced out to the street. A freshly waxed black hearse sat out front, already attracting a crowd. One man cupped his hands around his face, trying to peer through the dark, tinted windows. Nick shook his head. It was as if the circus had come to town. He closed and locked the door before his two guests drew attention his way. Turning to them, he smiled and spread his arms wide. "Welcome to The Chamberlain Theater."

Both nodded their appreciation before turning away.

Claudia wandered further into the lobby, the sound of her high-heeled boots echoing throughout the quiet lobby. She pivoted her focus to the ceiling. With her head tilted back, her flowing auburn hair cascaded all the way to her black, leather-clad rear end. She ambled about the room, eyes glued to the ceiling. Concentration hardened her face as she peered into every nook and cranny. It was as if she were looking into the lobby's soul.

Nick joined the woman in her observation of the ceiling. All he saw were the white, decorative ceiling tiles, sections of intersecting silver ductwork, and two large fans that kept the lobby about fifteen degrees cooler than the outside. He sidled up to the concession counter, leaned against it, and crossed his arms over his chest.

"What's she doing?" he asked, keeping his voice low.

The husband, Börne, hovered nearby. "Getting a sense of their temperament."

Nick's brow wrinkled. "Their?"

Börne nodded. He pulled a pewter pocket watch from a slit in his vest, then replaced it seconds later. "The spirits."

Nick's attention returned to the ceiling. "Really? You think there are spirits here?"

Börne slid his sunglasses up onto his head, nestled them in his spiky blond hair.

"If they're here," he said, nodding, "she'll find them."

Nick frowned. "But… here in the lobby? Nothing's ever—"

The sound of an opening auditorium door severed the end of his sentence. The wooden door squealed enough to alert Nick and the Forresters to its movement. Everyone stopped what they were doing and turned in the auditorium's direction.

Seconds later, a bright light broke through the open doorway and illuminated the auditorium. Music sprung through its speakers. It seemed as if the auditorium was trying to capture their attention, if not lure them in.

"Anyone else here?" Börne asked, now standing beside Nick.

Nick stared at the door, dumbfounded, and shook his head.

"Excellent." Claudia's booming voice echoed throughout the empty lobby. "When can we start?"

Nick turned to Claudia. Though he was certain she'd asked the question of him, her eyes were alert and focused on her husband. Börne returned her gaze with eyebrows raised.

"Um… The first show of the day is in less than an hour, if you'd like to sit in," Nick offered.

Claudia thought about it. At least it looked like she was considering it. Her mind appeared hard at work on something. She drew in her bottom lip. She glanced again at the auditorium's open door, then gave the lobby another once over. She shook her head.

"I don't think so." She sauntered over to the counter and curtsied in Nick's direction. "But thank you all the same." She pulled her sunglasses out of her fiery mane and placed them back over her eyes. "Tonight, though, you shall be closed, yes? We will return around eleven o'clock. I assume that works for you?"

Nick was about to answer that yes, due to a city ordinance restricting how late downtown businesses could remain open, eleven o'clock would indeed work for him. But his answer was deemed unnecessary when Claudia started toward the door without waiting for one. He returned a nod from Börne, who had also replaced his sunglasses, and followed the husband-and-wife team to the front door and out onto the steps.

"See you guys at eleven, then?"

Claudia tossed a queen's wave over her shoulder as the Forresters glided down the concrete steps toward the sidewalk and their awaiting hearse.

Nick assumed that meant they were indeed on for eleven o'clock. Then he cautioned himself. He could already tell that making assumptions with these two would most likely not serve him well.

They hadn't even wanted to see the auditorium.

After signing a few autographs and kindly dispersing the crowd that had gathered around the hearse, Börne unlocked the passenger door and opened it wide.

"That didn't take much convincing."

Claudia stepped up to the car, but stopped short of getting in. She turned and looked up at The Chamberlain's marquee. The façade was old, grey stone in need of a good power washing. The tall, red letters were showing their age in spots. Its glass doors and ticket booth window, however, gleamed in the sunlight, making mirrors of both.

"Let's just say I got a feeling," she said, turning and climbing into the passenger seat. "This one'll be worth the trip."

Börne shut the car door, then nodded and waved to the few lingering onlookers as he made his way around the front of the hearse.

"Yeah?" he said once he'd climbed behind the wheel and shut his door. "You mean, I did good this time?" He started the car's engine and pulled away from the curb toward their hotel.

"You did good, my dear." Claudia rested her hand on Börne's thigh. "Though after the Wrigleyville debacle, the bar's been set pretty low."

Börne snickered. "I'll never live that one down, will I?"

Claudia smiled. She closed her eyes and rested the back of her head against the headrest. "Not as long as I'm around."

TWELVE

Nori Park clicked on the 'send' icon and sat back in her chair. After several starts and stops, her latest article was finally on its way to her editor for review. The mayor and city council were butting heads on budgetary matters. Specifically, how to pay for a much-needed sand dune restoration project. It wasn't Black Lives Matter. It wasn't #MeToo. It wasn't anything exciting or even noteworthy to most. But someone had to keep the townsfolk—at least the few who cared—apprised of what went on in their town. No matter how mundane those matters may be. And, for better or worse, she was that someone.

The sky through the newsroom windows had been blue when she'd started her article. She'd watched it morph into a rich orange, then purple, and finally a deep black. One by one, the tiny offices along her corridor had also gone dark. About an hour ago, a dull ache had settled in her lower back. She'd been sitting too long. Her rumbling stomach was a reminder that her social life wasn't the only thing she'd been neglecting. But that's how it went when she was up against a deadline. All non-essentials were eligible for sacrifice.

Nori picked up her cell phone and checked the time. *9:23*. Mrs. Chang, the owner of the Chinese restaurant near her apartment, shut down her woks at 10:00, sometimes earlier if business was slow. She needed to get moving if she was going to make her date with the couch, a glass of white wine, and a steaming bowl of shrimp lo meine. It wasn't the food of her homeland, but it was a close second. She also wanted to squeeze in at least a couple hours of Netflix before shuffling off to bed. She was tired of plugging her ears when people in the office started talking about the latest episode of the shows she liked. She was about four episodes behind on her current series and needed to fix that.

Nori closed her email and brought up the Reuters news website one last time. It seemed things were happening all over. Turkey was waking to another terrorist bombing. A nightclub shooting in Texas. Wildfires in California. All big stories, all terrible events for anyone involved. Anyone except those in the media. A necessary evil, bad news put food on their tables, gas in their cars. It covered the rising costs of healthcare. And nobody on Nori's side made any apologies for it, no matter how much they were judged and sometimes derided for it.

There were times she dreamed of being in the thick of things, reporting on the stories the entire country, if not the world, were tuning in for. However, because that kind of work could take an emotional toll, there were also times she was thankful she wasn't.

Then sometimes she felt lost. Neither thankful, nor preoccupied with what could be. Lately, boredom had set in. So much so, the tendrils of indecision were infiltrating her thoughts, consuming them. She had three options: remain content with the quiet life and uninteresting job; move somewhere more exciting where reportable things happened; or find a new profession altogether. No one option outshined the others. Each had its pros and cons. She knew her parents' preference. Short of moving back home to South Korea, they would love for her to stay right where she was, living life out of harm's way. To them, boring meant safe. To Nori, it simply meant boring.

"Hey, Park!"

Callie Lipton, her best friend and the newspaper's junior editor, popped her head through the newsroom door. Hailing from

New York City, Nori often wondered about the career choice Callie had made. Moving away from arguably the biggest, most news-active city in the world, she'd settled in little old Angler Bay, North Carolina, home to beautiful sand and surf and little else. Heck, they'd only recently gotten a Starbucks. Callie claimed to welcome the peace, the slow-paced lifestyle. For the first fifteen years of her career, she lived through and reported on everything the Big Apple could throw at her. Survived it, as she liked to tell it. Now she relished her position as Number Two at the Angler Bay Standard, the sleepiest rag on Earth. All newspapers had the occasional slow news day. For The Standard, it was like one long, never-ending slow news day.

Mr. Dingle's wayward cats were bigger celebrities around town than the Kardashians.

"Jason and I are heading over to The Galley for drinks and a late dinner," Callie said. "Apparently, he's in the mood for oysters. So, you know what that means."

Her wink and smile told Nori everything she needed to know about how the Liptons would be spending their evening once they got home. Nori and Callie had had more than one conversation about Jason, his oysters, and how they affected his libido. Not only was it more information than Nori needed to know, but also the reason she had to hold in her smirk every time she saw him.

"Think I'll take a raincheck." She glanced at the time before shutting down her computer. "You kids have fun, though."

"Oh, you know we will," Another wink and smile. "Maybe this weekend?"

"As long as aliens don't invade our little town, or anything else interesting enough to keep me glued to my desk."

"Cool!" Callie said. "Jason's talking about taking out the boat, cruise up the coast. If it goes anything like usual, he'll fish, and I'll lay in the sun drinking mango hard seltzers until he gets frustrated with not catching anything and we head home. It's a whole thing.

You're coming along this time."

"Sounds like an offer I'd be crazy to refuse." Nori rose from her chair and started gathering her things. "My doctor's been hounding me to work more mango hard seltzers into my diet, anyway. Works out perfectly."

"Outstanding!" Callie flashed her signature smile. A model's smile. A movie star's smile. It was Nori's belief her friend should be making headlines, not reporting them. "Talk more tomorrow?"

She answered with a simple nod.

Callie danced her fingertips on the doorframe before vanishing.

Slinging her satchel up onto her shoulder, Nori swiped her cell and keys.

Callie reappeared in the doorway. "Hey!"

Startled, Nori jumped and dropped her keys on the floor. "Shit, Callie!"

"Sorry." Callie chuckled. "Almost forgot, though. Heard some chatter this afternoon that might interest you. Sounds like there's something going on over at The Chamberlain."

THIRTEEN

It had been a quiet day at the theater. Even by The Chamberlain's standards. Nick hadn't sold a single ticket. Hadn't bothered to show a film. Around 2:30, a woman poked her head into the lobby, but only to inquire about using the restroom. He couldn't even interest her in a snack for the road. Losing money on this latest business venture was becoming a full-time job. An occupation he was all too familiar with, and unfortunately, getting good at. So far, he had ignored the phone calls from his accountant. Unless he had a rich uncle, who'd kicked the bucket and left him his fortune, she wasn't calling to pass along good news. He didn't return her texts, nor open her emails. Avoiding one's accountant wasn't the best way to run a business. But then, could owning a theater that never saw asses in its seats be considered "running a business?"

For at least the second time that day, he wondered if calling in the paranormal investigators would make a difference. Did he even believe in ghosts? It was a question he'd never considered until he'd been forced to. He still didn't have an answer, couldn't explain the things happening in the auditorium. Ultimately, he'd let them take a look, do whatever it was they did, and see what they had to say. It couldn't hurt either way. Nothing else, perhaps he'd get some publicity out of the whole thing.

It was 10:55, and Nick was sitting on the concession counter munching his way through his second bag of Twizzlers when he saw the members of F.A.U.S.T. walking up the front steps. Bathed in the harsh light from the overhead marquee, their pale features appeared even more opaque. Nick hopped down from his perch and met them at the door.

"Good evening, Mr. Fallon."

He nodded to Claudia, then Börne as they passed through the doorway. "Good evening."

He closed the door behind them, his attention immediately drawn to Claudia. He couldn't help it. Her transformation commanded it. The black leather pants and boots from earlier in the day were gone. Her black top, too. She'd swapped it all for a long, flowing white gown that concealed her feet and trailed like a shadow in her wake. She didn't walk across the floor as much as glided across it as she made her way around the lobby, refamiliarizing herself with the nearly century-old room.

Mesmerized, Nick couldn't tear his eyes away.

"I could use a hand."

He started at the voice beside him. "Sorry?"

"My equipment," Börne said. "From the car? I could use some help to bring it all in." He seemed annoyed, causing Nick to wonder if he hadn't been staring at the man's wife a little too long. Or too admiringly.

"Right. Sure."

He followed Börne out, leaving Claudia staring off into space. For the first time since they'd arrived, he noticed Börne, who had also dressed more elaborately than he had that morning. Black was still the order of the day, from his top hat to his boots. He draped himself in a long black frock with silver buttons down the front and tails that hit behind the knees. Only his ruffled white dress shirt and burgundy red vest stood apart from the black of everything else. To Nick, the guy looked like a gothic superhero. The two of them were sure to draw attention anywhere they went in Angler Bay.

In contrast, Nick felt more than a little underdressed in his khakis, light blue button down, and sensible loafers.

"So, do they always hang out near the ceiling?" he asked as they descended the steps to the street.

"What do you mean?" Börne asked.

"She's always looking up at the ceiling," Nick explained. "This morning you said she was gauging the temperament of the spirits. So, I was wondering if they typically hang out up there?"

Börne shrugged as he swung open the rear door of the hearse. "Not usually."

"But she is looking for spirits…"

"Could be." When Börne looked up at him for the first time since stepping outside, a smirk pulled at the corner of his mouth, and he winked. "Could be my wife studied gothic architecture at university and likes old buildings."

Two trips to the car.

Four black cases, a laptop bag, and a duffle bag.

By the time they were done, they'd erected a mini pyramid of paranormal research and video equipment in front of the concession stand. It seemed the Forresters weren't ones to travel light. Or waste time. Börne began rooting through his duffle bag. Claudia ventured down the hallway toward Nick's office and storage room.

And Nick stood there, hands in his pockets, caught somewhere between anticipation and skepticism.

"So." Börne pulled out a laptop, flipped it open, and started tapping away at the keyboard. "We did some research. Your theater has some interesting history, Mr. Fallon. One incident stood out. I mean, *way* out. Like a nun at a gentleman's club. Tell us what you know about Floyd Cropper."

The couple's roles had switched since their visit earlier in the day. This morning, Claudia had been the only one of the two investigators who spoke. Except for a brief exchange between him and Nick, Börne may as well have been a mute who'd had his tongue removed. Now, though, he seemed to run the show. The F.A.U.S.T. team had been there ten minutes, and Claudia had yet to utter a single word.

"I'm sorry," Nick said, remembering Börne's request. "Who?"

Börne repeated the name.

Even after hearing it aloud a second time, it still didn't ring Nick's bell. *Floyd Cropper.* Seemed like he'd heard the name before, somewhere, but he had no idea who it belonged to. His lack of poker face must have betrayed his ignorance, because Claudia spoke up. And when she did, Nick wondered if he should be taking notes.

"In all the years since The Chamberlain has existed," she said, floating through the lobby, "Angler Bay has seen only three tragic deaths. What I would consider tragic, at least. Deaths above and beyond a simple car crash here or there. Two young boys, ages ten and twelve. Took their boat out one night and were never seen again. Talk is they drowned or were washed out to sea. Never found the boat, either."

Nick nodded. "The mayor's boys."

"I'm sorry?"

He looked up at Claudia. "Stephen and Mitchel Blackwood. They were the mayor's sons. Though he wasn't the mayor yet. This was back in the eighties, I think. Story goes, it was Mitchel's little rowboat. Got it for his birthday. They apparently couldn't wait 'til morning like they were told, so they snuck out at night to try out the boat." He shrugged. "And, like you said, were never seen nor heard from again."

"Damn," Börne said. "That's enough to kill a man."

"Or render him senselessly mean," Nick said.

Börne nodded. "Or that."

"There's still a debate around town," Nick continued. "Some people say losing his sons made the mayor the way he is. Others argue his demeanor is why he lost his sons."

Claudia gazed at him, brow furrowed. "I don't follow."

"Rumor is," he continued, "Blackwood was pretty hard on the boys. Would knock 'em around some. Especially when he'd been drinking, I guess. Some swear the boys didn't drown at all. They ran away."

"And what do you believe, Mr. Fallon?" Claudia asked.

Nick shrugged. "Don't know. It was all before I got here. And I've learned first-hand how rumors work in a small town like this. Stick around long enough, and I'm sure you'll hear one or two about me and The Chamberlain."

"Which brings me to your town's third tragedy," Claudia said. "The Chamberlain's previous owner."

"Floyd Cropper," Börne re-iterated, pointing out front. "The old man who started a fire out on those steps, using himself as kindling."

"Oh." Nick exaggerated his nod, trying hard to sell it. "*That* Floyd Cropper." He felt foolish. He continued to nod, a piss poor attempt at stalling. He should offer more, but what could he say? He knew little of the theater's previous owner. Only what Börne had shared. Mr. Cropper had lost the property and set himself on fire in protest. Right or wrong, it was all Nick knew. All he cared to know. Self-preservation and all.

"Seems to me," Börne said, looking up from his laptop, "Floyd Cropper would be a good place to start the conversation, Mr. Fallon. You know, about what's going on in your theater."

"Please, call me Nick. And do you really think so?"

Claudia approached the counter.

"Makes sense, doesn't it? The man had nothing, Nick. No family, other than his wife. No kids. No grandkids. Seems the theater was all Floyd Cropper had. Right up 'til he lost it."

"Literally *and* figuratively," Börne interjected.

"He's so crushed over the loss of his beloved theater," Claudia continued, "that he kills himself violently outside the front door.

Seems to me that's exactly the type of spirit that would want to stick around and cause problems for the next owner. Practically text book."

What was it about Claudia—*her accent?*—that made her so alluring? Not to mention, distracting?

"Uh, yeah," Nick said, clearing the queries from his mind. "I guess you're—"

A sharp rap on the glass door stalled his thought.

Everyone jumped, startled, including the two who dealt with scary things for a living.

Nick joined Claudia and Börne in a chuckle. At least he had an excuse. He wasn't used to all this ghost talk. Still, they hadn't even started yet. Something told him he better get used to it all real quick.

Don't be such a chickenshit, Nick.

But a moment later, when he saw who was pressing their face against the glass, he knew he had cause for worry.

"Shit," he whispered. With a deep sigh, he addressed the husband-and-wife team of F.A.U.S.T. "Excuse me."

He strolled to the front door, taking his time. The taste of Ms. Park's unflattering opening night article crept up the back of his throat like acid reflux. There were a hundred reasons the reporter might knock on his door, but only one of those reasons made sense.

She pulled away from the glass—hands still cupped around her eyes—as he approached.

"Can I help you?" Nick held the door open a mere six inches. It was enough to look the journalist in the eyes, but he wasn't about to give her space enough to slip through.

"Aw, don't be like that, Nick." As she addressed him, Nori's eyes were everywhere but on him. She weaved side to side, up and down, trying to see past him. "You're not still upset about the article, are you?"

His jaw came unhinged. "Seriously? That article is part of the reason there's no one here this evening."

"Oh, there's someone here, alright." She stopped evading him and met his gaze head on. "Their hearse is sitting right there!"

And there it was. The reason the journalist was knocking on his door out of the blue. And at such a late hour.

"Oh, no," he said, shaking his head. He turned back to Börne and Claudia, who appeared to be watching him, and smiled. Then he turned back to Nori, where his smile died. "You're not coming in here. And you're sure as hell not talking to them. Not if I can help it."

Nori bit her bottom lip. Her expression softened. She tugged on her right ear. "Come on, Nick. Maybe I can help."

He feigned a laugh, reminded himself to stay strong. Historically, intelligent and attractive women had been his kryptonite, and he already had one of those on the case.

"Oh," he said, conjuring a bit of sarcasm, "I think you've helped enough, thank you."

"Think about it, Nick." The reporter in her was not easily deterred. A personality trait he recalled from opening night. "Word's gonna get out they're here. It already has. How do you think I found out? So why not let me help publicize the fact? I can put a positive spin on it from the get go."

He thought about it, then thought better of it. "Thought that was the plan a couple months ago. And look how that turned out. You roasted me."

"I absolutely did not." Nori shook her head. "The story we ran was not the story I wrote. My editor made changes. Made it more salacious. In his mind, more interesting. You know what they say, Nick. 'If it bleeds, it leads.' He just made your story bleed more than you would have liked. This, though, this is different. This could be great for you and the theater. Ergo, the town. I'm picturing an in-depth interview up front, get their insights on what's going on in the theater. Then I can chronicle the work they're doing here.

And if all goes right, we put their stamp of approval on The Chamberlain, and let everyone know it's okay to come back."

Nick could feel his defenses crumbling like a sandcastle at high tide, and Nori Park was a rogue wave. It wasn't even her intelligence, or any perceived attraction on Nick's part. Problem was, the points she'd made were more than valid.

"And if all doesn't go right?" he asked.

"Aw come on, Nick." She smiled. "Have some faith."

Nick chuckled, but it wasn't because he found what she'd said humorous. If there was one thing he lacked, besides customers, it was faith. He didn't have faith F.A.U.S.T. could fix what was broken inside the theater. Didn't have faith people would return simply because they said it was okay. And he sure as hell didn't have faith in Nori Park and The Standard doing a one-eighty where their views of him and The Chamberlain were concerned.

But he found it impossible to poke holes in the iron-clad case she was making. The only thing for him to do was admit defeat.

He took a step back and opened the door wide.

"Outstanding!" Nori wasted no time sliding through.

He had to hand it to her. She was nothing if not ambitious. She was already introducing herself to the Forresters by the time he'd shut and locked the front door. As he rejoined them, a little voice told him he would come to regret letting the reporter in. He didn't know when or why, but it was the one thing in which Nick had faith.

"So," Börne said, turning his attention from Nori back to Nick, "can we see this theater?"

FOURTEEN

It was like the intro to a joke: Two paranormal investigators, a journalist, and a failed entrepreneur walk into a theater…

Nick just hoped the joke wasn't on him.

They left the equipment behind and made their way to the heavy oak doors separating the lobby from the auditorium. Traditionally, he kept the doors open right up to the time the previews started. Recently, however, circumstances trumped routine, and he left the doors closed. At all times. Call it superstition, call it a former scout being prepared. Confining the theater's phenomena to one area seemed like plain old good sense.

With his hand on the door handle, Nick hesitated. "Everyone ready?"

Everyone nodded except Nori, who suddenly didn't seem as sure about what she'd signed up for. Understandable. As eager as she was to cover the story, she'd been there on opening night. No doubt she'd also heard the multitude of rumors since. In a small community like Angler Bay, rumors spread like the most aggressive of diseases. Sometimes with the same catastrophic results.

"Yeah," she said. "I'm ready." Though the sullen look in her eyes said otherwise. Nori took in a deep breath, held it for a second, then just as slowly let it out.

Nick exchanged looks with both Börne and Claudia, then turned back to the doors and gave them a tug.

They didn't open.

Didn't even budge.

If anyone had been hoping for a grand reveal, they were disappointed. Nick gave both handles another hard pull. It was as if someone much stronger was on the other side, holding them shut.

"Locked?"

Nick considered Börne's question. They shouldn't be. He never locked the doors. Ever. Not since opening night. And not since keeping them closed had proven sufficient. He looked the doors up and down. Nothing seemed amiss. It made no sense. He let go of the handles and reached into his pockets for his keys. He pulled them out and began sorting through.

Was it possible the doors had locked on their own? It didn't seem likely. It would be a new wrinkle if they had.

"They shouldn't be locked," he said. "Haven't locked them since—"

The sound of creaking wood interrupted him. When he looked up, he couldn't believe his eyes.

The doors stood ajar. As improbable as it was that he'd been unable to open them, it was just as improbable they had opened on their own.

"Interesting." Börne said, exchanging a look with Claudia. "This ever happen before?"

Nick shook his head, bit his lip. "Not at all."

Nori seemed to find the situation just as peculiar. Her eyes narrowed. A storm cloud of concern churned behind them.

Welcome to The Chamberlain, Nick thought.

"Now, before we enter," Claudia said, "I must ask. Nick, are you a religious man?" She turned to Nori. "You?"

Nick and Nori both shook their heads.

"In that case, please humor me as I ask for protection over us."

Nick's eyes widened.

"Protection?" Was she serious? Or was this simply a dramatic part of their act? He looked at Börne to see if he was being put on. The man's expression spoke of utmost seriousness.

"We find it's better to be safe than sorry," Börne said. "And if you don't believe in prayer, that's okay. Sometimes people use this as an opportunity to put themselves in a positive frame of mind. Trust me, keeping an open and positive outlook can be beneficial to the process."

Nick checked in with Nori. Her eyes studied the floor. He turned back to Claudia. Her eyes were closed, her hands stretched out toward them, patiently waiting.

Not without some hesitation, he reached out and took Claudia's hand. Nori caught sight of what was happening and took the other. Börne took Nick and Nori's other hands, closing the circle.

"Saint Michael the Archangel," Claudia began, "defend us in battle. Be our protection against the wickedness and snares of the devil. May God rebuke him, we humbly pray…"

As the prayer continued to flow from Claudia, Nick lifted his head so he could see Nori. It appeared Claudia's insistence on prayer wasn't easing the journalist's anxiety any more than it was his. If anything, it was making it worse. *Protection?* Nori's face had lost all but a hint of color. Twice she turned and looked toward the lobby. He thought she might bolt for the door, which, all things considered, might not be such a bad idea. When she remained rooted where she was, he offered her a tiny smile. She returned a half-hearted smile before lowering her head.

"…all the evil spirits who prowl about the world seeking the ruin of souls. Amen." Claudia's eyes opened. She nodded ever so subtly while releasing their hands. "We are safe to enter."

First protection, now mention of safety.

Before tonight, Nick had never considered he needed either. The activity at The Chamberlain had been a nuisance. A hindrance to making a profit. But now? Things suddenly felt different. It had taken bringing in the experts for him to feel threatened for the first time. A chill tickled his spine.

Silence was the soundtrack to the moment until Nick realized all eyes were on him.

"Oh, by all means." He pulled the doors open and gestured for everyone to enter. Claudia did. Börne followed, hot on her heels. After one more top-to-bottom inspection of the doors, Nick joined the pair inside the auditorium. Only Nori lagged.

"I think I'll observe from here," she said from outside the doorway.

In contrast, Claudia strolled down the center aisle like she owned the place, like fear was as foreign to her as time travel. Her eyes scanned the ceiling, repeating her behavior from the lobby. Halfway down the aisle, she stopped. A moment later, she turned to Börne.

"*Meine Liebe.*"

Their eyes met and held for several seconds. That was all it took to send him away. Börne returned a moment later, carrying two of his black cases. He set one case down inside the doorway. He carried the other around the back row of seats to the far rear corner of the auditorium.

Nick watched with interest, wondering what was in the cases. On the mayor's recommendation, he'd recently watched the movie Ghostbusters late one night when the stress of the job had rendered sleep obsolete. He doubted Börne would pull out a proton pack from either case, but one never—

"Floyd Cropper."

Nick jumped.

Claudia's voice in the otherwise silence was startling. It echoed throughout the room before fading into the void where all echoes go to die. She and her flowing white gown made their way down front, where she stopped at the bottom of the aisle. Her head perked up. She tilted it to one side, then remained still for a moment. "Are you here, Floyd?"

Another chill rippled down Nick's spine as a thought occurred to him: what if the old man actually answered?

Approaching the screen, Claudia ran her hand along its shimmering surface. "Floyd? Are you with us?"

The floor trembled.

"What the…" Nick uttered.

The vibration was subtle. It started in his feet and ran up his legs. He grabbed the seat back beside him and looked at Claudia. Then Börne. Neither appeared to notice the rumbling beneath their feet. If they did, it didn't faze them in the least.

The mild quake coursed through the seats. They rumbled. The overhead lights rattled, then began swaying back and forth. A high-pitched creaking of metal filled the air. A faint hum joined in as machines kicked on overhead. An instant later, those machines spit a fine spritz of water. A swift breeze circled through the auditorium.

Nick took in a deep breath. *Stay calm.* None of this was out of the ordinary. At least not by The Chamberlain's standards. Ironically, this was the very phenomenon some folks were coming to witness. The exact atmosphere Nick had paid a lot of money to establish. The difference now? No movie was showing to correspond with the effects. There was no trigger. No reason for any of it to be happening other than the mere presence of the four individuals there to bear witness.

And that Claudia was summoning the ghost of an old man.

He checked in with Nori. She remained inside the doorway, experiencing her first taste of the phenomena. Both hands covered her mouth. Her wild eyes darted around the large room.

"Nick?" Börne asked. "Are you…"

Nick raised his hands in a show of innocence. "Nope. Not doing anything. And it's not part of the—"

A loud pop cut him off.

Everyone's attention hastened to the ceiling where light bulbs flickered. One by one, those bulbs exploded. Tiny diamond-like shards of glass rained down upon the seats and floor. The showers were sporadic at first, centralized. One sprang up down front by Claudia. Another in the back to his left. As light bulbs all throughout the room snuffed themselves out, they quickly formed one large storm of raining glass.

Covering her head with her arms, Claudia rushed up the aisle, glass crunching underfoot. Nori greeted her at the doors. Nick soon joined them, and a moment later, so did Börne. Everyone was breathing heavily. Everyone shook bits of glass from their hair.

"Now, that," Nick said, watching the chaos unfold, "is new. At least to that… extent."

They stood in the relative safety of the doorway, watching darkness devour the auditorium. The popping of light bulbs sounded like a child with an endless supply of bubble wrap. Chaos reigned in the fading light. The mist continued to fall. The wind continued to gust.

When the last bulb burst, an eerie calm settled over the nearly pitch auditorium. The only remaining lights were the red glow of the exit sign down front and the handful of ambient sconces mounted along the back and side walls. None of which dispensed with enough light to see much of anything. The mist had stopped. So too had the wind and violent trembling.

The faint scent of smoke wafted through the doorway. Barely noticeable at first, the odor grew stronger. Soon, there was no denying its existence.

Börne's voice floated over Nick's shoulder, a hint of excitement present in the investigator's voice. "Smoke."

Nick nodded in acknowledgement while trying to steady his heavy breathing.

"Think it's from the light bulbs?" Börne asked.

"I don't think so," Nick said, wiping sweat from his forehead.

"It's always been—"

Nori's cough interrupted the conversation. She wrinkled her nose. The stench was growing stronger. Like someone had set ablaze an invisible campfire in their midst.

"Screw this," she said, and slammed the two heavy doors shut. She turned and faced the others with a sheepish gaze. "Sorry. But, you know, enough's enough."

Claudia raised a hand. "It's quite alright." She turned to Börne, adrenaline in her eyes. "Tell me you got that."

Börne shook his head. His expression mimicked a sad puppy dog. "Happened too quick," he said. "I wasn't set up yet."

"Got what?" Nori asked. "I mean, what was that?"

A smile pulled at Claudia's lips. "I believe we just received a formal hello from our Mr. Cropper."

FIFTEEN

"Well," Nick said, "that was more fun than my usual Tuesday nights."

He didn't smoke, but he could have used a cigarette right then. His hands shook, so he slid them into his pockets. He thought of the tiny packet he used to keep there. The pills he no longer courted. For good reason, he reminded himself. He considered the bottle of bourbon stashed in the desk drawer in his office. Considered it, then let go of the idea. Maybe later. For now, he'd have to calm himself organically. A tall order. Not since opening night had he seen The Chamberlain come so alive. Back then, it had all been in his head. This time, however, he was pretty sure it had really happened.

"The shaking seats are one thing," he said. "A shattered light bulb here and there. Problems with the projector. But that…"

Claudia reached up and put her hand on his shoulder. She ran it up and down his arm. "Well," she said, in a soothing voice, "we've got Mr. Cropper's undivided attention. Something you didn't have before. Things were bound to escalate once we connected."

Nick shook his head. He couldn't help but feel a little foolish. Like a child being comforted by his teacher.

Nori hugged herself and rubbed her shoulders. "That was a little scary. Not too proud to admit."

"It can be," Claudia continued. "Mostly, spirits just want something. That's why they hang around. Some want a wrong to be righted. Some just want us to recognize the fact they existed."

"Hell of a way to get recognition," Nick said, jabbing his thumb toward the auditorium. "I've seen toddlers throw lesser tantrums."

"Um, speaking of recognition," Börne said, "are we going to gloss over the fact it smelled like something was on fire in there?"

Everyone took a collective step away from the set of doors. Everyone, that is, except Nick.

"It's alright," he said, giving the all clear with his hands. "It just smells that way sometimes. I don't know why. Sometimes the smell is so strong, so thick, it feels like you're about to be overcome by smoke. But there never is any. Not actually. Not that I, or anyone else, have found a source for. Somehow, it's just the smell."

Börne exchanged a look with Claudia. "So… where's the smell coming from then?"

"Damned if I know," Nick said. "Maybe you two could figure it out while you're here."

The group fell silent, everyone lost in thought. For Nick, the events of the past twenty minutes layered themselves atop those of opening night. There were similarities, which bothered him. Was it simply a hallucination he experienced that night? Or could the rumors of a premonition hold some merit?

"So now what?" he asked, eyeing the auditorium doors warily, expecting them to fly open at any moment.

Börne bit his bottom lip and appeared to contemplate. "Contact rarely occurs so quickly," he said. "So, I suggest everyone hang tight while I finish setting up the equipment. Then we'll try it again. In the meantime, use the restroom, grab a Coke and some snacks. Get ready for the next show."

Nori snickered. "Well, if the second show is anything like the first, I'm gonna need something to mix with that Coke."

Nick pulled the bottle of bourbon from the bottom drawer of his desk. Drinking at work was a rarity but keeping it on hand was one of two pieces of advice he retained from business school. You saw it all the time on television and the movies. Though, in all his years of doing business, he rarely had an occasion to get it out and offer a guest a drink. As for the other piece of advice, he never did learn to play golf.

"Hope this'll do," he said, twisting the bottle's lid. The seal broke free with a tearing sound in the otherwise quiet office.

"Works for me." Nori sat on the edge of his desk with her ankles crossed. She handed him her red and white paper cup, already half full of Coke and ice. "And don't be shy."

Nick added a generous splash of Kentucky's finest.

"So," he said, handing the cup back to Nori, "what do you think about all this? I mean, we've never gotten the chance to talk about any of it. Not after… you know."

Nori stirred her drink with her middle finger, then slid the digit into her mouth and sucked the liquid off.

"Well," she said before sipping from her cup, "this is definitely a first for me."

Nick laughed. "I assume you're not talking about the drink."

"Ha, ha. No." When she smiled, it wasn't the schmoozing smile of a reporter chasing a story. This time her smile was genuine. Friendly. "I've seen some weird things in my line of work. Being an investigative reporter and all. But this…" She shook her head. "Never seen anything like this."

They both grew quiet.

Nori stared into her cup.

Nick cast his eyes to the floor. The dark grey carpet, while only a couple months old, was already showing signs of wear. A faint path split the room in half. He would need to find somewhere else to do his nervous pacing before he ruined the carpet altogether.

It was several minutes before either of them spoke again. When she did, Nori's soft voice floated between them, loud enough for only Nick to hear.

"Do you remember what you asked me on opening night? When you were showing me around?"

He didn't and said so with a shake of his head.

"Before you left me alone in the theater," she continued, "you asked if I scared easily." She took another long sip of her drink, tucked a strand of hair behind her ear. "When I told you no, it wasn't a lie. But... I'm sorry to say that's all changed now. This has me completely unnerved, Nick. It feels... I don't know... personal somehow. Do you feel that way?"

He allowed the chill in his blood to run its course while he gazed at the floor. When he looked up and met Nori's hollow eyes, he had to fight back his initial instinct to take her by the hand, run away, and leave The Chamberlain for good. But life wasn't that simple. It never would be.

Instead, he screwed the cap onto the bottle of bourbon and slid it back into the desk drawer.

"We should probably get back."

SIXTEEN

By the time they'd returned to the auditorium, the double doors stood open again. Claudia wandered the lobby, mumbling into what appeared to be a digital voice recorder, and Nick found Börne in the back of the auditorium, setting up equipment in the narrow space behind the back row of seats. Nori veered away from the auditorium and headed toward the concession counter in search of something to go with her drink.

Everywhere he looked, the floor sparkled with shards of broken glass. Only a few of the overhead lightbulbs remained intact. He shook his head while trying to estimate how much it was going to cost to replace the others. The ornate sconces mounted on the walls every twenty feet appeared to work fine. They provided only a modicum of light, but at least they kept Börne from having to work in the dark.

"Looks interesting."

"This?" The investigator wore a headset. He swung the microphone away from his mouth and held up a chunky green box that looked like a 90s-era cell phone on steroids. "It's an EMF meter."

"Oh." Nick considered playing along like he knew to what Börne was referring but decided against it. Can't learn anything if you act like you know everything. His father had taught him that when he was a child. Besides, he had no clue what an EMF was, much less an EMF meter.

Börne detected as much.

"EMF. Stands for electro-magnetic field," he said. He crouched and held the green box near an electrical outlet. Red and green bars zipped across the screen. White numbers blipped. He stood and offered Nick a better look at the box. "It's believed the conscious mind contains an electromagnetic field that leaves residue behind, long after we're dead. This meter lets me know when a spirit is close. Before I can take readings of spirits, though, I have to take a baseline of all potentially elevated areas in the room—electrical outlets, light fixtures—so when I do get a spike, I can tell which are spirits and which are me standing too close to a known power source."

Nick turned the box over in his hand, taking great effort to appear as if he was checking out specific features. In reality, he only hoped to put on a convincing show. He was anything but tech savvy. He knew next to nothing about high-tech gadgetry. Even the blue shirts at Best Buy intimidated him. With a nod of feigned approval, he handed the meter back to Börne. "Cool," he said.

And he was being honest. Exploding lightbulbs aside, Nick was finding the entire experience with Börne and Claudia more interesting than he'd expected. He only wished he didn't have so much riding on it.

Börne turned and made his way along the back wall, broken glass crunching beneath his every step. He followed the wall as it curved around the last seat in the row, then led down along the side toward the front of the theater. Each electrical outlet and wall sconce he came to got its EMF field detected and recorded into the microphone on his headset. It was important to document everything, Börne had also explained. Time, location, every minor aspect, no matter how minute and inconsequential it may seem. The information would prove crucial in pinpointing any anomalies that may occur during the review of data and footage.

As the process of setting up and testing equipment grew more technical, Nick grew increasingly less interested. At some point, Claudia had left the auditorium, so he was about to leave Börne to his work and go see what she and Nori were up to when the sconce above Börne's head went bat shit crazy.

The lamp grew brighter than normal. Nick shielded his eyes, as looking at it became unbearable. Then, just as quickly, the light returned to normal before softening to the point of barely staying lit. The bulb now produced little light at all. It did this several times. Back and forth in rapid succession. Soon others joined in. All around the room, wall sconces teetered between extremes, high and low.

Nick scowled. *Not those, too.*

It was as if the theater was either excited about something or trying to get their attention.

Then the wall sconce near Börne snuffed out. It didn't blow or shatter like the overhead lights. It didn't burst with a loud pop. It merely went dark, and this time, stayed that way.

Nick stopped at the doorway and scoured the room. In search of what, he didn't know.

Then, lest anyone think the first was a coincidence, one after another, all the wall sconces went dark. The lights were controlled by switches located inside the door, but to Nick, it was as if someone was making their way around the auditorium, systematically flipping switches. Within a minute of the first light going out, the last of the sconces extinguished itself. The Chamberlain had faded to black as if a film were about to start. Only there were no films scheduled.

"Um, ladies?" he called into the lobby, though his gaze remained on the action in the auditorium. "You might wanna see this."

Light filtered through the open doorway. The emergency exit sign down front glowed a subtle red. The room was otherwise pitch. Börne had made his way to the emergency exit and now stood beneath its sign. His upper body was awash in red. He appeared to be drenched in blood. A male version of Stephen King's *Carrie*.

Darkness suddenly closed in around Nick.

When he turned, the heavy wooden doors slammed in his face. He stood frozen in place as the concuss reverberated throughout the darkened room. His heartrate shot up. A chill tickled his neck. The message wasn't hard to read. It was coming through loud and clear. Someone—or some*thing*—either didn't want them there or didn't want them to leave.

Neither option fit into Nick's plans.

He looked to Börne beneath the exit sign. The red glow reached all the way to the floor. Börne was gone.

The earlier chill now ran the length of Nick's spine, and he shivered from the sudden cold.

"Börne?"

He got no response from the investigator. His EMF meter, however, had plenty to say. Somewhere in the pitch, it was working overtime. The high-pitched bleating echoed throughout the auditorium, sounding as if the damn thing was about to pop a gasket. Tracing its location, however, proved impossible.

The stench of burnt wood ignited around Nick and assaulted his nose.

"Börne!"

Still no answer. Making matters worse—or better, depending—the EMF meter fell silent. An unsettling hush joined the darkness in engulfing the room.

Where the hell was Börne? And why wasn't he responding?

A loud pop from somewhere down front reached out and grabbed Nick's attention. The darkness made it impossible to pinpoint where the sound had come from. Then Nick noticed it. There was no longer a red glow near the emergency exit. Something had happened to the exit sign. By the sound of the pop, the damn thing had exploded.

Nick felt a presence encroach upon his personal space. The energy quickly gained strength. A faint buzz tickled his ears. His arm hair stood on end. The smoky odor grew more intense, more concentrated.

Remembering the set of doors behind him, Nick reached through the dark for a handle.

A hand grabbed his forearm. Only it wasn't Börne's hand. Nor was it like any other. This hand was hot. Branding iron-hot. The grip seared his skin. The fetor of singed hair reached his nose. Sizzling flesh, his ears. Nick cried out in pain, ripping his arm free. From whom or what, he didn't know.

In shock, but burning with a need to remove himself from his situation, he braved the consequences. He reached out into the darkness a second time. This time, nothing grabbed him. This time, he found a door handle and pushed.

Déjà vu.

The door didn't open. Wouldn't budge. He found the other handle and garnered the same result. Flashes of opening night came flooding back.

He pounded on the doors. Pounded until his hand hurt. The stench of smoke grew so strong, it was as if he, himself was on fire.

"Claudia! Nori! Somebody open the damn doors!"

He pounded harder.

The stench of smoke—*but not actually smoke?*—continued to saturate the air, leaving little room for anything else. He breathed it in, having no other choice. The last bit of calm drained from his body. He knew what he'd told Börne. *There's never any actual smoke. It's just the smell.* But he'd never experienced the smell this strong. He envisioned a cloud of smoke engulfing him, reducing him to a coughing fit, hands on knees, his chest heaving, gasping for any hint of clean air.

Strangely, it never came to that.

His throat never burned like he'd expected. It never

constricted. He continued to breathe fine just fine.

Still, Nick pulled his collar up over his nose as he pounded the door.

When one of the doors opened, Nori stood to one side, Claudia peering over her shoulder. The new flood of light swarmed Nick and caught Börne in its spotlight. The man marched up the center aisle, halfway to the doors.

Nick didn't wait for him.

He rushed through the open doorway and took up post across from Nori. As soon as Börne burst through, she slammed the door home, sealing off the auditorium and containing the smoky stench inside.

Only then did Nick's thoughts turn to the agony inflicting his arm.

Four ugly red streaks curled around his forearm. Burn marks resembling tiny fingers scorched his skin. He turned his arm over. On the underside, a perfectly shaped thumb imprint to match the others.

"What the fuck?" He looked to Börne and Claudia, who were exchanging a look of their own. Concern etched their faces, like the lines on a roadmap to Hades. Börne, too, was gasping for air.

"What?" Nick asked, somehow doubting their concern was for his injury. "What are you guys thinking?"

The husband-and-wife investigative team exchanged another brief glance before Claudia's eyes met his. She took a deep breath.

"I think we need to get some ice on that arm," she said. "And then, we need to talk."

SEVENTEEN

"Let's talk about spirits."

Nick sat on the concession counter balancing a bag of ice on his wounded arm. In his hand, he held a drink twice as potent as the one he'd made Nori. It was the most effective pain reliever he allowed himself. Leaning against the counter beside him, Nori chewed the end of her straw, eyes glued to the floor. The Forresters sat facing them in the two chairs Nick had retrieved from his office. Börne drank from a bottle he had run down and purchased from The Sand Dollar. He'd lamented the store's unimpressive selection of German imports but didn't seem hindered by the choice he'd had to make. He was already on his second beer.

Claudia was the only one of them not imbibing. She'd declined a drink, wanting to keep her mind clear and focused. Such was her state of being as she gave Nori and Nick an education on spirits of the non-alcoholic variety.

"Call them what you will—ghosts, phantoms, apparitions— these spirits were human at one time. For reasons no one is clear on, aspects of their humanity remain in this world. Lingering. Maybe they have unfinished business. Perhaps they're holding on to an unrequited love. We refer to these types of spirits as residual. Residuals may not even know they were supposed to have moved on. It's believed a residual's energy results from a traumatic experience, often attaching itself to an object or location having to do with that experience."

"Like a theater?" Nori asked.

Nick felt the brush of a cool draft. He glanced over to make sure the only door to the outside was closed. It was, and he'd known it would be.

"Possibly." Claudia nodded. "Either way, these spirits generally pose no harm to the living. They go about their business, their actions repeating on a loop with no implications to us, short term or otherwise."

Nick lifted the bag of ice and surveyed the burn marks stretching across his forearm. *No harm, my ass.*

"So," he said, "can we go back to the unfinished business part? What do you mean by that, exactly? Like, they had things at the dry cleaners they never picked up, or what?"

"Revenge," Börne said. He gave Nick a wink before taking a long pull from his bottle of quickly disappearing *Kolsch.*

To Nick's surprise, not to mention alarm, Claudia offered no contradiction to her husband's statement.

"Sometimes." She put her hand on Börne's knee as if to remind him to tread lightly. "And sometimes it's only the continued pull of an unrealized dream. Maybe they passed before closing an important business deal."

"Yeah," Börne chuckled. "The business of revenge."

Claudia tilted her head toward Börne and, this time, shot him a disapproving frown. He stopped laughing. He tipped his head back and filled his mouth.

Nick let out a chuckle himself. Albeit a sarcastic one. He knew what Börne was trying to do. He was trying to scare him. Even if just a little. Though he hated to admit it, Börne's venture was a successful one. Hairs all over Nick's body stood on end. That Floyd Cropper was still hanging around his beloved theater could no longer be denied. Claudia had gone as far as calling the guy out by name.

And damned if he hadn't responded.

Silence hung like a plague over the lobby.

Börne's use of the word revenge resonated in Nick's mind. As far as motives went, it couldn't be ruled out. Especially considering how despondent Floyd had been over losing The Chamberlain. Torching himself on the steps? Hell, it made perfect sense really. And who could blame him? After what Blackwood did to him? What Nick had done? After all, he hadn't skipped a beat in swooping in and purchasing the place before it had even gone on the market. He'd been as eager to find a theater and get the ball rolling on his new idea as Blackwood had been to offer it up.

Nick swallowed hard against the fiery ball of lead forming in his gut.

"What about demons?" Nori asked.

Nick dropped his bag of ice, and his jaw dropped with it.

Claudia gave Nori a studied look. "Why do you ask?"

The reporter shrugged and began tugging at her ear. "I don't know. It just… I guess I don't understand why the phenomena is happening inside the theater, when Floyd killed himself out on the steps. Just wondering what else might be doing it."

"Whoa! Wait a second?" Nick dropped to his feet and retrieved the squishy bag of melting ice. He placed it back on his arm. "Demons?"

"Non-human spirits," Claudia said, picking up the conversation. "Their energy is not of this world. Same with angels."

"So, you're telling me these things are real. Demons? Really?"

Börne pointed to the auditorium. "As real as those lights that blew themselves up." This time there was no hint of merriment in his voice. His face was stone. His eyes cold.

"Shit." Nick uttered the word, soft and breathy. Perspiration broke on his forehead. "Holy shit." The fiery ball of lead in his stomach sprang a leak. He didn't feel well. He looked all around the lobby, from floor to ceiling, in every corner. "Suddenly, the idea of a ghost doesn't sound so bad."

"Right?" Nori quipped. "I say, bring on the effing ghosts."

He couldn't help but laugh. Nori had offered the first spark of levity they'd experienced in some time.

"Even if it's a vengeful ghost?" Börne asked.

Nick stopped laughing.

Börne fixed his eyes solely on him as he spoke. "They can be pretty nasty." He nodded, gesturing toward Nick's arm.

He could no longer tell if Börne was pulling his leg. He looked to Claudia for help. Her hesitation before nodding felt like she was deciding whether to answer truthfully.

"For what it's worth, Nick," she said. "I believe that's what we're dealing with here. Not a demon, but a vengeful spirit. They do exist, even though they're not common."

"Shit," Nick said again.

"So, vengeful, residual, non-human, whatever kind of spirit it is," Nori said, "my question, and I'm sure I speak for Nick here, is how do we get rid of it?"

Nick turned to Nori as she returned to chewing on her straw. Her use of the word 'we' hadn't gone unnoticed. She'd said it like they were a team. Like he wasn't in this alone. He liked both the sound and the thought of it.

"Well," Claudia said, "if this energy is connected to an object, you remove the object. Take it elsewhere and the spirit follows."

The ice on his arm had melted at this point, and Nick tossed the bag of water into a nearby trashcan. "And if it's connected to a location?" he asked.

Börne exchanged another look with Claudia before answering. "You move."

The rest of the evening proved uneventful. No more outbursts or busted lights, no more scent of smoke. Even Nori grew comfortable enough to join them in crunching up and down the auditorium's aisles in search of the paranormal. While Börne's equipment stood at the ready, eager to capture something either on film or audio, nothing of real importance made its way onto a recording.

It was as if the theater knew cameras were rolling.

It was after four in the morning when Nori helped Nick toss the last of the broken glass-filled trash bags into the dumpster out behind The Chamberlain. The ground was damp. The alley was empty and still. And as Nori said good night and disappeared back into the theater, Nick realized how long of a day it had been. He was exhausted, too tired to think about anything except his warm bed. Not ghosts. Not the unexplained burn marks on his arm. Not even the burgeoning feelings he was having for Miss Nori Park. Sleep, and lots of it, was the only thing on his agenda.

EIGHTEEN

The dream starts with Nick seated at the desk in The Chamberlain's office. He's running the week's numbers. It doesn't take long. Music flows from the tinny speaker on his cell phone. It could be day; it could be night. The atmosphere inside the windowless building is the same either way.

A sound from out in the hallway steals his focus.

It's not quite a laugh, but a raspy giggle.

As far as he knows, he's alone.

He slides his chair out, rises, and cautiously makes his way to the door. So far, the sound hasn't repeated. He questions whether he truly heard anything. He pokes his head through the doorway to be sure.

The hallway is dark.

The hallway is empty.

He exhales, unsure what he expected to find. All the theater doors are locked.

A sense of responsibility, the need to be thorough urges him further. It propels him up the short hall toward the lobby. It, too, is empty. He checks the front door and finds it locked, as it should be. Without explanation for the giggling he heard, he retreats back down the hall to his office.

An old man sits at his desk.

Nick gasps.

The old man turns. As startling as his presence is, it's his appearance that alarms Nick the most. All the flesh on the man's face is gone. What remains of his skin resembles stringy and shriveled flypaper. Singed black and crisp. The sinewy muscle underneath is roiling and angry. A sound like bacon sizzling permeates the room. The smell isn't as pleasant. The top half of the old man's button-up shirt has been burnt away, exposing ruined shoulders that match the face. The lower half of the shirt hangs in midair. It covers his torso, suspended in midair. This seems impossible, yet somehow is not. The fabric's ragged edges are black. The fringe smolders with scarlet embers, emitting a putrid smoke.

The old man sneers.

"This?" His voice is thick, full of charred gravel. A skeletal hand holds up the laptop in which Nick keeps track of his finances, or the lack thereof. "This is what you stole my theater for? This… pittance?" Spittle flies from the man's blackened lips.

Nick's mouth doesn't work. Words refuse to form in the face of judgment. The day has come. He knows who the man is. He can finally put a face to the name, as horrifying as that face may be…

Floyd Cropper.

"I… I…" Words continue to abandon him. They scatter like cowardly friends facing a fight.

When the old man rises, Nick's feet succeed where his mouth fails. He takes a step back. When the man steps toward him, he matches it, retreating a step further. He's back in the hallway. A quick glance in both directions reveals an unfortunate truth: he is alone. A circumstance that proved reassuring earlier, but unnerving now.

Heat intrudes on his personal space.

He turns back to the old man.

Floyd Cropper has taken great strides, and now stands before him. Heat radiates from the man. He's a fire in a barrel.

Nick sucks in a sharp intake of air. The intense heat sears his throat. The closer the man steps, the hotter the surrounding air grows. Standing face to—*face?*—the heat proves unbearable. It's as if the man is still on fire. Yet, there are no flames.

Sweat breaks across Nick's body.

He coughs.

He turns to run.

The once short hallway is suddenly much longer. It can now only be described as a corridor; its length having stretched to at least twice its original. He can barely make out the lobby's faint glow at the other end. Sanctuary feels impossibly far away.

A blaze erupts along both sides of the corridor. The sconces illuminate the walls, chasing away the inky blackness. Only the radiance doesn't come from their bulbs. The lamps don't glow with their normal 40 watts.

They rage with fire.

Within seconds, the flames creep up the walls. A stifling heat overtakes the corridor. He coughs. His throat pays a painful price. Normal breathing becomes a memory.

Nick takes the first step toward the lobby. His second step shows more urgency. Soon, he is running up a corridor made of flame. The blaze licks at him, swipes at him as he passes. Sweat pours down his face. The distance between him and the lobby, however, doesn't change. The gap doesn't shrink, despite his best efforts. Sheer curtains of fire now drape the walls. Wallpaper sags, melts, and then drips onto the floor.

The mounting heat becomes all-consuming.

The inability to breathe overcomes him. His face stings like the worst sunburn. The skin of his arms starts to sizzle. The acrid stench of blistering skin infiltrates his nostrils. He gags. He shields his face the best he can as he sprints further up a hallway that feels longer with every step.

He stumbles.

He reaches out but doesn't hit the floor. Instead, his outstretched hands find the backs of two theater seats. The once-tight vinyl has become soft, molten. It gives way under his grip. Liquid vinyl oozes through his fingers, burning his hands. He cries out, letting go of the seats.

He staggers back. The walls of flame are gone. The hallway, too, is gone. He finds himself at the front of the auditorium, the silver screen to his back. Despite his change in location, he doesn't feel safe. He doesn't relax. An energy resonates throughout the auditorium. The room is alive with electricity. The air crackles and spits. It feels like only a matter of time before—

The seat in front of him bursts into flame. It proves to be the first of many. Within seconds, a dozen individual fires have ignited throughout the auditorium. Their numbers double. Soon, full rows of the once plush seating are transformed into meandering bonfires. Their flames reach high into the air, their serpent tongues licking the ceiling.

The temperature in the room swelters.

Sweat soaks his clothes. His skin bubbles. Smoke chokes back the air in his throat, burns his eyes. Terror becomes all-consuming, and he begins to panic.

Every seat in the house is now engulfed in flame.

The roar is deafening.

The inferno scales its way up the walls, its flames devouring drywall like famished piranha. Insatiable. When rain falls from the ceiling, he's momentarily relieved. When drops hit the back of his neck, that relief is replaced by a searing pain.

The sprinkler system hasn't kicked on.

The situation is not getting better.

The aluminum light fixtures hanging from the ceiling have melted. Black, metallic precipitation falls throughout the auditorium. It soon covers the seats, the floor, anything unfortunate enough to be in its path. The liquid metal scorches the top of his head and burns holes in his clothing.

He cries out.

Flames, like hands, reach out from all directions, coaxing him into their embrace. He takes a step back. There is nowhere to go. At least no place that isn't alight with soul-scalding fire and rain. Even the towering screen behind him is aglow with orange conflagration. Bent, hands on knees, he chokes down what little oxygen he can find as everything around him burns.

A hand grabs his arm, yanking him upright.

Floyd stands before him, the man's naked body engulfed in an orange blaze. Head to toe. No part of his body is free of dancing fire. He is a human torch.

Unfazed by his own burning flesh, the man sneers as he thrusts something toward Nick.

The something crushes his stomach, robbing him of precious air. His eyes are now swollen. He looks down through slits and can barely make out the object in Floyd's fiery hands. The old man laughs. His laughter overtakes the inferno's roar. It echoes throughout the room, swallowing the last of the auditorium's oxygen.

Then the old man is gone.

Nick is left surrounded by a world on fire, holding an empty gas can.

He can only breathe smoke. There is no clean air left. There is only fire and smoke and unbearable heat. He drops the metal container and stumbles toward the emergency exit. His skin melts, slides off muscle and bone. His vision is nearly gone. The door leading to the alley is indiscernible. A phantom portal hidden among a giant fiery wall.

Nearly blind, he staggers, then falls to his knees, engulfed in flame. He puts his hands to his cheeks. He finds only a hot and mushy mess. His fingers sink knuckle-deep into his flesh before he can pull them away. Strands of skin, like stringy melted cheese, come away from his face. His vision has completely abandoned him. His world is dark and loud and burning out of control.

He collapses.

Then he awakens.

Nick finds himself curled up on his bedroom floor. He's wrapped like a cocoon in his sheet, cloaked in sweat. He gasps for air. His mouth is hot and dry. It feels like he's been eating cotton swabs roasted like marshmallows over a campfire. The sunlight through his window warms his face. And as he realizes it's all been a horrible nightmare it's the lingering ghost of smoke in his nose that leaves him the most shaken.

NINETEEN

Nick dragged his feet getting to the theater the next morning. There were no showings scheduled until the afternoon, and despite the amount of work awaiting him, he was in no hurry. It had, after all, been a long night. Sleep hadn't come easy. And then there was the dream. It still had him rattled. A single cup of coffee usually got him through most mornings, but he was halfway through his second by the time he gathered his wallet and keys. After chugging the last of the cup's offering, he set it in the sink and headed for the door.

The air was already thick. He was still getting used to summer in the south where the heat and humidity rarely took a day off. Perspiration peppered his forehead. As was often the case, he'd want a second shower by the time he reached the theater. Nothing else, the intense sun would help wake him. If he was lucky, it might even burn off the remnants of that horrible dream.

Burn off?

He shuddered at the thought.

As he locked the door behind him, his mind changed gears, and he ran through the day's to-do list. He had replacement light bulbs in the storage room, though he couldn't recall how many. Surely it wasn't enough. Who could have predicted he'd be replacing them all at once? As for the exit sign, his initial hunch had been correct. It was a lost cause. For both items, he would have to swing by the hardware store on his way in. He wasn't entirely put out by the detour. The Chamberlain wasn't going anywhere. Neither was its uninvited houseguest.

With the thin white box tucked under his arm, Nick unlocked the theater's front door. He'd been lucky. Not only had he scored the last exit sign the hardware store had in stock, but he could install it before they delivered the four cases of light bulbs later that morning. Special delivery: one of the last vestiges of old school customer service still found in a small town. He was only surprised he hadn't gotten more of a reaction from Gene, the owner of the hardware store, when inquiring on the bulk supply of light bulbs. Not that it should surprise him. The people of Angler Bay hardly blinked at The Chamberlain's strange happenings anymore.

Nick gave the key a twist and pushed the door open.

A refreshing rush of frosty air greeted him as he stepped inside and pulled the door closed. The lobby's climate was a welcome contrast to the tropical conditions outside. He carried the box over to the concession stand and laid it on the counter. He reached for a napkin to wipe the sweat from his face. And that was when he noticed it.

"What the…"

Cool AC wasn't the only thing in the air.

He scowled, turning to gaze upon the auditorium's wooden doors. Closed, as usual. But it wasn't enough to keep the muffled strains of a soundtrack from reaching the lobby.

"Now what?"

Tossing his keys onto the counter, he strolled toward the auditorium. The music grew louder. As did the sound of a man's voice. He recognized it as that of the narrator of the kids' movie he showed during matinees. The hour-long film about the wonders of the planet Earth was the only kid-friendly movie he had for the 4-D experience. Plans for more had stalled because of budgetary constraints. Not to mention the fact few residents were bringing their kids around, anyway. For this film, the cameras explored all corners of the planet with effects to match: a cool puff of air as the helicopter scaled the Himalayas; a fine mist as the audience trekked through the Amazon rainforest; slithering eels and graceful stingrays rippling through the vinyl seats as their submarine cruised along the Great Barrier Reef.

It was all great family fun.

Question was, why the hell was it playing?

Nick approached the doors, took a handle in each hand, and with a deep exhale, pulled them wide.

The best he could tell in the dark, row after row of seats sat empty. They were solid, too, and not molten. He knew it had been a dream, but having visual proof of the fact eased his mind further.

What did not set his mind at ease, however, was the silver screen down front, set aglow by a shaft of light beamed in from the tiny control room window. On the screen, a helicopter's view as it flew above the Texas plains ahead of an approaching storm. Thunder rumbled through the overhead speakers. A bolt of lightning flashed across the churning sky. The only reason the lights above weren't strobing in sync with the lightning on the screen was the lack of functioning bulbs.

He turned and peered up at the control room window.

The fact he was the only one who knew how to operate the system was also concerning.

He'd only just gotten there.

Backpedaling from the auditorium, he made his way down the short hallway and up the steps to the control room. As far as he could remember, he'd never witnessed strange phenomena in the control room, so he left that door unlocked. A practice he might have to revisit given the circumstances.

He flung open the door and stepped inside.

The tiny room presented itself as empty as the auditorium. The control panel, however, was lit up and in full working order. Several icons were illuminated in red, showing which particular functions were in use. A miniature-scaled version of the film played in a small window at the bottom right corner of the control panel screen.

The faint odor of smoke lingered in the air.

Nick waved the stench away and approached the panel. The lack of an engineer had forced him to get out the manual and learn the system. At least Manny had been right: it was easy. He wasn't sure a kindergartener could operate it, like Manny had said, but with kids' knowledge of technology these days, he probably wasn't far off. After a couple of taps on the screen, the film stopped. The auditorium went dark. The speakers fell silent.

With a furrowed brow and a shake of his head, he looked through the small window, out over the vast sea of empty seats.

"Strange."

And it was. But then, strange summed up the daily existence of The Chamberlain Theater.

Nori climbed off her exercise bike. Perspiration ran down her neck and soaked the collar of her Gwen Stefani concert tee. While she shook the circulation back into her wobbly legs, she grabbed her towel off the hook.

Thirteen miles.

Not her best, but certainly not her worst. Anything in double digits was acceptable. A full twenty miles would have been nice, but considering the paltry amount of sleep she was running on, she was happy with thirteen.

Tilting her head back and taking a long drink from her water bottle, her thoughts turned to Nick. Something that had been happening with frequency since she'd awoken. She wondered how he was faring this morning. How was he faring period? The stress of it all. The failing theater. The bizarre phenomena. Pressure from their asshole mayor.

And then there were the drugs. She knew he had a history with them, though he said those days were behind him. She wanted to believe him, as much as anyone wanted to believe a former user when they said drugs were no longer a problem. She also knew the stress he was under had to feel like a ten-ton brick on his shoulders and his shoulders alone.

Hang in there, buddy.

She had just stripped out of her damp workout clothes and turned on the shower when her cell phone chimed. The notification would have to wait. The steaming hot water played tug-of-war with her weary muscles, and her cell phone was on the losing end. She stepped into the shower and pulled the curtain closed.

The hardware store had sent just enough light bulbs. Which was nothing more than sheer luck since Nick had had to guess how many he needed. Twenty-four brand new incandescent bulbs hung poised and ready to show patrons to and from their seats the next time The Chamberlain showed a film.

If there *was* a next time.

He was replacing the plastic cover on the new exit sign when an abrupt beep filled the otherwise quiet auditorium. He clung to the ladder with one hand, while checking his pocket for his cell with the other. It wasn't there. Which was nothing new. He hated being tied to that device twenty-four seven. If he had to guess, his cell probably sat on the counter with his keys.

The beep rang out twice more.

What the hell?

Nick turned on the ladder as much as he could without losing his balance and scanned the large room. With the lights on, shadows lingered anywhere the light couldn't reach. As far as he could tell, he was alone. And as far as he knew, none of the 4D equipment made a beeping sound.

A tickle started at the base of his neck.

I am alone… right?

The next time the beeping sounded it didn't stop. The shrill bleating reverberated throughout the room.

Nick made his way down the ladder. With the emergency exit at his back, he once again scanned the large room, this time from ground level. Row after row of red vinyl seats stared back at him. The rear double doors at the top of the center aisle stood open, awaiting a quick exit if need be.

After folding the ladder and tucking it under his arm, he made his way across the front of the auditorium. It wasn't long before he detected the faint smell of smoke. The closer he drew to the center aisle, the more prevalent the smell. And the louder the beeping.

At the center aisle, the beeping reached a crescendo. Nick searched the surrounding seats. He propped the ladder against a nearby seat back, then stooped and searched the floor. That's when he saw it. A small green box the size of a 90s era cell phone on steroids.

It was Börne's EMF detector he'd used last night before the ensuing chaos forced their retreat. He must have dropped it amid all the craziness.

Nick reached under the seat and retrieved the device. He wasn't sure what all the beeping meant, but the meter sure seemed intent on alerting someone of something. Green and red lights flashed across the top. The number 68.8 flashed in white on a tiny screen. What the hell did it all mean? Was that good? Bad? Then Börne's words came back to him: *this meter lets me know when a spirit is close.*

The tickle that had flitted the base of his neck shot down Nick's entire spine.

He dropped the green box and let it crash to the concrete floor. The beeping didn't stop.

He took a step back and bumped the ladder. It, too, clattered to the floor. He took another step up the aisle as cold sweat broke out across his face.

The EMF meter didn't die with the fall. It continued to beep.

Nick took two more backward steps up the aisle before turning and running the rest of the way.

As he neared the back row of seats, the beeping stopped. His blood froze in his veins. As thankful as he was for the EMF meter to go quiet, the fact filled him with more fear than joy. Why had it stopped beeping? That was the question on his mind as he neared the doors.

Why?

He gave up wondering where the spirit may have gone. One after the other, he slammed the heavy doors closed behind him. And as he stood there, back against the doors, one thought came to mind.

I should've just stayed in bed.

TWENTY

Hunched over the men's room sink, Nick cupped his hands under the faucet. When the water reached capacity, he splashed it onto his face. He did this three times before reaching up and shutting off the water. A stack of folded paper towels sat nearby on the counter, and he grabbed two off the top.

With his face patted dry and the crumpled paper towels deposited in the nearby trash can, he placed both hands on the countertop and leaned in toward the mirror. The weary man staring back at him eventually grinned. He shook his head.

"Crazy."

This entire experience with F.A.U.S.T. and–dare he say it—Floyd, was becoming a bigger deal than he could have ever imagined. Maybe more than he bargained for. More and more, Nick was finding himself needing a drink. More and more, he fought the urge to call in a favor from his doctor for a bottle of tiny red saviors.

"Stay strong," said the man in the mirror. "We'll get through this." Then he chuckled. "I mean, what more could happen?"

Nick was imagining the possibilities of what more could happen when adolescent chatter reached the men's room. *Kids? Really?* He considered the idea he might be imagining things, but the sounds of unabashed youth grew louder.

When he opened the restroom door and popped out, he was met by a parade of rambunctious school-age children marching through the lobby toward the auditorium. At the front of the line,

Mayor Blackwood led the charge like a hulking pied piper.

When he reached the double doors, Blackwood swung them open and motioned for the children to enter.

"Mayor!" Nick shouted, rushing toward the platoon of children set to invade the lobby.

He was too late.

One by one they marched through the open doorway and down the center aisle. A harried young woman bought up the rear of the first group. When they reached the front of the auditorium, she ordered her little soldiers into the front row of seats. By the size of the group and the way the woman acted toward them, Nick could only assume they were a class of schoolchildren, and she their stressed-out teacher.

That didn't, however, explain what they were doing there.

"Mayor, what the hell?"

"Nick!" The mayor's boisterous voice played well to the theater's engineered acoustics and may as well have been playing through the theater's high-tech speakers. "Been looking all over for ya."

"Wanna tell me what's going on?" Nick asked.

"It's called a field trip, Nick." The mayor's massive hand found his shoulder, a gesture Nick had come to know and despise. "It's where students leave the classroom and get some real-world education. I'm sure you've heard of it."

A young man in a tie, black-rimmed glasses, and skinny jeans followed the next troop of school children into the auditorium. When they reached the front row, he motioned his class to take seats on the other side of the aisle from the first class. The young man didn't seem as stressed as the first teacher. But then, his line of students wasn't as uniform as hers, either. It was clear he wasn't as much of a stickler.

With the events of the previous night still fresh in his mind, not to mention the EMF meter's terrifying reading only moments ago,

Nick's stomach turned over on itself.

"Not really sure what these kids can learn here at The Chamberlain, Mayor."

Another, more disciplined, line of middle schoolers approached the auditorium, led by a stern-looking older woman. Her set jaw would have rivaled the most hardened of drill sergeants.

Blackwood leaned in so only Nick could hear.

"That The Chamberlain isn't haunted and is perfectly safe to patronize." The mayor nodded and winked at the teacher as she passed. Her sour expression spoke to ill feelings about being at the theater. It also explained why her group of kids were much better behaved than the others. "Then they'll go home," the mayor continued, "and tell their parents how much fun they had at the movies. Safe fun, that is. Family-type fun. The kind of fun that makes it rain."

The mayor swiped at a stack of invisible money from one hand with two fingers of the other.

The teacher took an open seat next to the last child in the row. Nick was certain she'd rolled her eyes as she passed by the mayor, but he couldn't be sure. If she did, the mayor hadn't seen either.

Nick cast a wary glance toward the ceiling and swallowed hard. Twenty-four new light bulbs stared back at him, reminding him of the stakes. "And you're thinking this will bring people back?"

"In droves."

Nick didn't agree, but he also didn't have time to debate the mayor on the merits of his idea and whether he thought it would work. He had more important problems. With each child that entered the auditorium, more alarms sounded in his mind. The words *vengeful spirit* flashed off and on behind his eyes like a neon sign on the Vegas Strip. The scent of smoke, while no longer fresh in his nose, still hovered in his subconscious. And then there was his forearm, wrapped in white cotton gauze. It was enough to send slivers of ice churning through his veins.

Children continued to filter into the theater. So young. So innocent. And so many. Blackwood must have brought the entire school with him. Nick imagined there were a small fleet of yellow school buses lining the street out front.

Damn it!

He turned back.

"Uh, Mayor?" he said. "This really isn't a good idea. Last night—"

"Aw, bullshit, Fallon."

Another teacher who was passing by shot the mayor a disapproving look. Surprisingly, and most likely because this teacher resembled Halle Berry with the perkiness of an over-caffeinated Starbuck's barista, the mayor offered a half-hearted apology for his language. When he spoke next, his voice was a little softer and didn't carry so far.

"Nonsense, Nick. This is exactly the kinda thing to turn business around at the Chamberlain." The mayor put his arm around his shoulder. "Word'll spread. You'll see. These kids here? They're gonna have a great time. Little shits'll have so much fun they'll piss themselves. Now give 'em a few minutes to settle in, then start that movie." The mayor's grip on his shoulder tightened as he spoke the last part. Interpretation: don't question me on this.

Nick's knees buckled.

His stomach soured.

The wall sconces flanking the double doors flickered.

He noticed the lights but lacked the time to deal with them directly. Even though he interpreted the mayor's threat as intended, question he must. Blackwood's plan was a disaster in the making.

"Mayor, seriously," he said, speaking as sternly as he could. "This is a mistake. Last night—"

Mayor Blackwood spun, eyes squinting, lips pursed. He leaned in until his forehead hovered within inches of Nick's and spoke with as much purpose as Nick had ever heard.

"I don't give a flying fuck what happened last night." His cold eyes searched Nick's for the seed of fear he hoped to plant. "What I do give a fuck about is showing these damn kids a fucking movie. Do you understand me, Fallon? Nod once for yes, and fuck off for no."

And with that, Blackwood exited the auditorium.

Mic drop.

Nick couldn't match the mayor's intensity or ferocity. He didn't have it in him. The battle was lost, his defenses crushed. The battlefield lay in smoldering ruin. With a sickening sense of dread souring his gut, he started down the aisle toward the ladder and Börne's little green box, wondering what else he stood to lose that morning.

TWENTY-ONE

The burden of the students' safety weighed heavily on his shoulders. He envisioned an angel on one side, urging action; her horned nemesis perched on the other, recommending Nick grab a tub of popcorn, find a seat in the auditorium, and watch what was about to unfold.

If the mayor insisted on giving these kids the 4D experience, then they would get one, alright. Just not the full experience. Thankfully, the technology was configured in a manner that allowed him to shut down certain mechanical features if he so chose. And today he so chose.

His entire being teemed with dread.

Nick crested the aisle, holding the ladder high so as not to decapitate any kids with it along the way. His laundry list grew more extensive with each child he passed; things he'd need to take care of before he could even think about starting the movie. If he was going to keep these kids safe—if that was even possible—precautions would need to be taken.

Sweat broke out under his collar as he dropped the ladder in the hallway with a clatter. He wiped his hands on his khakis and started toward the control room.

A thought hit him. A memory from the opening night fiasco. Nick spun on his heels and returned to the ladder. A moment later, it sat propped against the back wall *inside* the auditorium.

Just in case.

"Hey, Nick!"

He recognized the voice, though its normally soft tone was gone. A sharpness replaced it. Like razor wire.

"What the heck's going on?"

Nori's face wore a mask of concern as she made her way through the lobby, playing caboose to the train of students barreling toward the auditorium. Once the last pre-teen disappeared through the double doors, she joined Nick in his rush to the control room.

"Blackwood had one of his bright ideas," he said, sweat streaming down the side of his neck. It was as if the devil on his shoulder had relieved himself in disgust at his decision to side with the angel. He ran his gauze-wrapped forearm across his brow. "Feel warm in here to you?"

Nori didn't answer. He wouldn't have heard anyway. His mind was taxed at the moment. It could only do so much thinking at one time.

At the door to the control room, he hesitated and turned to her with a frown. "What are you doing here, anyway?"

Her gaze turned back to the auditorium doors, the previous night's events no doubt on her mind as well.

"The mayor sent me a text," she said. "Told me something was going on here I'd want to report on." She shook her head, eyes wide and cavernous. It seemed her journalism classes hadn't covered how to report on innocent children put in harm's way by a town's sworn leader. "I had no idea he was doing something like this."

Nick opened the door and scaled the two steps to the control room.

"The children," she continued, right on his heels. "How could he… why would he…" They were not questions in the usual sense, nor were they statements of fact. They were simply a reporter verbally processing the situation laid before her. Nick had no answers to offer, though he doubted she was seeking any. At least, not from him.

For the second time that day, he brought up the touch screen control panel. He started swiping and tapping, turning the effects on and off, making judgment calls on each one. Given the circumstances, misting machines spraying anything onto the kids seemed like a bad idea. He shut them off. Armrests that sent a brief and buzzing shock? Nope. Shut those off, too. About the only thing he couldn't control ahead of time were the light bulbs. If they decided to blow themselves up again, all he could do was try to get everyone out as quickly as possible.

"Do me a favor," he said, fingers swiping through a catalogue of options.

Nori didn't hesitate. "Anything."

He handed over his set of keys, holding out a shiny silver key in particular. "Down the hallway, past my office, is the storage room. There are metal cases containing old movie reels stacked in the corner. Grab the biggest, heaviest one you can carry, and meet me back at the auditorium."

Nori disappeared without further instruction.

Nick turned back to the control panel. What to do about the seats themselves? They rocked a little. Jostled up and down. Had mechanical sensors hidden in the cushions that, when triggered, made it feel as if you had sat on a small animal. Comparatively speaking, the seats seemed the least likely to pose a threat. Besides, he had to leave the kids something to experience, right? How else were they supposed to—in the mayor's words—piss themselves with laughter?

Better than pissing themselves with fear.

He shook his mind free of the thought.

Satisfied he'd done everything in his power to keep the kids safe, Nick cued the movie. Of course, keeping the kids safe was not entirely within his control. He could shut off all the effects he wanted. If The Chamberlain or its previous owner's spirit got a hair up its ass to lash out…

The movie took a moment to load. Once it had, it still wouldn't start until he pressed play. Good thing. He wasn't ready for it to start just yet. Grabbing two spare electrical cables from a nearby cardboard box, he exited the control room.

They met again at the auditorium's double doors. Nori had done as he'd asked. She held a large grey metal case, both hands through the handle. The previous owner had left behind the films. Not knowing what to do with the oversized paperweights, Nick had allowed them to continue collecting dust in the storage room until he could find a use for them.

A use had finally presented itself.

"Trade ya." He took the case, and in exchange, handed Nori the cables. "Be right back."

While the town's children were discovering the stereoscopic effects of their 3D glasses, Nick made his way down the aisle toward the front of the theater. Turning right brought him to the emergency exit. He pushed open the door and wedged the reel case between it and the doorjamb. By propping open an emergency exit door, he was assuredly violating a fire code. He didn't care. Nor did he have time to research it even if he did. Legal or not, it was necessary. If the kids needed a quick way out, they would damn sure have options. Key word: unrestricted. A door that couldn't close, sure as shit couldn't lock.

Nori remained in the doorway where he'd left her, cables in hand.

"Thanks," he said, taking one of the thick, black cables from her. He fashioned a loop with one end and slid it around one of the door handles. Pulling it tight, he wrapped the other end of the cable numerous times around a nearby wall sconce. Keeping the double doors open would allow an annoying amount of light in. There was sure to be grumbling. But at least it would keep the exit clear. The kids would just have to deal with it, as it was for their own protection.

Protection.

He shuddered at the thought of them needing it.

"Good idea."

"Huh?" In his haste, he'd forgotten Nori was still hanging around. It reminded him of how difficult it had been to lose her on opening night. This time, her persistence was a Godsend. Despite their rocky start, the reporter was proving a valuable ally. Whether this showing resulted in a positive story, he wouldn't have wanted to guess. Nor could he predict how long this budding kinship would last. For now, he was glad she was on his side. "Oh, thanks."

Nick took a deep breath and tried to calm his racing heart. After running through his mental list, the conclusion he came to was this: the kids were as safe as he could hope to make them. Short of outright disobeying the mayor and refusing to show the movie altogether, there wasn't much more he could do.

"If you could secure the other door the same way," he said, handing the second cable to Nori, "I'll go start the movie."

TWENTY-TWO

Nick took in a deep breath.

Beyond the control room's tiny window, the auditorium was nearly full. Under normal circumstances, it was a situation for which he would have traded an appendage. However, these weren't normal circumstances. These circumstances had the potential to become dire really quick. After the previous evening's conversation with Börne and Claudia, he couldn't believe he was actually going through with this.

If there's a repeat performance of last night...

He closed his eyes, forced the thought into the dark recesses of his mind. It would scar the kids for life if that happened. He also didn't see where he had a choice. There was no getting out from under the mayor's thumb on this one. Not if he wanted to keep The Chamberlain long enough to turn it around. He'd seen how easily the mayor had pulled the theater out from under...

Cropper.

Nick exhaled slowly.

With a single tap to the control screen, the auditorium's lights dimmed. The room's chatter devolved into a hush, save for a smattering of giggles that required a teacher's hard "shh" to quell. Another deep breath, another pensive exhale. He tapped the screen once more and exited the control room.

The mayor stood outside the auditorium's open doors talking to Nori. From all appearances, the conversation wasn't going well.

The mayor kept adjusting his tie. Nori looked even more perturbed than she had a moment ago.

Nick braced himself as he approached.

"What's up?" he asked.

Nori jabbed a thumb at Blackwood. "Mayor here's skipping out on the movie."

Nick looked at Blackwood who appeared as sheepish as a man with a four-hour erection walking into an emergency room.

"Sorry, Nick." The mayor tapped his watch. "Got a meeting at noon. Only came along to make sure you understood the plan here." He shot a quick glance into the darkened theater where the opening credits were already rolling. His façade cracked and his anxiety showed through. The mayor tapped his watch again. "Gotta get back to the office."

"But Mayor—"

"Sorry, Nick." The mayor turned, gesturing with half a wave. "Places and people."

And then he was gone, the heels of his loafers click-clacking through the lobby.

When Nick turned back to Nori, the brief interaction with Blackwood had only stoked the flames of the inferno behind her eyes.

"You believe that guy?" she looked as angry as the mayor had looked anxious. "He's got balls enough to fill the theater with innocent children, but not enough to sit in there with them? Meeting my ass." She raised a middle finger toward the front door. "Tell you what, Nick. If I was his kid, I would have run away, too."

If he had to pinpoint the moment he first detected honest to goodness feelings for Ms. Nori Park, that would have been it. The break from her usual poised and mild-mannered way of carrying herself was refreshing. There was a realness to it. Her furrowed brow rivaled the most melodramatic of toddlers. The flared nostrils and pursed lips. All genuine. All cute as hell. He'd heard people say, "you're adorable when you're angry," but it wasn't until that moment he understood what they meant. He had to stifle a grin.

He must not have completely succeeded.

"What?" she asked.

He did his best to play it straight. "Sorry?"

"You had a look." Her eyes narrowed, then relaxed. "Like you had something to say."

He shook his head. "No, not really."

"Okay. Never mind. Sorry." She exhaled and dropped her shoulders. "And sorry for that back there." She gestured toward the door in reference to her outburst over Blackwood. "But sometimes that man…"

The sound of calliope music wafted through the open doorway.

Nick reached up and touched her elbow. "It's fine. Trust me." Second guessing the gesture, he pulled his hand back. "I'm right there with you."

Inside the auditorium, a man's voice started talking over the music.

Nick raised his eyebrows. "Here we go."

Nori nodded and mustered a slight grin. "It's gonna be okay."

He returned the gesture, knowing full well she didn't believe it.

That was okay.

Neither did he.

And from the doorway of the auditorium, Nick and Nori held their breath and watched the opening scenes of the movie, one eye on the overhead lights, the other on over two hundred and fifty of Angler Bay's youngest and brightest.

The film was only four minutes old when the first scream erupted.

From the open doorway, Nick and Nori exchanged a look.

Their expressions mirrored each other's emotions: fear, dread, horror.

Nick bolted into the auditorium, Nori within his shadow.

The scream had come from down front and somewhere to the left. A young girl, by the sound of it. A cluster of students and a few teachers rose to their feet in the front row. Murmurs filled the air. A commotion poised to spread like a California wildfire.

Alarming scenarios ran through his mind, each contributing to a growing queue of questions. What had caused the scream? Was it something he'd seen before? A phenomenon familiar to The Chamberlain? Or was it some fresh horror to add to its catalogue?

He filed them all away. The what's and how's weren't important. He focused foremost on reaching the girl whose scream had turned his stomach inside out.

The film continued to play on the screen.

Nick's pace slowed as he neared the bottom. Over the music and narration, he could hear Nori's footsteps behind him. At the front of the auditorium, he turned left. It wasn't until then that he realized the oddest of truths: the scream and now giggling had both come from the same area.

Turned out, it was the same girl.

"Sorry," she said, as he approached. The girl with long brown curls and a Harry Potter t-shirt had returned to her seat, hands folded over her lap. In the glow from the nearby screen, an embarrassed grin graced her face. "The ripples in the seat," she continued. "They scared me is all."

The mob of whispering gawkers dispersed, and everyone returned to their seats.

Nick rubbed his forehead and released a deep exhale. Relief deflated his rigid shoulders. His heart rate, however, would take longer to normalize. *Guess I should've turned off the damn seats, too.*

On the screen behind him, a killer whale rose out of the sea before twisting and splashing back down.

He looked skyward. Normally, the overhead misters would have kicked on at that moment, spraying water—hopefully—over the crowd. Thank God, he'd shut them down. He turned to Nori, whose face showed more relief than annoyance.

"False alarm?" she asked.

He nodded.

She ducked down and started back toward the center aisle.

Nick looked to the cowering girl once more. She mouthed the word 'sorry.' He replied by mouthing, 'it's okay,' and gave her a thumbs up. When he turned to leave, the teacher sitting at the end of the row offered an apologetic smile. He nodded and hurried up the aisle.

The following fifty minutes of film played on without disturbance. Without a hitch, as the mayor would have said, had he the nerve to stick around. For nearly an hour, Nori and Nick stood in the doorway, tense as sentries, poised to organize an emergency retreat if the need arose. Several times their eyes met. Several times they exchanged a raised eyebrow. That everything was going so smoothly surprised them both. Especially Nick. It seemed anytime he set foot in the auditorium anymore something bizarre, or at least out of the ordinary, happened.

But, as two hundred and fifty raucous students and a dozen relieved teachers filed out of the auditorium toward their awaiting buses, The Chamberlain felt like any other movie theater in any other town. A cool place to while away the hours on a hot summer day. Relaxing. Fun. Safe.

And that caused concern to tie his stomach in a knot.

Whatever spirit was calling The Chamberlain home had just shown its ability to pick and choose when to go bat shit crazy and when not to. That meant the spirit wasn't only vengeful, but it had the ability to scheme.

And Nick couldn't imagine a more frightening scenario.

TWENTY-THREE

"Whatcha lookin' at, *meine Liebe*?"

Swaddled in a terrycloth white robe, wet hair wrapped in a towel, Claudia sat on the edge of the bed sipping the hotel's finest dark roast from a paper cup. Her transformation was just beginning, from the everyday Claudia Forrester who cherished yoga pants, oversized t-shirts, and DIY landscaping shows on Saturday mornings, to the elegant and mysterious paranormal investigator and one half of F.A.U.S.T. The entire process—hair, makeup, wardrobe—took most of two hours.

Börne, whose transformation took less time, sat at the room's narrow desk with his laptop open in front of him.

An episode of *Big Bang Theory* played on the television in the background.

"Floor plans." He sipped Matcha tea and checked his watch. "8:40, by the way."

Claudia didn't acknowledge his gentle prod. "Floor plans, huh? Finally building me my dream home?"

Börne tilted his head and eyed his wife over the rims of his glasses. The way the hotel's standard issue robe draped her slender form gave new meaning to the word "complimentary." She hadn't tied the robe together. She rarely did unless someone came to the door. He often questioned why she bothered wearing a robe at all. Other times, he simply enjoyed the view. Like now. Her damp cleavage and baby soft naval taunted him to no end. The sheer black panties that peeked out when she uncrossed, then re-crossed her legs made matters worse. In his mind, he imagined himself rising from the chair and going to her, sliding his hands inside the folds of terry cloth and sending the robe to the floor.

But, only in his mind. They had some place to be. Things to do.

If only they hadn't made plans with Nick.

He shook the fantasy from his mind and turned back to the laptop. "The Chamberlain, my dearest Claudia. I've been comparing these original floor plans from 1912 to what the theater looks like now. At least from what I can remember."

"And?" She unwound the towel and shook her head. Damp, red ringlets cascaded over her shoulders. "Find anything interesting?"

He leaned in and squinted at the laptop's small screen, wishing he had access to his much larger desktop monitor at home. "Not yet."

Claudia slapped at the mattress. "Well, keep at it. I'm sure you'll find something."

She swung her legs off the bed and got to her feet. In the process, she allowed the robe to slip off her shoulders. The garment gathered in a heap on the floor. Not trying all that hard to conceal a wicked grin, she sashayed around the end of the bed. Halfway to the bathroom, she cast a glance over her shoulder to see if Börne was looking.

He was.

Then he was on his feet and headed her way.

It was almost an hour before Claudia made it to the bathroom to continue her transformation.

The last showing ended at 10:35 pm.

For the film's entire ninety-three-minute run time, The Chamberlain held not a single soul. Floyd Cropper's notwithstanding. So far, the mayor's plan to generate business had yet to produce results. In all fairness, it would require time for word to get around. If the plan was to work at all. Bad news travelled quickly in small communities like Angler Bay. Good news? Not so much. It wasn't as interesting, didn't demand the same urgency.

Unfortunately, Nick didn't know how much time The Chamberlain Theater had. Bills were piling up, and his dwindling rainy-day fund wouldn't get him through a light sprinkle. With that in mind, he had to give Blackwood at least a little credit. And only because things had gone so well. It wasn't necessarily a poor plan, just ill-advised. They had gotten lucky.

Had things not gone so well…

While he waited for Claudia and Börne to arrive, he went about shutting things down in the control room. With three quick taps, the screen went dark. The system's soft humming came to a rest. The theater fell as quiet as an underground cave. The only exception being the occasional rumble of thunder somewhere out in the night.

He looked through the small window and out over the still auditorium. For the hundredth time that day, he tried wrapping his head around the events of the morning. Or to be more exact, the *lack of* events. He couldn't even remember smelling smoke while the students were there. It all left him with so many questions. Why had Floyd's spirit not shown itself? Why not rear its ugly head? It had been daytime. Did that matter? Did the time of day have bearing on when a vengeful spirit acted out? He didn't think so. Especially when it was virtual nighttime twenty-four seven in the auditorium because of the lack of windows.

He flipped off the light in the control room and closed the door behind him. He was eager to get F.A.U.S.T.'s thoughts on what had and had not transpired that morning. They were, after all, the experts.

Nick started down the hallway, but hearing the opening and closing of the front door stopped him in his tracks. He glanced at his watch. The paranormal investigators were also prompt, it seemed.

He continued down the hallway toward the lobby, making a mental note to grab the broom and dustpan. He may not have had any paying customers that day, but in hosting an auditorium full of pre-teens, there was no shortage of cleaning to be done. Nearly twelve hours later and he was still finding stray candy and gum wrappers lying around. And he hadn't even sold the students any concessions. Kids were resourceful that way.

He chuckled to himself. Perhaps that was the reason the morning's showing had gone off without a hitch. Maybe ol' Floyd was too frightened by the prospect of a theater full of unpredictable kids.

Nick couldn't blame him.

He was still finding the idea amusing when he rounded the corner and came face to face with an empty lobby. His grin dissolved. He could have sworn he'd heard the front door open, then close. Outside, rain was coming down at a good clip. The throng of wind and rain while the door had been open had been unmistakable.

Right on cue, a clap of thunder rattled the roof above.

"Hello?"

Nick looked all around the deserted lobby. Despite what he thought he'd heard, he appeared to be very much alone.

The first hair on the back of his neck rose.

He shook the sensation off.

Maybe he'd simply been too slow to make an appearance. Maybe Börne and Claudia had arrived after all. They'd poked their heads in, and having not found him in the lobby, retreated to their car to grab their equipment. *Of course.* That was it. The most likely scenario.

At the front door, he placed his forehead against the glass and cupped his hands around his eyes. The outside world was shrouded in night and saturation. The street glistened with falling rain. Buildings shimmered with the light of nearby streetlamps. Rainwater ran down the theater's steps, converged into a flowing current, and swept the gutter clean.

What he didn't see was a hearse.

Or any other vehicles, for that matter. The street was empty. Not a single soul scuttered about. The brewing storm was keeping everyone huddled at home. Everyone except—

"Nick."

His feet left the ground. His heart left his chest. He spun around.

Mayor Blackwood stood in the doorway of the men's room. *Leaned* was maybe a more accurate description. Propped. Only one foot supported the man's heft. His shoulder lodged against the doorjamb afforded him the ability to remain upright. His nose was red, his hair damp, and the way his necktie was loose and pulled to the side spun a tale as old as time. His light blue button-up poking through his fly backed up the story.

There was apparently one person in town whose good time wasn't being hampered by the weather. And by all appearances, Mrs. Blackwood hadn't been in on the fun. Which was a shame, because Valarie Blackwood was by far the best and most palatable aspect of the mayor. Nick didn't envy her having to deal with the mayor when sober. He couldn't imagine having to deal with the man after an evening spent in the bottle.

Blackwood let a world-class belch escape, then smacked his lips, savoring his bourbon a second time.

Nick pursed his lips. Forget the man's wife. Right now, he didn't envy his own damn self. "Mayor. What can I do for you?"

"You got shit to eat around here, Nick? And for fuck's sake, call me John."

Nice try, but no thanks.

He wasn't falling for it. Not again. The night he'd signed the paperwork acquiring The Chamberlain, the mayor had taken him out for a celebratory dinner and drinks and showed him the proper way to punish one's liver. What the mayor's liver had ever done to deserve it Nick had no idea. But damned if the man hadn't given it a sound beating. It was at some point during the assault he'd instructed Nick to stop calling him Mr. Mayor. Or even Mayor. Said it was too formal for the two of them at this stage in the game. Two days later, though, when they'd met up to do a walk through and discuss prospective plans, he made the mistake of calling the mayor by his first name. Nick received a head spin and a stern, third-degree scowl for his efforts. Blackwood didn't say anything. Didn't have to. Nick could tell by the man's reaction that addressing him informally was hereby frowned upon.

"The usual," Nick said. "Twizzlers, Sno Caps, Raisinets. Didn't make popcorn tonight. Didn't have the demand for it." He spread his arms wide, gesturing toward the lack of customers roaming the lobby. "But I could whip some up if you'd like."

He held his breath while awaiting an answer. He just knew the mayor would make him fire up the popcorn popper. Then he'd be here all night cleaning out the damn thing. Surprisingly, the mayor declined the offer.

"No, no." Blackwood shook his head and mumbled. "Won't be here long. Jus' wanted to stop on my way home, hear how well the showing for the kids went."

How well?

Nick sighed.

Assumptions were a heavily wielded weapon in the mayor's arsenal, always on his hip, always at the ready. They informed you that, not only was he right, but any attempt at disagreement would be futile. In Angler Bay, Blackwood was akin to the chef of a mob-run restaurant, always proclaiming his meatballs were the best, most authentic in the city. Who's going to argue with the chef of a restaurant backed by the mob? No one, that's who. The same no one who was going to tell the mayor his assumptions were wrong.

"Surprisingly, it went well," Nick said. "No casualties."

The mayor righted himself and shuffled toward the concession counter.

"Jesus H, Nick." A chuckle and sour breath exited the mayor's mouth. "Certainly, you weren't actually expecting… casualties."

Nick moved behind the counter to serve the man if he changed his mind, and not simply turn him loose on his inventory.

"It's not like we haven't had our share of chaos around here." As if he needed reminding, the burn on his arm started to itch. He thought about sharing the news of his injury with the mayor but dismissed the notion. "Very real chaos the last couple days. Claudia calls them manifestations. Whatever you wanna call it, something's definitely not right here. Or, not happy, if you believe those two."

"And do you?"

"What?"

"Believe those two?"

Nick shrugged. "Well…"

The mayor vomited laughter.

It wasn't the response he'd expected. He also couldn't claim to be surprised. He was dealing with the man who, on opening night, while Nick sat shaken and bleeding, asked how soon he could be up and running again. He shook his head at the memory, truly blessed to be graced with the man's inebriated presence on this glorious evening.

He started to speak, to defend either F.A.U.S.T., himself, or both, but saw the uselessness of it. *Fuck it.*

Nick was about to reach for his broom and act like he was too busy to chat when an honest to goodness blessing walked through the door. A blessing in the form of Börne and Claudia Forrester.

"Thank, God," he muttered.

TWENTY-FOUR

Turned out, Nick wasn't the only one eager to get Börne and Claudia's thoughts on the morning. Nori was hot on the Forresters' heels. When the door closed shut behind the trio, she and Claudia were already in mid-conversation.

"It was a false alarm," Nori said. "Something about the seat startled her."

"And that's it?" Claudia walked further into the lobby with her head cocked. The investigator was literally lending Nori an ear. "Nothing else?"

Claudia's flowing white evening gown, along with Börne's 'Goth butler about town' attire, must have struck the mayor's funny bone, because he snickered.

Nick's stomach seized.

"Ho-ly shit. Would you look at that? Halloween come early this year?" As words continued to spill from his mouth, the mayor seemed intent on *not* putting his best foot forward. "And what, may I ask, is your name, love? Or shall I just call you, Beautiful?"

Embarrassment turned Nick's stomach. He felt bad for the Forresters. If there was one thing he'd learned about Claudia, it was she could stand up for herself. But here was the mayor, hitting on the man's wife right in front of him.

Nick unbuttoned his collar, responding to the room's sudden rise in temperature.

As expected, Claudia handled the situation, and the mayor, with her usual aplomb.

"My name is Claudia Forrester," she said. "And this is my husband and partner, Börne." She offered no smile of greeting. It would have been fake if she had. "And you can only be Mayor Blackwood."

The mayor beamed, oblivious to the slight.

"Why, yes," he said. An arrogant grin broke across the mayor's flushed face. The besmirching of his reputation had sailed over his head without so much as putting a dent in his sloppy smile. His red-rimmed and bloodshot eyes didn't so much as blink. Even as he asked Claudia how she knew his name, it was obvious the man was more than pleased she did.

Claudia answered, "I've heard enough about you, Sir."

Nick smirked. *Classic.* Not 'I've heard *a lot* about you,' but 'I've heard *enough* about you.' Enough to form an opinion, apparently.

If he wasn't still reeling from the mayor's earlier repugnance, he might have cracked a smile. Börne fixed scornful eyes on the mayor. Nori rolled hers, and Claudia set hers on anything and everything except the mayor. Awkward was the name of the game. Nick loved The Chamberlain. It was his home away from home. But, at the moment, he would have rather been anywhere but standing in its lobby.

And to think, he had been looking forward to the evening.

"So," Nick said, turning to the Forresters and doing his best to ignore the mayor's presence, "sounds like Nori's been filling you in on our morning."

"She has." Even as he answered, Börne's stare remained on the mayor, who leered at Claudia. "Sounds like our friend has a soft spot for children."

"I'm sorry," the mayor said, his leering eyes finally breaking off Claudia. "Our friend?"

"The spirit haunting The Chamberlain," Claudia said. "Floyd Cropper's spirit to be exact."

"Someone," Börne chimed, "with whom I'm sure you're well-acquainted."

Another gut-busting bellow exploded from Blackwood.

Nick shook his head, looked to Claudia, and mouthed the words 'I'm sorry.' To the mayor, everything coming out of either Claudia or Börne's mouth was apparently the funniest damn thing. Nick shouldn't be surprised. Adding alcohol to an asshole generally makes for a bigger, more tactless asshole. He was embarrassed. Slightly ashamed. But, not surprised.

"Ridiculous," the mayor said, once the last of his chuckles died off. "First of all, yes, old Floyd loved kids. Shame he and Helen never had any of his own. But you think the old guy's haunting this place? Never heard something so absurd. I mean, don't get me wrong. Floyd Cropper loved this damn theater more than most men love their wives. Even more than they love their mistresses. But I don't think he had ambition enough to spend his afterlife running around causing problems for ol' Nick here. Ambition to that degree would have kept The Chamberlain from going under while he was alive."

One after another, Nick met everyone's gaze. If they weren't all thinking the same thing—*was this guy really the mayor of a town?*—they soon would be. The man never went too long without putting his size eleven foot in his mouth.

"Look," Blackwood said, circling the group, taking measure of each of them. "You two come in here dressed like you just walked off the set of a seventies B-Movie, filling Nick's head with stories of spirits and grandeur. No wonder he can't make any money. He's too busy looking over his shoulder for the ghost of owners past to concentrate on running this damn place, let alone come up with any kind of real business strategy."

Nick's eyes widened while his stomach soured.

Blackwood had sobered at an astonishing rate. He no longer resembled the town lush, stumbling and fumbling. He spoke clearly and with purpose. He was now the captain of his ship, and everyone else in the room, his vassal.

"And you," the mayor said, stopping behind Nori. He leaned in as if to whisper in her ear, but the words came as loud and biting as his previous. "You're perpetuating this nonsense? Clouding Nick's head even more? Arming him with even more lame-ass excuses?"

"But Mayor—"

The mayor silenced her with a raised finger. He was on a roll, stonewalling to maximum effect, hardly a waver in his gate.

"I would expect more professionalism from you, Ms. Park. Perhaps I should give my pal, Preston, a call. Ask him why he doesn't have better control over his journalists."

Everyone stood there stunned and seething at being lectured like schoolchildren caught smoking behind the bleachers.

Nick looked at Nori. Her head shook with irritation. Her teeth held her bottom lip hostage. She wanted to say something; wanted to rage against the Blackwood machine. He wished she would. But his threat of calling her editor had teeth. She had already written one story about The Chamberlain, her shred-piece about the opening night fiasco. There was no upside to a second story about the failing theater. So far, she was working the follow-up on her own time, out of her own curiosity. One call from the mayor's office had the potential to kill a new story before she could determine whether there even was one. Much less pitch it. A journalist's worst nightmare.

The storm churning behind Börne's eyes told Nick all he needed to know about the man's introduction to Angler Bay's beloved mayor. Guy was pissed. Like, ready to pack up his shit and go home, pissed. Which would be a death blow, for sure. The final nail in The Chamberlain's coffin. Nick was out of ideas. Bringing in F.A.U.S.T. had been his Hail Mary.

Nick was about to speak up and try to stop the bleeding, turn the tide back in his favor, when Claudia opened her mouth and poked the bear.

"Well, then, Mr. Mayor," she said, "I don't suppose you'd like to meet this spirit for yourself?"

A guffaw. That's what they call a spontaneous eruption of laughter. This was also what came out of the mayor's mouth. If it had been anything but hot air, it would have soiled his shoes.

"Darling, I think I've got better things to do with my evening than to hang around here playing ghostbusters." The mayor straightened his tie, the universal gesture of someone important, with somewhere important to be, and something important to do. He may have been okay, if only he'd stopped there. "Nick, if this is how you want to spend your time and money, well, I can't stop you. But there are two things I know about my bank: it closes every day at five; and if they don't get the lease payment from you, they'll gladly get it from someone else."

The mayor turned on his heels, shirt still sticking out of his fly like a blue tongue and headed toward the door.

Nick fumed. He didn't know where his line lay, but somewhere during his speech, Blackwood had crossed it. He needed to speak up. Stand up for not only himself, but all of them. Someone had to put the son of a bitch in his place.

Since it turned out not to be him, he couldn't have been happier it was Nori.

"What's wrong Mayor?" she called out before the man could reach the front door. "Afraid to face Floyd after what you did to him?"

The soles of Blackwood's loafers sent out a sharp squeak as he stopped abruptly. He didn't turn around immediately. He just stood there with his back to them. When he finally did turn to face them, his face was the color of a Mexican chili, his temper just as hot. He pursed his lips, but it didn't stop him from speaking through them.

"Let's get on with it."

TWENTY-FIVE

"Black tourmaline." Claudia reached out her hand. "Its protection against negative energy and spirits have always served me well." Two strands of black leather cord, identical to the ones hanging around her and Börne's necks, hung from her fingers. A stone, about an inch and a half long, swung at the bottom of the cord. It was rough-edged, resembling a piece of jagged black chalk. She looked around the group, concluding her survey with Blackwood. "Though I'm afraid I only brought four necklaces, Mr. Mayor. I didn't know you would be joining us."

The mayor chuckled.

"That's quite alright, Miss." The smirk on his face affirmed that not receiving a gemstone was indeed alright. He didn't need the protection any more than he needed alcohol counseling. "I'm good."

Nori took a necklace.

Nick followed suit. He hadn't given a moment's thought to things like crystals, oils, or anything else of the spiritual persuasion. As far as he was concerned, only people who liked to dance naked in the forest under a full moon believed in their powers. And while the image of Claudia dancing naked among the trees tried to enter his mind, he blocked its entrance. He ignored the mayor's ridicule of the gemstone and didn't feel the least bit foolish slipping the necklace over his head. Not until he noticed the man's derisive expression now aimed in his direction.

Nick turned away.

"The black tourmaline," Börne said, "is considered one of the most effective gemstones for protection. At least it's the one we feel most confident using. Stones and crystals work differently for different people, but these have always served us well."

Nick ran his fingers up and down the length of the course stone. "And how many times have you dealt with a spirit this… vengeful?"

"A time or two," Claudia answered, but only after exchanging a look with Börne.

"What?" It was Nori who noticed. "What is it?"

Claudia reacted like a teenager caught kicking a secret-holding friend under the table. "What do you mean?" she asked, feigning indifference.

Nori looked to Börne with her reporter's eye, then turned it back on Claudia. "Feels like there's something you're not telling us."

Claudia checked in with Börne again. After a moment's hesitation, he gave her a slight nod. She cleared her throat while everyone, including Blackwood, looked on. "It's just… well… to be honest, we've never experienced manifestations this… pronounced. This tangible."

Nick's jaw squared. "This pissed off, you mean."

Börne answered with a nod. "Which is why we're forgoing the EMF meter and much of the other detection equipment tonight," he explained. "There's really nothing to detect at this point. We already know it's here. We've seen its handiwork. This spirit is being anything but subtle."

"Floyd's spirit," the mayor mocked.

"As far as we've seen," Börne continued, "nobody has ever caught evidence of the afterlife like what we've seen here at The Chamberlain on video. Not like this. Most images captured on film have to be interpreted. And I mean interpreted to determine whether the image is something, or just an anomalous trick of light everyone hopes is something. So, the next time the shit hits the fan in there," he pointed toward the auditorium, "we're catching said shit on video." He bent and pulled two hand held camcorders from a black duffle bag. He handed one to Nick.

Nick turned the device over in his hands and started familiarizing himself with its controls.

"What about sage?" Nori asked. "I've heard of people burning sage to cleanse a house."

Nick looked to Nori with eyebrows raised. "Is that an option?"

"Two problems," Claudia said. "In order for sage to work, there must be windows in the space. Somewhere to flush the spirits, allowing them somewhere to escape. As the theater has no windows, I don't think burning sage would do anything but fill the room with a pleasant fragrance."

Nick stopped fiddling with his camera. "And the second problem?"

Claudia sucked in her bottom lip, wedged it between her teeth. She cast pensive eyes in Börne's direction. "*Meine Liebe*?"

"The thing is," Börne said, having a difficult time hiding the mischief creeping into his grin, "we don't want to get rid of the spirit. Not yet."

Nick's eyebrows drew up in high arches.

Nori's eyes narrowed.

The mayor belched, otherwise remaining uncharacteristically quiet and indifferent.

"Wait a second," Nick started.

Börne raised the camera for all to see. "Not until we get some footage." He met everyone's gaze one by one, reading their reactions, before settling on one in particular. "Nick," he continued, "I'm not exaggerating when I say this could be huge."

Nori, ever the probing reporter, was quick to interject. "For your website, you mean."

"For all of us," Claudia said.

"I don't know." Nick dropped the camera to his side. "Riling up this spirit to get some video of it? Sounds a little risky to me. Not to mention irresponsible. Kinda like pouring gasoline on a fire so you can see it better. I'd as soon get rid of this damn thing, whatever it is, and move on with our lives."

"We will," Börne assured. "But—"

"Aw, come on, Nick," the mayor busted in. "Where's your sense of adventure?" He looked Claudia and Börne up and down. "These two are obviously professionals. If they think we're sitting on something big here, then by God, why are we standing around with our dicks in our hands debating it?"

Börne's grin stretched to a full-on smile. Not because of the mayor's sophomoric humor, but because he had convinced at least one person in the group to see the value of his plan. Keyword being *value*. In Nick's experience, if the mayor saw dollar signs in a particular plan, that was all the dangling carrot he needed.

"Let's get on with it!" The mayor clapped his meaty hands and lead the way toward the auditorium doors. The rest of the circle broke rank. Börne followed hot on the mayor's heels, a puppy shadowing a toddler with a cookie. Nori didn't seem as anxious. She trailed a few steps behind, her investigative mind no doubt processing the change in F.A.U.S.T.'s plans.

Only Claudia and Nick hung back, watching the others walk away. He had his reasons for not following. He assumed Claudia had hers. With that in mind, he made the most of the one-on-one time.

"You don't seem as excited as your husband." He searched Claudia's face for a telltale sign. Something foreshadowing an explanation. His investigation came up empty.

"Let's just say I take the paranormal a little more seriously than my beloved." Claudia continued to watch the group retreat as she spoke. "Specifically, the dangers it can present."

Nick swallowed hard. His hand went to the pendant hanging around his neck. If she was trying to put him at ease, she was off to a piss poor start.

"Um… dangers?"

She nodded but remained silent. Nick sensed there was a story behind the silence. A story he decided he wanted to hear before stepping foot in the auditorium again.

"So," he said. "You've only felt the need to use the crystals for protection, what, a time or two? Have they ever failed you?"

"Once," Claudia said, meeting his gaze. "They've failed me once."

Nick eyed her warily. The sudden softness of her voice. The lack of confidence in her green eyes. It was all out of place. A side of the paranormal governess he had yet to see. It filled him with unease. Enough so, it caused the contents of his stomach to whirlpool with nausea. "I'm almost afraid to ask, but what happened?"

Her expression was that of a time traveler's journeying back to a memory as she looked away. "It didn't go well."

He expected a loud clap of thunder to erupt outside, the lobby lights to flicker, or a phantom orchestra to play an ominous dun, dun, dun. Something to portend a dramatic revelation. Neither happened. This wasn't a movie, after all. He checked in on the group standing near the closed auditorium doors. Closed doors was the new protocol. He saw no benefit in leaving them open anymore. Only the mayor appeared impatient. He wasn't used to people keeping him waiting and cast Nick a questioning glare. Nick ignored the look and turned back to Claudia. "Wanna tell me about it?"

She shook her head, let out a sigh. "Not exactly."

The nausea in Nick's stomach solidified into a greasy mass of dread. "Okay, then," he said, running a hand through his hair. "Maybe we should just—"

"Her name was Shelby Ann Creek." Claudia's voice was meek, her words a virtual whisper. "She was my mentor. My teacher. Most of all, she was my friend."

The repeated use of the word 'was' didn't slip by unnoticed.

"She taught me everything I know," she continued. "Investigation after investigation, I soaked up every bit of knowledge I could. Under her guidance, I honed my own skills and sensibilities. She was an encyclopedia of information. Of strategy." She paused, casting her eyes down. "Then Dieburg happened."

Another pause, eyes now closed.

His mind raced. What healthy alternatives did former addicts turn to when anxieties mounted? What did herbal tea taste like, anyway? He waited a reasonable amount of time before prying. "What's a Dieburg?"

Claudia raised her eyes. "It's not a *what*," she said, "but a *where*." She placed a trembling hand to her temple, seemingly uncomfortable with having to relive the experience. "She should have seen it coming, should've known. But she was overconfident. We thought we were ready. We had no idea. The spirit was too powerful. More powerful than Shelby Ann had ever encountered."

"And the spirit here at the Chamberlain…"

"Let's call him by his name, shall we?"

He nodded. "Floyd. Is it, or is *he* as powerful as others you've encountered?"

Her down-turned look told him everything.

Nick's pulse quickened. His neck sprouted baby beads of sweat. All while his mind broke in ten different directions, reeling with this new information. Truth was, they were all in potential danger. He knew that now.

He should warn Nori. He should excuse himself and hide in his office, letting Börne videotape to his heart's content. For a moment, Nick even thought about calling off the whole damn thing. No videotaping. No summoning of spirits. No prayers for protection required, because nobody was going in. *No way in hell.*

He took a deep breath.

The only thing stopping him from cancelling the investigation were the consequences of doing so. If this thing didn't work out, if Claudia and Börne couldn't rid The Chamberlain of Floyd's pissed off spirit, then he was toast. Finished. Through. The doors would close on the theater, possibly forever, and Nick Fallon would add one more busted business venture to his ever-growing resume of failures.

"So," he pressed, but cautiously, "what happened in Dieburg?"

A visible shudder made its way through Claudia's shoulders. Her eyes remained closed.

How far back in time was her mind having to travel? He glanced over at Nori. She remained at the auditorium doors, talking to the other half of F.A.U.S.T. He wished he could hear their conversation. Was Börne expounding on his wife's fears? Was he sharing with them the potential dangers they faced? Nick doubted it. Why risk shitting on a plan that had little support to begin with? Especially when the only one showing said support was Mayor Blackwood. Not exactly an immoveable object. As eager as the man was to make a buck, he didn't come across as an adventurer-type, and would probably turn tail if he was privy to what Nick was learning.

Screw the herbal tea. Healthy alternative or not, he considered the bottle of bourbon sitting in his desk down the hall.

Claudia took in a deep breath and exhaled, pulling his attention back around.

"The details don't matter," she said. Sucking in her stomach, she smoothed out the lace of her white gown, straightened her posture. "What is inherently important is I made it out of that house before it crumbled in on itself. Shelby, God rest her soul, did not."

And there it was. The danger of which she had earlier spoken. *The house crumbled in on itself.* Nick shivered from a phantom breeze. Who knew that was a thing? Who knew a spirit could do more than flicker a few lights and slam a door or two? Who knew they had the means to cause actual harm?

Me, Nick thought, eyeing his bandaged arm.

You know damn well.

"Okay," he said. "So, I'm thinking—"

"Hey, Nick!" The mayor's voice split the quiet of the lobby, causing Nick to jump. "Stop hitting on this man's wife, would ya? I need to get home before mine locks me out."

TWENTY-SIX

Asshole!

Nick couldn't remember ever wanting something to happen inside the theater. Until now. Nothing too big. Nothing too dangerous. Nothing like Claudia's story. But an occurrence big enough to shake the mayor's arrogance and put the fear of—*Floyd?*—in him. New light bulbs be damned. As he and Claudia walked toward the auditorium, Nick felt the need to apologize for the mayor's lack of human decency. But with his blood boiling, he wasn't sure he could open his mouth right then without making an equally damning impression.

They joined the rest of the group at the auditorium doors.

Somewhere in the night, thunder rumbled on its way out of town.

"First things first," Claudia said, reaching out her hands. "We didn't offer a prayer of protection the last time, and Nick's arm suffered the consequences. It was irresponsible of me. I insist we return to that practice considering the spirit's temperament."

To the surprise of no one, a derisive chuckle escaped the mayor's lips.

Nick bit his lower lip. He was over the mayor thinking everything about the evening was funny. He assumed everyone else was, too. He wouldn't acknowledge the guy's rudeness, however, and risk giving him an opening for more.

In an uncharacteristic moment of weakness, Claudia didn't, or maybe couldn't, let it go.

"Something amusing you, Mr. Mayor?"

Blackwood raised his hands, the international sign of apology.

"Sorry," he said through droopy eyes. "But temperament? I wasn't aware ghosts had good and bad days."

Awaiting Claudia's retort, Nick considered the mayor's remark. It sounded legit, but was that truly the mayor's strategy? Was he wanting to have a serious discussion about spirits? Or was this yet another attempt at mocking the situation? Veiled as it might be.

"Mr. Mayor," Claudia said, dropping her outstretched hands. She bit her lower lip, mining the right amount of tact. "There are different types of spirits. And as they did while alive, all possess distinct personalities. Behaviors. Temperaments. Whatever you want to call it. They do not differ from any other creature in nature."

"No different?" The mayor looked all around the group. "So, you're telling me these so-called spirits are as natural as you and I? As Ms. Park? As... I'm sorry. Your name again?"

"Börne."

"As natural as good old Börne here?"

Nick remained a fly on the wall, watching the tennis match play out between Claudia and the mayor. It was both fascinating and, more than likely, far from over.

"We refer to the supernatural," Claudia continued, "as that which is beyond our scientific understanding of the laws of nature. At least, as we know them thus far. However, just because we can't wrap it up in a nice little package with these laws, does not mean they are any less a natural force. There are many forces of nature we don't have a complete grasp on. The supernatural is just one such force."

"A force to be reckoned with," Börne chimed in. Then he added, "at times."

Everyone took a beat, processing Claudia's explanation. Even the mayor seemed lost in thought. Though he may have simply been too drunk to process all the information he'd been given.

After several moments, and without further comment from any of them, Claudia reached her hands out to the others. Without hesitation, Nori took one. Nick took Nori's hand, and so on. All members of the group formed a circle except one.

"That's quite alright," the mayor said. To emphasize his lack of interest, Blackwood shoved his hands deep into his pants pockets. "Think I'll pass on the talking to God portion of the show. Never been much of a believer."

"In what?" Claudia inquired. "God or the supernatural?"

Blackwood nodded. "Yes."

"Interesting." She took a moment, appearing to turn something over in her mind. "Normally, I'd say your lack of belief in our vengeful spirit might be enough to protect you. It's a popular theory that how much credence we give spirits determines their strength."

The mayor cocked his head. "Normally?"

"I'm sorry?"

"You said *normally* my lack of belief might protect me." An uncomfortable grin broke across his face. "What did you mean?"

It was Nick who answered. "Like I keep telling you, Mayor. The situation here is anything but normal."

"Now," Claudia continued, seemingly satisfied with Nick's answer, "I usually say the prayer, covering the group." She glanced around, making eye contact with everyone. "This time, however, I would prefer if everyone said it with me. Everyone who believes, that is."

Only one of them abstained from nodding their agreement.

"Please, repeat after me." With eyes closed and head tilted back, Claudia took a deep breath and let it out. "Saint Michael, the Archangel, defend us in battle…"

Everyone did as she had asked, repeating her prayer line for line, word for word. Despite a devout upbringing, Nick teetered on the fence. He was still unsure whether he believed in God. He'd always found the arguments both for and against His existence compelling. Each swayed the needle in their direction at different times in his life. Each had felt right. Tonight, however, he took no chances. He said the prayer and said it well. Said it like a sinner in church the morning after a less than righteous Saturday night.

To the mayor's credit, he did nothing to disrespect their invocation. No awkward coughs, no clearing of his throat meant to distract. No guffaws. For all anyone knew, the man was silently repeating the words right alongside them. Perhaps all the talk about spirits had changed his mind after all.

Or more plausibly, maybe the drunk was sobering up.

"Alright," Börne said once they'd finished, "video recorders out, set to record." His smile, if the group wasn't careful, had the potential to be contagious. "Let's make history!"

TWENTY-SEVEN

Nick flipped the switch turning on the camcorder Börne had given him without first asking if he wanted it. An excellent move on the investigator's part. Had he asked, Nick wasn't sure he would have consented. If Börne was looking for someone to hang around and film the shit as it hit the fan, he probably wasn't the guy. He would have bet money on it. At least Börne's reasoning had been plausible. He didn't want to risk missing something by having only a stationary camera setup somewhere in the theater. With the mobile cameras, they could cover the room from both sides, capturing all angles and corners. Fairly logical as far as game plans went. Börne only regretted not having a third camera for Nori. Though she didn't seem put off by not having one. Otherwise, he would have gladly relinquished his.

The camcorder clicked and buzzed its way to life. The shutter snapped open. A roving white light came on. Nick swung the camera around, taking turns bringing everyone in the group within its grainy viewfinder.

"Mr. Mayor, since you are without a black tourmaline necklace," Claudia said, "I'd suggest sticking close to someone who possesses one."

Blackwood showed appreciation for her concern as only he could: with a wave of his hand and a show of his backside as he sauntered down the center aisle toward the front of the auditorium.

In the doorway, Nori and Nick exchanged a look. Both

shrugged, then went their separate ways. She went with Börne to the left, while he took a hard right and made his way behind the back row of seats.

As soon as he'd entered the auditorium, Nick smelled smoke. He checked the ray of light coming from the hallway. He saw no trace of it hovering in the air. Only his nose alerted him of its presence. Was it possible he smelled it only because he expected to at this point? He couldn't say for sure. For all he knew, the charred stench had seeped deep into the theater's pores, promising to linger there until the day The Chamberlain was torn down.

"Floyd Cropper?" Claudia's voice sliced through the quiet like a Katana blade. "Are you here?"

It was the second time she'd caught Nick off guard, nearly giving himself whiplash spinning in her direction. *Shit.* Maybe he was too jumpy for this kind of work. Ten seconds in, his heart rate was already off and running. He forced himself to take a deep breath. *Damn it, man! Calm yourself.* It was too early in the evening's festivities to freak out. There was no telling what they might encounter in the next few hours.

His hand went to his chest and found the gemstone beneath his shirt. He should have asked Claudia if she and her mentor had possessed black tourmaline the day that house had come down. It suddenly seemed like an important detail.

"Floyd?" Claudia's voice sounded a tad different from a moment earlier. It held something not previously there. It wasn't fear. It wasn't anxiety.

It was caution.

Nick swept the camera around the room twice, then brought it back to her.

"If you are here, Floyd, please make your presence known."

A long, drawn-out silence followed, stretching for thirty seconds. Then sixty. The auditorium remained at rest.

Nick brimmed with unease. That feeling of knowing

something was coming, but not knowing what or when. His spine tingled. A growing energy permeated the air. Be prepared for anything, he told himself, counting on the others to do the same. Except for Blackwood. He knew better than to count on that guy for the simplest of things, much less preparedness.

Proving Nick's point, the mayor plopped into a seat in the front row and kicked back, legs out, ankles crossed. He clasped his hands behind his head. Like a regular paying customer, settling in for the show.

Nick expected nothing less.

It took a flickering of the lights to change the mayor's posture.

The brief strobe brought the mayor upright in his seat. He turned around with an exaggerated chuckle.

"Nice try, you assholes." Blackwood's deep voice broke through a tension that had suddenly befallen the room. "Gonna take more than jacking with the lights to scare me."

Nick spoke up. "Nobody's jackin' with anything, Mayor."

"It's actually becoming quite common here at the Chamberlain," Nori chimed in. "Welcome to the show."

Once, then twice more, the sconce lights on the walls blinked off. The new overhead bulbs followed suit, extinguishing themselves. Extinguishing, but not exploding. Nick held his breath and hoped they remained that way. It wasn't all good news. The darkened auditorium proved unsettling, despite the commonality of the occurrence. For Nick, it hardly got easier with each manifestation.

What he *was* growing accustomed to was the pace at which his heart now thumped. What was normal anyway? And would his heart remember it once this was all said and done?

A moment later, all the lights came back on.

"Floyd," Claudia continued, now looking to the ceiling with eyes open. "Is that you making—"

Visibility was a short-lived luxury. This time, all the lights snuffed out simultaneously. The sconce lights. The overheads, too. The auditorium had once again plunged itself into sheer darkness. Only two scant sources of light saved the room from going pitch: the soft red glow of the new exit sign in the front corner; and the narrow shaft of light coming through the doors to the lobby.

Neither reached into the back corner where Nick stood, and he lowered the camera to his side, his heart throbbing in his ears.

No one said a word. The room was still and quiet, like a morgue at midnight. It was Börne who finally broke the silence.

"Hey, Nick?" His words travelled through the inky blackness from the other side of the auditorium, somewhere down front. "There's a tiny button south of the on/off switch. It'll turn on the night vision. Probably shoulda mentioned that beforehand."

Night vision, huh? That would be handy.

Nick fumbled in the dark, jostling the camera in search of the night vision button. He felt sorry for Börne. Or Claudia. Or anyone else who might have to watch his footage later. He envisioned them growing seasick from all the jarring.

It took him a few seconds to find the button, click it, and right the camera. On the screen, objects in the room lit up in washed-out shades of eerie green. It looked as if a glowing, toxic liquid had swept through the auditorium, staining everything in its wake. The lighter colored the object, the more the green clung to it. Claudia's flowing white gown looked as though the contaminant itself cascaded over her shoulders and down the entirety of her body. Across the sea of seats, Nori and Börne's faces took on a soft green pallor. Their eyes, however, gleamed a stark white. Almost alien-like.

The auditorium itself remained a shadowy black.

As Claudia once again attempted conversation with The Chamberlain's resident spirit, Nick slowly panned the camera down the sloping rows of seats, toward the front of the auditorium.

Was this what Börne wanted him to do? Just work the camera over the room in the hopes of capturing something on film? He did not know. Börne had given no instruction, after all. Simply handed him the camera and turned him loose.

Despite the change in atmosphere, the mayor remained in his front-row seat. The way he sat slumped with his head back against the headrest, Nick couldn't tell if the man had settled in for a show or a quick nap.

It didn't matter. The theater came alive before he could enjoy either.

The rows of overhead lights began to swing. Like fingernails on a chalkboard, the sound of metal wrenching against metal twisted the muscles in Nick's neck. The riggings swayed. They pitched forward then back, their momentum growing with each arc.

He took a deep breath.

His pulse doubled.

Here we go.

The smell of smoke grew stronger in his nose, lest he try to forget. He checked the camera's viewfinder, hoping the infra-red technology was picking up what his eyes couldn't. Unfortunately, that wasn't the case. There was no sign of smoke on the screen, white, green, or any other color. Yet, the growing stench was undeniable.

"Anyone else smell that?" he asked the darkness.

Nori's voice emerged from beneath its veil, sounding a million miles away. "How could we not? Smells like a campfire."

A sizzling sound joined the screeching metal coursing through the auditorium. Static-like. The air buzzed with energy. Light suddenly burst forth from the rows of overhead bulbs.

Nick yanked the camcorder away from his face. The bright light didn't play well with the infra-red. Even without the camera, he found himself squinting against the auditorium's brilliance. The bright lights caused the temperature to rise. Sweat soon peppered his forehead. He wiped his face on his shoulder. The heightened illumination would soon push the bulbs beyond their capacity.

Then, in one joint maneuver, all the overhead bulbs fizzled and went dark, once again plunging the auditorium into pitch black.

Nick held his breath.

For several seconds, no one said a word. Everyone waited to see what would happen next. Unlike the evening before, the tinkling of glass hitting concrete never came. The exit sign remained intact. When it became obvious this newfound darkness was their new normal, it was Claudia who spoke first.

"Everyone alright?" When her voice reached through the dark, Nick detected a shakiness in it. A fracture in the normally confident façade. He didn't like it. It chipped away at his confidence, his mind replaying Claudia's story.

We thought we were ready. We had no idea.

A chorus of murmurs answered her question. Everyone was alright, but too on edge to form words. Too preoccupied corralling their fear.

Nick's hand trembled as he slowly raised the camcorder. Trying his damnedest to keep it steady, he scanned the auditorium in pursuit of whatever might come next.

The room flooded with bright light.

Damn it!

Nick once again ripped the camera's viewfinder from before his eyes. Too late. The blinding light had already burned white circles in his vision. He blinked, squeezed his eyes shut. Blinked some more. "Make up your mind already! We gonna have light or not?"

"Nick?" Nori inquired from across the room.

"Nothing," he replied, then took a deep breath. "Just talking to myself."

Once his eyes regained focus, Nick realized something strange. Something different. The brilliant light illuminating the auditorium wasn't coming from its new overhead bulbs. The light was coming from down front.

The large, sixty foot by twenty-foot movie screen glowed a ghostly white.

He frowned and turned to the control room window. For the screen to be lit up, a shaft of light had to be projected from the control room. But there was no shaft. There was no light.

How the hell?

Nick turned back to the screen that glowed as if a film was about to begin. But how could that be? It had no power source of its own. No electricity ran to it. It was a simple vinyl sheet with a silver, paint-like coating.

Yet somehow…

"Um, Nick? Buddy?"

Nick ran his free hand down over his chin, wishing he had a beard to stroke for times like these. "Yeah, Börne?"

"Wasn't aware there was a showing scheduled."

"There's not."

"Then…"

"I have no idea."

TWENTY-EIGHT

Nori had either read his mind, or she'd done her own math and had come to the same conclusion. "It's not coming from the control room is it, Nick? How is that possible?"

Nick shrugged, though no one could see him in the dark.

"Floyd?" Claudia's voice was shaky but controlled. "Floyd, are you manipulating the screen?"

The auditorium remained quiet.

With the night vision switched off, Nick swept the camera to the back of the large room where Claudia stood fingering the stone round her neck. He allowed the lens to linger, capturing her unease. A moment later, when she looked his way, he turned the camera toward the front and settled in. If anything was to happen, the chances of it happening near the phantom-lit screen were as good as any.

Call it a hunch.

"Floyd?" Claudia continued. "Floyd, are you wanting to show us something?"

Nick's heart rate held steady as he tried to anticipate the spirit's next move. Bypassing the auditorium's lighting to somehow illuminate the screen? Forget the how. Why? What was the plan? Where was all this leading?

Still seated down front, the mayor didn't appear the least bit concerned. His posture hadn't changed. Even after the events of the last few minutes, Blackwood remained slumped in his seat, unstirred. Was he asleep? Couldn't be. Who could sleep with everything going on?

There was only one logical explanation: the mayor's evening of excess had caught up with him. He'd given in to liquor's sweet embrace and passed out. It was unbelievable, really. The man was nearer the screen than anyone, yet unaware it had come alive.

Crazy.

It was Börne who saw it first. His words coming slow and breathy. "Holy shit."

Nick brought the camera around to him, zooming in on his open-mouthed gape. He didn't see what the commotion was about at first. It took several seconds and the lowering of the camera's viewfinder. Then his jaw dropped. He voiced an expletive to match Börne's.

The screen down front...

Claudia must have seen it, too, because when she spoke, Nick wasn't sure if she was encouraging the group as a whole or herself. "Everyone stay calm."

A series of shadowy impressions had appeared on the screen. Not so much on the screen, but *within* it. Finger-like protrusions pushed against the material, as if stretching it outward from behind. Though they weren't normal sized fingers. These were nearly the size of baseball bats. A simple flick from any of them would do substantial harm to life and limb. As the fingers stretched further outward, the hands they belonged to soon emerged, growing out of the screen. The aluminized piece of vinyl gave no more resistance than a large bed sheet.

"Nick? Are you getting this?"

There was a genuine excitement in Börne's voice that Nick couldn't match. The butterflies in his stomach were anything but enthusiastic. He'd settled into more of what he'd call an alarming sense of trepidation.

Further shadows emerged on the screen. A second pair of hands. Four in all. They stretched the vinyl, reaching for something beyond Nick's imagination. It wasn't until the hands drifted to the left that he understood their intention.

Their apparent target slumped in a seat a mere fifteen feet away.

"Mayor!" Nick shouted. If Blackwood heard, he offered no acknowledgement. Not a stir. Not so much as flinch. Nick tried again. "Blackwood!"

Still no response.

"What the hell?" Nori said, no longer down front with Börne but making her way toward the doors. And wasting no time in doing so. "Why isn't he moving?"

Nick offered no answer as he wondered the same thing.

A loud thumping sound started in his ears. It took bewildered and startled looks from both Claudia and Nori for him to realize the pounding wasn't his own heart. It came from somewhere deep inside the theater. Rising in decibels, the heartbeat soon shook the walls, the floor, and every row of seats. The screen wasn't the only thing that had animated.

The whole damn auditorium was alive.

"Börne?" Claudia asked, sounding strange. The concern in her voice had risen to a level Nick hadn't heard before. Anxious. Borderline fearful. *"Börne, meine Liebe! Komm schon!"*

Twenty steps separated Nick from the doors. It might as well have been a hundred. He couldn't move. He stood transfixed, eyes darting between the hands reaching from the screen and the man they reached for.

"Blackwood! Damn it!"

Though her attempt was higher-pitched and shrill, Nori's shout proved no more effective. Four of the largest hands the world had ever seen crept toward the mayor like a pair of stealth hunters. Still, he remained oblivious. God only knew what their intentions were once they reached their prey.

From the dark, something grabbed Nick's arm.

"Nick!" Nori shouted while shaking him. "Come on! Let's get out of here!"

He looked first to Nori, then to Claudia. His lead. The one running the show. But she was too busy to lead anyone by example, shouting to her husband in words he could only guess at the meaning of. Her pleading expression, however, was universal.

The auditorium continued to rumble and tremor beneath Nick's feet. It's heartbeat continued to thump.

He turned back and locked eyes with Nori. He saw fear. He also saw confidence.

"Okay," he said. "Let's get out of here."

She turned and started up the aisle toward the doors.

He took a step to follow, then stopped. "Wait! Nori!"

She stopped and turned but made no move to return to his side.

"What about the mayor?" he shouted.

"What about him?"

"We can't just leave him!"

Nori threw up her arms, looked to the man still slumped in the front row. Seconds later, when she turned back to Nick, she'd made her decision. "Screw him!"

Nick's chest deflated as he watched her continue up the aisle toward the doors. Her reaction wasn't what he'd expected, but he wasn't surprised. There was no love lost between Nori and the mayor. Blackwood threatening to call her editor had set a match to that already crumbling bridge.

Still...

"We can't just leave him," he repeated, mostly to himself. Despite his protest, Nick's feet moved forward, putting distance between himself and the mayor. At the open doorway, he stopped and took a quick head count. They were still shy two people. He'd thought it might be only one at that point. "Where's Börne?"

TWENTY-NINE

Claudia clutched her pendent in a white-knuckled fist and nodded down the center aisle.

Nick soon discovered the target of her fearful gaze. A Börne-shaped silhouette crept across the brilliantly lit screen down front, headed straight for its enormous hands. As far as Nick could tell, Börne still had his camera running, capturing everything. At such close range, the footage was bound to be extraordinary. He envisioned a smile stretching across the man's face despite the potential for danger.

Ten feet away, the mayor remained motionless, painfully unaware of the circumstances surrounding him.

"Shit." Nick bit his bottom lip, pondering the decision he faced. On one hand, the relative safety of the lobby called his name. He also knew Börne might need a hand extracting the mayor from his seat, if that was indeed the plan. After all, Blackwood wasn't a small man, and there was no telling the state he'd be in once awakened.

Damn it.

"Here." Nick handed the camcorder to Nori with a half-hearted smile. "If I die epically, make sure you get it on film."

She didn't share in his levity. Her face was stone as she took the camera. "Be careful!"

With adrenaline fueling his pace, Nick hurried down the center aisle. The closer he drew to the screen, the stronger the stench of smoke. The air also thickened by a degree. He found it harder to breathe. His throat burned. He brought a fist up to his mouth and coughed.

By the time he met up with Börne, the phantom fingertips were only inches from Blackwood. Astonishingly, they all but ignored Börne as he ran the camera with one hand and shook the sleeping mayor with the other.

"Asshole!" he yelled. "Wake the fuck up!"

Nick winced as Börne pulled out all the stops. He didn't have it in him to speak to the mayor that way. Even though, speaking to the mayor that way was apparently what the situation required.

The mayor finally showed signs of life as one of the ghostly hands snaked in between him and Börne and latched onto his leg. His eyes flared open. Shock expressed itself all over his face.

He screamed.

Thin streams of white smoke billowed up from beneath the hand clutching the mayor's pant leg. A sound like sizzling bacon accompanied the smoke. His grey slacks turned black, then to ash, then disintegrated.

"Son of a..." Börne handed the camera to Nick. Then after a deep breath, he grabbed ahold of the glowing white arm. Alarm registered on his face as soon as he came in contact. He clenched his teeth, powered through, and wrenched the hand free of the mayor.

Eyes wide and clutching his injured leg, the mayor gazed up at the two of them.

"Come on, damn it!" Nick urged. "Don't just sit there!"

The mayor's attention jolted back to the four hands poised to engulf him. After seeing the pain one hand had inflicted, Nick couldn't imagine what would happen if all four got ahold of someone. Knowing the mayor was probably thinking along the same lines, he feared the old fool might be too frozen with fear to move. Thankfully, that proved not to be the case.

Already slumped deep in the seat, Blackwood slithered the rest of the way out, underneath the grasping hands and onto the floor. Crawling on his hands and knees got him to the aisle. Börne grabbed him under one arm. Nick grabbed him under the other. Together, they lifted the mayor to his feet and held him until his legs stabilized. Once the man's legs seemed up to supporting his bulk, they cautiously let go.

"Come on!" Nick shouted.

Neither he nor Börne looked back as they scaled the center aisle. Neither thought to check on the mayor, either. Not until they were at the doorway. If they had, they would have realized the mayor had only made it to the aisle's midway point before the silvery hands reached out and halted his progress.

The fingers of one hand wrapped themselves around the mayor's substantial belly, singeing and burning his suit jacket. Another finger curled around his face, covering his mouth and nose. Even in the relative darkness, Nick saw the mayor's eyes bulge in their sockets. Smoke formed a cloud above him. Anywhere the hands touched sizzled.

Blackwood cried out in muffled agony.

"Oh, my God!" Claudia gave voice to everyone's thoughts as they all sucked in a collective breath.

"What do we do?" Nick looked to Börne for the answer. A purely reactionary move. The man had proven himself a natural leader, and Nick was comfortable in his role as devoted follower.

It didn't surprise him when that leader once again stepped up.

Without a word to any of them, Börne turned back down the aisle, digging into his vest pocket as he picked up the pace.

"Here!" Nori handed Nick the camera, then followed in Börne's footsteps.

Nick raised the camcorder on a scene his eyes dared him to believe. The four hands resembled half an octopus, clutching one part of the mayor or another. Each tentacle-like arm worked independently. The mayor's attempts at screaming were stifled. His movement, bound. Smoke continued to waft from his body as the hands began dragging him back toward the screen. His attempts at grasping the seat backs for leverage proved futile.

A haze of honest to goodness white smoke enveloped the auditorium.

It wasn't until Börne raised his hand high over his head that Nick realized what the investigator had retrieved from his pocket. The object glinted in the light from the screen. When Börne brought the knife down, the blade sliced through the arm holding its hand over the mayor's mouth. The arm disintegrated, vanishing into a puff of grey smoke, and took the hand with it.

The mayor gulped air like a tarpon in a cooler.

Nori grabbed the mayor by his arm and started pulling. He didn't come free, but she was able to slow the screen's progress.

The screen's progress.

It was a bizarre thought, for sure. But that was the only way Nick could think of it. It was the *screen* that wanted the mayor. Not a spirit. Not Floyd.

The. Fucking. Screen.

Börne took a swipe at the arm holding the mayor's shoulder. Like the previous, the second appendage also disintegrated. Light from the screen caught evidence of its demise like dust in a sun's ray coming through a window.

Nick continued to run the camcorder, capturing all of Börne and Nori's heroics. Up to that point, four phantom impediments had prevented Blackwood from making his exit. Börne had now cut that number in half.

Nori climbed her way up the aisle, pulling the mayor with her. Each limb Börne severed made her task that much easier. Blackwood continued to sob and cry out in either pain or fear. Nick only hoped he stayed on his feet long enough to make it out of the auditorium. Once in the lobby, with the doors shut behind him, he was free to collapse if he so chose.

Several seconds and two more arcs of Börne's blade freed the mayor from the screen's grip. The ordeal had left the man injured and weak. Nori and Börne all but carried him the rest of the way up the incline toward the waiting doors. Though his feet went through the motions of taking steps, it was clear his wobbly legs weren't supporting his weight.

As they struggled to keep the mayor on his feet, Nick felt foolish standing there running the camera. He also knew Börne wouldn't have it any other way. To the investigator, the footage of the mayor's rescue was likely more valuable than the mayor himself. To some degree, he had the more important job.

"Come on!" he urged, tearing his eyes from the trio to check the status of the screen down front. He half expected to see more hands—*reinforcements?*—reaching out from the flat surface. Thankfully, there were none. It was a plain old movie screen. As it should be. It was as if the hands had never been there.

But they had.

And he'd captured them on film. The burns on the mayor's suit and face were proof enough, regardless. Scorch marks darkened the grey fabric in several spots. A pink handprint stretched across his face like a sunburn. And as he passed by on his way through the double doors, the fetor of burnt flesh and smoke and soot assaulted Nick's nose.

Claudia and Nori slammed the doors shut. And as the clamor echoed throughout the otherwise silent lobby, one thought registered in Nick's mind. Much like the mayor's once-pristine suit, none of them would be the same after that night. They now shared a scar, so deep and so unfathomable, it would never fade.

THIRTY

"Mr. Mayor?" Claudia was the first to speak, while everyone else stood wide-eyed and mute. "Mayor Blackwood. Are you alright?"

For his part, Nick couldn't have been more shell-shocked by the evening's events if he'd just witnessed a car wreck that left the ground littered with white sheets. Even the lobby remained silent, as if holding its breath in anticipation of what might happen next.

The mayor exchanged sheepish glances with everyone huddled around him. The skin on his face was already turning ten shades of pink and red. Either he also suffered from the group's collective loss for words, or the burns on his face made it too painful to speak. Tears filled the man's eyes. They rolled down his scorched cheeks as he leaned against the wall for support. And to top it all off, the front of his grey slacks, all down one leg, was darker than the rest. Not from the burns, but from fear.

"Nick?" Nori asked. "Do you have a first-aid kit around here?"

He nodded. "Yeah, I think so." Stepping toward the mayor, he asked, "John? Are you okay?"

Even addressing the mayor by his first name didn't elicit a reaction. The man only stared hollowly at the others, his mind seemingly in a different dimension, in another time. Gone was the arrogance he wore like a fraternity pin. Gone was the aura of brute strength. Much like a two-year-old stallion wearing a shiny new saddle, the man had been broken.

"Can't be," he muttered to no one but himself. "Not... not

possible."

Nick turned away, embarrassed to be witnessing someone's rock bottom.

Beside him, Börne subtly reached for the camcorder, which Nick was only too happy to surrender.

It was when Nori reached out and touched his elbow, that the mayor pushed himself off the wall and turned away from the group. Without another word, and no indication where he was going, he stumbled his way through the lobby and out the front door. Like a shadow after sunset, he disappeared into the night. He'd given them no opportunity to say, "we told you so." Not that anyone would have. Cruelty of that level lived in none of them. Even as despicable as the mayor had been only a half hour before.

For several minutes, no one said a word. The calm of the lobby was a sharp contrast to the mayhem of the auditorium. And very much welcomed. Nick was still trying to process everything he'd seen, and assumed their silence meant everyone else was as well. All of them dumbfounded in light of everything.

Everyone, that was, except Börne, who was already fiddling with the camcorder.

When Claudia broke the silence, her uncharacteristic use of profanity provided some much-needed levity. "These fucking doors. Do we have to stand so close?"

"Way to be prepared," Nick said, as he and Börne followed the ladies further into the lobby. "The knife, I mean. Must have seen some scary things in your line of work to make you carry one of those, huh?"

Börne shook his head. "Not really. I've carried a pocketknife since I was eight. Grandfather gave me my first. A small Solingen Bulldog with a bone handle. I'd recommend it. Never know when you'll need one."

Nick glanced over his shoulder at the closed auditorium doors. "Guess so."

Börne drew in a deep breath, then released it. He shook his head. "Never seen anything like that, Nick." A hint of adrenaline still permeated his voice. "Surprised I didn't piss *my* pants."

When they reached the concession stand, Claudia embraced him, burying her face in his chest. He wrapped his arms around her shoulders and planted his chin atop her head. Soothing words passed by his lips.

A few feet away, Nori took Nick by the arm. Her slim fingers gently stroked the soft skin of its underside. "You okay?"

He nodded, offering a wan smile. "I'm alright. How about you, Wonder Woman?"

Nori's smile was as weak as Nick's. "Never better."

Nobody said anything more for several minutes. The storms, both outside and inside the auditorium, had passed, taking their theatrics with them. The night was calm. Peaceful.

When Nick finally spoke, it broke a seal that bound them all. "Anyone want—"

"Screw it," Nori interrupted. "I'm just gonna ask. What in holy hell was that?"

"And did you see how it went right for the mayor?" Claudia asked. "In all the years—"

"It reached right past me!" Börne chimed.

"It went after the mayor like it knew him!"

"Like it had a score to settle."

"Kinda makes sense," Claudia said. Everyone stopped talking and looked her way. "I mean, I can see where Floyd might blame the mayor for losing the theater."

Everyone offered a nod as imaginations ran with that theory. Nick touched the black tourmaline hanging around his neck. He thought of the fact the mayor—the only one of them to be attacked—was also the only one of them without a piece of the so-called protective gemstone. Coincidence, or cause and effect? It would take more than one evening to sort that one out.

"And why did it burn when it touched him?" Nori asked.

"Right?" Börne, chimed. "The heat coming off the arms. My God, it felt like a coal furnace. Just glad my leather jacket…"

It went on like that for several more minutes. Questions came so fast no one stopped long enough to offer any answers. Once they'd run through their cache of queries, the group once again fell silent. They searched each other's faces for explanations. They came up empty.

"So," Nick said, "guess the only question left is, what does it all mean?"

He was greeted with more of the same blank stares. It seemed this latest question was another in a long line without answers.

"I think we need a break." Claudia reached up and tucked a loose strand of hair behind her ear. "Floyd, the spirit, however we want to refer to him, seems pretty riled up." Her statement came as a revelation to no one, and they greeted her with appreciative nods.

"This was the biggest… what do you call it… manifestation yet," Nori said. "And so aggressive."

"Right." Börne lifted one of his black cases onto the counter and started stowing away his camcorders. "Something was definitely different this time around."

The mayor? Nick doubted he was the only one thinking it.

"But, yes," Claudia continued, "I think we need to shut the investigation down. Just for a day or two. That'll give us time to do more research and think this thing through. I may even make a phone call or two. Get some colleague's opinions on the matter. I mean, seriously, this is…" From that point, she only shook her head.

Börne snapped the clasp on the black case and slid it off the counter. He stood there bobbing his head back and forth, glancing over to the front door. He appeared as impatient as a kid waiting for the okay to dive into their beggar's night haul. He finally turned to Nick. "Are you good with keeping the theater closed for a day or so?"

"Yeah, Nick," Nori chimed in. For the first time that night, a genuine smile cracked her stoic face. "Can you afford to lose that $22.50?"

Nick chuckled. He could afford to lose the little money he'd make over the next couple days a lot more than he could afford to lose his sanity.

Or worse.

THIRTY-ONE

"Four hands."

Börne was talking to himself again, working his way through the Chamberlain case. It was his way; how he did things. With his laptop open on the desk in front of him, he reclined in the hotel's sad excuse for an office chair. "What does that mean, four hands? Pretty sure ol' Floyd only had the two."

That they'd witnessed such a salient manifestation of phenomena firsthand was unbelievable in its own right. To capture it on film was remarkable. Beyond remarkable. Astonishing. Yet, here he was, sitting in a darkened hotel room watching that very footage.

The paranormal community—hell, the entire world—would collectively shit themselves once it caught a glimpse of what F.A.U.S.T. had captured on film.

He couldn't get enough. While Claudia snored softly in the bed beside him, he ran the footage back once more, slower this time. He sat up straighter. He leaned in closer. With elbows on the desk and chin in hand, he watched the evening's events play out for the eighth time since returning to the room…

First, the lights in the theater flicker, brighten and then went out. A moment later, the night vision kicked in and everything turned varying shades of green. Then nothing—everything was calm—until the moment the movie screen illuminated the auditorium.

And all the while, the mayor sat slumped in his seat down in the lower right corner of the monitor.

Börne shook his head. The mayor was something else. Ignorant and arrogant, a poor combination. Not to mention rude. Still, it was hard not to feel empathy for the poor bastard. The situation had progressed well beyond anything they'd prepared for. Much less prepared *him* for. Börne shouldered his share of guilt. Whether he deserved that guilt was debatable. In the end, the mayor was simply in the wrong place at the wrong time. It was out of anyone's—

In the video, the movie screen sprouted hands.

He leaned in until he felt the heat from the laptop on his face and slowed the footage even further. The hands, first one and then the other, appeared to press against the screen from behind. The screen itself stretched outward, pushed well beyond what its construction should have allowed. And as he watched the second pair of hands sprout a moment later, his thoughts turned to the Chamberlain's previous owner.

"So, what's the story, Floyd? It appears you have a friend we weren't aware of."

Nick's cell phone erupted on the nightstand beside his bed.

He pried his eyes open one at a time. The blaring ringtone had interrupted a delightful dream, the interruption made more irritating by the fact dreams had been few and far between as of late. At least good ones. His hand blindly searched the nightstand. He found the lamp, the empty bottle of bourbon he'd swiped from his work desk, and a near empty glass of watered-down sleep aid before eventually landing on his phone.

Despite sleep trying to draw him back into its clutches, he was able to find the talk button. He cleared his throat. "Yeah?"

"Nick, you up? It's Börne."

Nick sighed. The man didn't have to introduce himself. Even while half asleep he recognized the accent.

"Did I wake you?"

Nick lifted his head and glanced around his bedroom. The sky outside his window was pitch black. *Did I wake you?* He pulled the phone away, and after several blinks of his eyes, read the time on the screen.

"Börne. It's three o'clock in the morning. What do you think?"

The silence on the other end was answer enough, and he considered letting it drag out. Just maybe, given the opportunity, Börne would hang up and let him get back to sleep. It wasn't likely, assuming the man had a good reason for calling at that hour. He ultimately decided he wanted to know, had to know what that reason was. So, he asked what was so damn important it warranted the middle of the night phone call.

"I need you to come down to the theater," Börne said, excitement edging his voice. "There's something you need to see."

When Nick arrived at The Chamberlain, still groggy and bleary-eyed, Börne was waiting in the lobby. A camcorder and a paper cup sporting a hotel logo rested on the concession stand counter. Dressed for a Victorian funeral, Börne wore his usual black boots, black slacks, white button up, black and red vest, and a long black frock with large silver buckles running down the right side. It was the same outfit he'd worn the night before, which told Nick the man hadn't been to bed yet. Maybe giving him a key and after-hours access to the theater hadn't been such a good idea. When Börne had initially asked about investigating on his own, Nick hadn't seen an issue with it. Summoning him in the wee hours of the night might have changed matters.

"This could be huge!" Börne wrung his hands while shuffling

his weight from one foot to the other. His eyes were lively despite the early hour. Nick couldn't tell if he was excited, nervous, or if that cup of coffee on the counter wasn't his first. Börne stripped off his frock and laid it on the counter. He swiped the camcorder, and before Nick could ask what the hell was so huge, the investigator turned and started toward the auditorium. "Come on."

Nick watched him go, slow to follow. Unlike Börne, he hadn't had any coffee yet. He'd refrained from grabbing some on the way over, hoping to return to bed at some point. The lack of caffeine was also a convenient excuse. He was lagging because, quite simply, he wasn't mentally prepared to deal with The Chamberlain's auditorium just yet.

Especially if Börne really had found something 'huge.'

He covered his mouth with a fist and let out a massive yawn. He considered the cup of coffee Börne had left on the counter. Ultimately, and through a ridiculous amount of effort and will power, he decided against grabbing it.

"Aw, hell."

He dragged his feet along the linoleum floor, following the path Börne had taken.

"I couldn't sleep." Börne stood waiting outside the auditorium doors.

"Really?" Nick said as he approached. "I was doing fine." And he had, in fact, been sleeping well. It had just taken an unhealthy amount of bourbon to get him there. Which may have also contributed to him dragging ass.

Börne turned away, ignoring Nick's remark. But instead of entering the auditorium, he started down the long hallway where Nick's office and storage room were located.

"So, I thought I'd come over," Börne said, "and do a walk through with my EMF meter."

"You're a fun guy, Börne. I can tell."

Börne stopped, turned, and eyed him. "What do you mean?"

Nick chuckled, waved him off. "Never mind."

Börne shrugged and continued down the sloping hallway. "So, I'm walking around the auditorium, finding nothing of interest. Then I started thinking back to last night's events. You know, with the screen. Its behavior, I guess you'd say. So, I walked up to it—"

Nick stopped. "Wait, a second. The screen? Why the hell would you wanna do that? Just how short is your memory?"

Börne looked back at Nick.

"Uh, because that's how you investigate?" He smiled at his own sarcasm. "Don't worry. I propped the doors open and would have high-tailed it out had anything happened."

Nick shook his head.

Börne continued. "Anyway, I go up to the screen and the meter suddenly goes apeshit—"

Nick raised his hand. "Hold on. People in Germany use the word, 'apeshit?'"

"When they've lived in the States for over ten years, yeah. And," Börne smiled like a schoolboy who'd found out the girl on the monkey bars liked him, "when we come across something like this."

Their footsteps echoed through the dimly lit corridor as they continued down the narrow hallway. They passed the door to Nick's office first, then the one to the small storage room. Wall sconces lit most of the way, but as they neared the end, darkness awaited.

"Another stupid question for ya," Nick said. "If the screen made your EMF meter go apeshit, then why are we out in the hallway? Why aren't we checking out the screen?"

"Ah," Börne said, raising both his eyebrows and index finger. "Because I don't believe the energy was coming from the screen last night."

"No? Did you not see—"

"It was coming from *behind* the screen."

Nick's brow pulled off a classic furrow. "Behind it?" He shook his head. "Not possible. There's nothing behind the screen except a wall. Behind that, an alley. And I've been in that alley. Trust me, there's nothing out there except cigarette butts, broken beer bottles, and a trash dumpster that smells like something crawled inside and died."

"Well, my friend, I hate to contradict you. But I think you're wrong."

Nick guffawed. "Seriously. If you smelled it—"

"Not the dumpster," Börne said, resting his hand on the wall that ended the hallway. "I think you're wrong about there not being anything behind the screen."

THIRTY-TWO

"I think there's a room on the other side of this wall."

Nick stepped beside Börne and looked the wall up and down. It was difficult to see much of anything in the dim light. He could, at most, estimate its location in relation to the auditorium. Where they stood coincided with the front of the auditorium, down near the screen. Börne was right about that much. Nick turned to him.

"So…"

Börne nodded. "Behind the screen."

"Like some kind of—"

"Secret room." Even in the shadows, Börne's smile glowed. "In fact, I'd bet money on it."

Nick placed a hand on the wall, ran it back and forth over the red and gold striped wallpaper, now only a few months old. There had been no mention of The Chamberlain having a secret room; not that he'd ever heard. As far as he knew, the theater consisted of the lobby, auditorium, control room, office, and storage room. They would have detected an additional room during renovation, wouldn't they?

Not if it was a secret one.

He tried to find the seams in the wallpaper, but there were no raised edges where the strips met. No subtle humps or divots. No evidence of anything impermanent about the wall. He even rapped his knuckles against it. Solid. Like any other.

Börne raised the camcorder, flipped on the LED light mounted on top, and handed it to Nick. From his vest pocket, he pulled out a cell phone and brought the screen to life.

Together, they directed their lights at the narrow wall. Up and down, side to side. They left no corner or wallpaper seam undetected. Still, they found nothing. If there was a secret door or panel present, it was hidden pretty damn well.

"Guess that's why they call them *secret* rooms." Nick lowered the camcorder. "And not 'come on in and make yourself at home' rooms."

Börne turned to the right, slapped his hand on the adjacent wall running the length of the hallway. "What's on the other side of *this* wall?"

An easier question to answer. "Storage room," Nick said.

Börne raised his eyebrows. "Then let's have a look at this storage room."

Nick led Börne back to the last doorway they'd passed. Camcorder tucked under his arm, he brought his collection of keys up to its light and began sorting through. His father had been the maintenance manager for several area apartment complexes, and always wore an enormous key ring packed full of jangly keys. All combined, they represented a massive jumble of authority and pride in a young Nick's eyes. Now that he had amassed a respectable set of keys himself, he saw them for what they truly were: a time-sucking pain in the ass.

After finding the silver key marked in black Sharpie with a large "S," he unlocked the door and swung it inward.

Darkness welcomed them.

Nick ran his hand along the wall inside the doorway. Finding the light switch, he gave it a flip.

A fluorescent bulb illuminated a space not much larger than a walk-in closet. It felt even smaller because of everything one would expect to find in a theater's storage room. Cardboard boxes filled with everything from paper cups to boxes of candy to toilet paper and hand soap lined the walls. A tall garbage can full of rolled up movie posters sat in one corner, and towering stacks of metal movie reel containers sat in another, all left behind by the previous owner. All collecting dust for as long as Nick had owned the place, and who knew how long before that. The storage room, along with the office, had gone untouched during renovations. He'd concentrated his money on the areas of the theater that mattered most: the lobby, control room, and auditorium. After all, the 4D movie experience didn't come cheap.

Börne went to the stacks of film reels. One by one, he began sliding the heavy metal cases away from the wall. The scraping of metal against the concrete floor pierced the room's placidity and sent a shiver coursing through Nick's shoulders. He wasn't sure what the investigator was looking for. He wasn't sure Börne even knew. Still, he wasn't raised to stand around watching others do all the work.

Nick tossed his keys onto a nearby carton, slid the trashcan of movie posters away from the wall, and set about inspecting Börne's wall of choice from the opposite corner.

Within minutes, a determination had been made: the wall was as common as any other. They'd found no loose panels, no areas sounding hollow when tapped on. If there was a secret room beyond the wall, it was certainly living up to its name. Nick's doubt about Börne's theory grew with each passing minute, with each square foot of wall they inspected and subsequently ruled out. It wasn't like experts were incapable of being wrong. Especially experts on something as unsubstantiated as the paranormal.

Nick checked his watch.

His heart sank.

One would never know from inside the windowless room, or anywhere in the theater except the lobby, but dawn was approaching. Which meant his chances of catching a few more hours of shut eye were slipping away. There would be no going back to bed at this point. Caffeine suddenly shot up the priority list.

He was about to suggest a java run when Börne interrupted his thoughts.

"Wait, a second." Börne studied an adjacent wall where an electrical panel peeked out from behind cardboard boxes. He pointed to the room next door. "When we were in your office last night, didn't I see an electrical panel?"

He did. Nick had needed to access the panel several times in the waning days of the renovation. The new popcorn popper kept overloading and tripping the circuit breaker. An electrician had come in and performed an upgrade, solving the problem. Nick relayed this information to Börne.

The investigator's shoulders did a quick up and down. "We're a long way from most of your mechanicals. Not sure why the theater would need two electrical panels in this area."

Nick considered it. "There are two in the control room."

Börne nodded. "Makes sense in there. But back here?" His attention returned to the metal panel that now seemed not only out of place, but unnecessary.

A mountain of cardboard sat in front of it. They began removing boxes from the top of the summit. When they'd reduced the mountain to a small hill, he nudged it aside with his boot and studied the metal panel.

"Let's see what we have here." Börne reached up and stuck a finger in the panel's latch.

A low rumble reverberated throughout the room. The stack of film reels rattled against one another. Movie posters chattered inside the trash can.

Börne pulled his hand back from the panel.

The rumbling ceased.

Nick and Börne exchanged a look.

"What the...?" Nick let the question run out of steam. Eyes wide, he nodded toward the panel. "Again."

Börne placed his hand on the metal door.

This time, nothing happened. No vibration. No rumble.

Were their minds playing tricks? Were their imaginations getting the better of them? Neither was likely. They couldn't both be imagining the same phenomenon.

After a half-minute of inactivity, Börne shrugged, reached up, and opened the panel door.

The tiny hinges creaked, protesting the notion of being put to work for the first time in who knew how long.

What lay on the other side of the panel door were the insides of an ordinary electrical panel, only much older than most. Corrosion, dust, and more than one spider's handiwork covered the tubular fuses. The handwritten notations along the side, indicating which fuse was for which mechanical, had long since faded.

"Looks old as hell," Nick said, interrupting a well-developed silence. "Original?"

Börne frowned, seemingly unconvinced. "Maybe."

"Would explain things," Nick offered. "Probably easier to install a new panel than to go through the hassle of bringing this one up to code."

"Ordinarily, I would agree with you." Börne looked at him with a sparkle in his eye. "If this were an actual working panel."

Nick didn't understand the inference and said as much.

"This," Börne said, tapping on the panel's façade, "this panel is a dummy. A fake."

Nick wasn't sure he followed. It looked real enough to him. "And how do you know this?"

"Simple. Before Claudia and I decided to take this paranormal hobby full time, I spent my twenties as an electrician's apprentice." Börne ran his fingers along both edges of the panel, apparently searching for something. What that something was, Nick couldn't guess. He did, however, recognize the 'a-ha' moment on Börne's face when the investigator found it.

"Bingo."

There were two soft clicks and the squeal of metal sliding free as the electrical panel swung away from the wall. In its place sat a large cavity of mostly nothingness. No further holes in the wall, no wiring passing through. Just a black rectangular box with a long iron lever, its thick, grey paint chipped and peeling.

Börne looked back at Nick, his grin now a broad-based smile. "Tell me you're not dying to pull that."

THIRTY-THREE

Nick was familiar with hidden passageways and secret rooms. He was, after all, a product of the Scooby Doo age, where the use of such plot devices ran rampant. But he had never seen either in person, much less been inside one. When it came to passageways and secret rooms, he was an unabashed virgin.

And seemingly about to lose that designation.

He took in a deep breath, held it, and pulled the lever.

A series of three metal thunks echoed in the tiny storage room.

With a whoosh of air decades in the making, a section of the back wall separated itself from the rest. Two vertical seams ran from floor to ceiling. The section of wall, roughly the width of a door, sat inset from the main wall by a couple of inches.

Nick released his long-held breath, then looked to Börne. If the investigator's chest was pounding as hard as his, it didn't show through his getup. His eyes were on fire, though, and a child's eagerness played across his face.

He nodded to the camcorder sitting on the box beside Nick.

Nick grabbed the camera, raised it, and pressed the power button, despite feeling wholly unprepared for what its lens might capture.

Börne walked over and placed both hands on the moveable section of the wall. Looking over his shoulder he asked, "Are we ready?"

Nick was not. To be fair, he doubted he ever would be given

the unknown that awaited them on the other side of the wall. Börne, on the other hand, showed no signs of fear or anxiety. Only adrenalized excitement. The look on his face told Nick there was no turning back now. He was going to open that door whether Nick wanted him to or not. It was obvious the man was in the right business. It was just as obvious Nick had made the right choice in bringing in F.A.U.S.T. He only hoped his trembling hands wouldn't betray his fear when Börne reviewed the footage later.

He made sure the little red dot on the viewfinder was on, then nodded.

Börne took in and let out a deep breath of his own, then started pushing.

A sorrowful creaking filled the room.

Years of immobility giving way to progress.

Once the section of wall had slid back a few inches, the left side caught, seemingly locking into place. The right side, however, continued to swing inward. A moment later, Börne stopped pushing and took a step back. The opening stood large enough for an adult man to slip through.

Or two.

Which was Nick's fear, him running the camera and all. His empty stomach knotted. Not for the first time he fantasized about being back in his bed, lonely as it sometimes was.

"So, uh, should we say that prayer or anything?"

Mesmerized by the open doorway, Börne's attention never strayed from it as he shook his head. "That's kinda Claudia's thing."

Nick thought back to the night before and the mayor. "Tourmaline?" he asked. "'Cause I left mine—"

Börne shook his head. "Claudia."

Nick scowled. "So, what are you saying? You don't believe in that stuff?"

"Oh, I do," Börne said. "Just not as much as she does. And yes, it's become a topic of discussion around our house from time to time. She says if I knew what she knew, I'd take it more seriously. And it's not like I don't, it's just… well… I doubt we'll be needing it. If that makes you feel any better. I mean, all your theater's manifestations have occurred inside the auditorium. Am I right?"

Nick nodded in answer, despite the fact Börne wasn't looking his way.

When he did finally turn and look back at Nick, adrenaline blazed in his eyes. "So? Rock, paper, scissors?"

Nick shook his head. "Oh, hell no." He extended an inviting hand toward the opening. "Lead the way."

Without further encouragement, Börne brought up the flashlight on his cell, slipped through the gap in the wall, and was instantly swallowed by a blackness that now awaited Nick.

THIRTY-FOUR

The smell was the first thing to greet him. Even before the pitch-black. There was must. There was dust. The usual suspects one would expect from a room closed up for what could only be estimated at decades. There was also the overwhelming scents of residual smoke and charred paper that reached out like an overeager sales agent, grabbing Nick by the gut before he was even through the doorway. The brute force of it caused him to recoil.

"Son of a…"

Nick pulled his shirt collar up over his nose while searching the darkness for Börne. The room was windowless, void of all light, save for the meager light they brought in with their devices.

"Hey, man, where'd you go?" He swung the camera to the right, finding nothing but a shadowy wall. The room extended to the left, so he swung the camcorder in that direction. When he caught Börne's ghostly visage in his weak light, he jolted. The sight of the man in black standing there was jarring, even though he'd fully expected to see him at some point.

He took a deep breath, exhaled, and brought the camcorder back around, once again training the LED light on Börne.

The investigator raised his hand and shielded his eyes. "Nick. Seriously."

He lowered the beam so it no longer shown on Börne's face. "Sorry."

Their words bounced about the room in a hollow echo. The

space felt tight. Small, like a cave. A chill filled its air.

"Gotta be a light switch somewhere," Börne said, scanning his cell light around the doorway.

Nick turned his light on the rest of the room.

An array of charred and smoke-damaged wooden crates lined a wall on one side of the room. A few still sprouted traces of old packing straw. The tops of three round and ancient wooden tables leaned against one wall, their legs removed and stacked on the dingy concrete floor beside them. A heap of wooden chairs held the tables in place. It was oddly more furniture than would fit in the space. Fine layers of black soot and what looked to be ash covered everything. Including the structure standing against the far wall, which itself seemed to cut the room off at an awkward angle.

"Behold!" Börne said, causing Nick to jump. The man's impersonation was a near perfect Vincent Price. "The proverbial writing on the wall." Then, Börne dropped the Vincent Price voice, and in his normal voice asked, "any idea what this means?"

Nick didn't have to think about which voice he preferred. This expedition was creepy enough without either of them making it moreso. Shaking off the chill Börne had sent through him, he stepped up beside the investigator. He raised the camcorder and married its light with Börne's.

It appeared as if the stone wall beside the doorframe had once served as a chalkboard. Smeared chalky hieroglyphics covered a small section, still visible behind a thin layer of black soot and ash. When Nick leaned in and blew on the wall, the ashy powder flew away and disappeared into the dark. Words had been scribbled on the wall and subsequently erased and rewritten many times over. Four legible words remained...

Corn... brown... foot juice... butts...

"What the hell is foot juice?" Börne shined his light all around the large doorway. If he was searching for more words, his search came up empty.

Nick smiled on the inside. Not because he was thrilled about the stench of smoke that was currently permeating his clothes, but because he knew what the words meant. Add them to other items he'd seen in the room, and he basked in the opportunity to teach Börne something for a change. He had learned of these things in college. Specifically, in his course on Early 20th Century America. It was a 7:30 am class, which meant he'd slept through more than his share of lectures. There were a few subject matters, however, he'd found interesting enough to keep his eyes propped open. And in those days, one of the few topics that captured his attention more than pretty coeds had been alcohol.

"It's a shopping list," he said, turning and shining the camera's light around the room. "For a speakeasy." He turned back to Börne, whose face looked ghostly pale and shadowy in the camera's down-turned light. "That's what this room was used for at one time. That's why it was hidden and kept secret."

A furrowed brow asked Börne's question before he could voice it. "What the hell's a speakeasy?"

Nick chuckled. "Like a private club. A secret drinking establishment back in the 1920s and 30s. Back when alcohol was illegal."

Börne's jaw dropped. His eyes doubled in size. "Wait, a second. There was a time in this country when alcohol was illegal?"

Nick nodded. "We called it Prohibition."

"Wow," Börne said, nudging a nearby crate with his boot. The sound of clinking glass emerged from inside. "You Americans are way too uptight."

Nick snickered. "Says the guy dressed like Queen Victoria's butler."

Börne laughed. "Touché, my friend. Touché."

"Anyway," Nick said, returning the camera's light to the words scribbled inside the doorway. "Corn means bourbon. Brown is Scotch. Foot juice is another term for wine, I think. Butts would mean cigarettes."

"Scotch, bourbon, wine," Börne said. "Now that's my kind of shopping list."

Nick turned and shined the camcorder's light onto the far wall. "Might not have to go too far to do your shopping."

Covering the entire stone wall was a stout system of wooden shelving. From one end to the other, a good fifteen feet across, the shelves stretched from floor to ceiling. On those shelves, an array of black, wooden crates took up every square inch of space. And resting in those crates were, by Nick's estimation, several hundred glass bottles of Prohibition-era contraband. All of which wore a coat of black soot. Though, not a fine layer like that which covered everything else in the room. The soot and ash on the crates and shelves had been disturbed. Smudged. Even wiped clean in some places.

Börne's whistle brushed past Nick's ear. "Any chance they're still full?"

"Only one way to find out."

As Börne made his way over to the wall, Nick's tense shoulders deflated a bit. But not in a bad way. Discovering The Chamberlain did indeed possess a secret room had initially filled him with unbridled anxiety. His vivid imagination had devised many macabre and deviant reasons for the existence of one. Finding out it was used for drinking and gambling, and not a crazed killer's torture chamber, allowed some of that tension to ease.

"Empty," Börne said, dropping a bottle into one of the wooden crates. A hollow clank cut through the dark as the bottle settled back into its original resting place.

Relieved as he was, Nick couldn't part with all his anxiety just yet. The room still held further mystery. It still had more story to tell. The tables and chairs, crates full of liquor bottles, and the writing on the wall told of a run-of-the-mill speakeasy. None of it, however, explained the soot and ash that seemed to cover everything in the room. Everything except the floor. It had been cleaned to an extent. Possibly mopped. Hints of dark swirls lingered where the mop water had become too soiled to be efficient. Turning away, he left Börne to explore the vast inventory of bottles alone.

At the pile of stacked furniture, Nick ran his finger along the leg of an upturned chair. The tables and chairs showed the same thin layer of black as everything else. He smelled the residue on his finger. It smelled of paper or wood. All signs pointed to a small fire having taken place in the room. It would have made sense if some patrons in the speakeasy had been smoking in the room and caught something on fire. What didn't make sense was the soot and ash coating the tables and chairs where they sat against the wall. Like the fire had happened after the speakeasy had already been shut down.

But…?

Nick let it go. It didn't make sense, but it was too early in the morning to think that hard. In fact, now that they'd discovered the room behind the movie screen, he was ready to leave. They could return later with better lighting. And a shop vac. He was about to suggest as much when his thoughts were interrupted.

"Now we're talking!" Börne's voice cut through the quiet like a thrown axe. He held out an unopened bottle. "You a gin man, Nick?"

Nick took the cloudy bottle. Tilting it toward the camera's light, he read the yellowed label. "Booth's? Never heard of it. And I'm not sure I've ever tried gin."

At the edge of his light, Börne smiled like a kid separated from his parents and locked inside a candy store.

"Your life's about to change, my friend."

Nick set the eighty-year-old bottle of liquor on a nearby chair. "Ya know," he said, walking away from the stacked furniture to an adjacent wall. "I think you were on to something, Börne. Pretty sure we're directly behind the scree—"

Something brushed his ear.

He ducked, pictured a spider swinging by its ass string, and cringed. He despised spiders. No creature on Earth should have that many legs. He could practically hear the tip-tip-tip of those hairy legs crawling across the ceiling overhead.

He swatted the object away with the back of his hand. A second later, it swung back and hit him again. Without thinking, he reached up and grasped the object, intent on yanking it down and casting it aside. As soon as it was in hand, however, he realized what it was. It wasn't a spider. It wasn't a creepy crawly of any kind.

It was a pull string for a light bulb.

Relief washed through him like he'd just been released from jury duty.

He was set to give the string a tug when the darkness exploded. Not with light, but with sound.

THIRTY-FIVE

Börne's shout was brief, cut short by a deafening crash.

The shattering and splintering of glass and wood.

It sounded as if the room was collapsing in on itself.

Nick recoiled as shrapnel hit his legs. A bottle pinwheeled off his shin. He yelped and bit his lip and retreated from the chaos a couple of steps, losing the pull string in the process.

As the mayhem settled, he heard only two sounds: liquid dripping onto the concrete floor.

And his own heavy breathing.

"Börne!" Nick swung the camcorder back to where he'd last seen the man. He was gone. To Nick's horror, so was a large section of the shelving. Only a bare brick wall remained.

"What the…"

A brief clinking of bottles. A creak of old wood. A thick gurgling sound, like someone gargling with motor oil.

He trained the camcorder's light on the floor. A cold inhale caught in his throat. He couldn't see Börne buried beneath the mountain of shelving, crates, and broken bottles. He could only hear him. And the sounds turned his stomach.

"My God!" Nick used the camera's light to search for the pull string. He didn't even know if the lights inside the room still worked. He had to try. He would need both hands free if he had any hope of lifting the massive section of shelving. The structure itself had to weigh several hundred pounds, at least. That wasn't even counting the crates, some of which still held their contents. He also feared in what condition he would find Börne beneath it all. If there was ever a situation that called for being able to see what you were doing, this was it.

The gurgling continued to waft up from underneath the pile.

Nick caught the string in the camera's light and reached for it. In his rush, his trembling fingertips grazed it and sent it swinging.

"Shit!"

His heart pounded. Panic gripped him by the back of the neck. He continued to search the air. When found the now-swinging string again, this time he grabbed it and held on. Held on like Börne's life depended on it.

Because…

He wasted no more time and yanked the string.

The darkness was instantly reduced to scattered shadows. A row of three yellow light bulbs hung from the ceiling. Together, they illuminated the narrow room.

One bulb burst, extinguishing itself immediately. The room's light dimmed by a good measure. Seconds later, a second bulb followed suit, further cutting Nick's ability to see.

"Come on!" He shouted. The third light bulb had to cooperate. It had to stay lit. *Had to!*

He couldn't waste what little time he might have waiting to find out.

He set the camcorder on a nearby box and rushed to where the shelving teetered atop splintered crates, broken bottles, and Börne. The task seemed insurmountable. The structure, so stout. His mind flashed to stories of frantic mothers lifting cars off toddlers. He could only hope his own white-hot adrenaline would help add him to this list of legendary feats.

"Hold on, man!" He wasn't sure Börne could hear him. It didn't stop him from extending the line of communication. Until he knew differently, he would hold out hope. "Gonna get you out!

Just hold on!"

For a moment, Nick feared his assurance to Börne might be a lie. The wooden structure was slow to cooperate. Heavier than he'd expected. Even when pushing his back to its limits, the shelving raised only two, three inches at most. The wood released a groan of defiance. Bottles shifted in their crates. When he was unable to maintain his grip, the structure settled back onto the pile of debris.

"Shit!"

Sweat trickled down the back of his neck. It broke across his forehead, and he wiped at it with his bandaged arm. Was the room getting warmer? He wasn't sure. The stench, however, was growing stronger. Of that he could attest.

It was the sudden onset of silence that drove the room's changing atmosphere from his mind.

The gurgling had stopped.

"Börne?" His pulse raced. Blood pumped through his ears. His heart threatened to beat free of his chest. "Hang in there, buddy!"

Nick wiped his damp hands on his jeans before attempting to lift the unit again. This time, he knew what he was up against and bettered his grip. This time, there was progress. Glass tinkled to the floor as the structure rose into the air. He raised it maybe six inches, but it was enough. With his arms and back protesting the heavy load, he shuffled a few steps to his left, dragging the top of the shelving unit with him. Then one foot slipped. Then the other. A growing pool of liquid seeped from beneath the structure and made the trek a slippery one.

When his grip was about to give out, he lowered the shelving onto a wooden crate. It teetered precariously but remained in place. He stretched and relieved the ache in his back.

Then he gasped.

Börne's face.

It was unrecognizable. Slivers of glass and wood jutted in all directions. Crimson painted the man's pained expression, leaving no trace of skin unmasked. Blood bubbled from a gash across the bridge of his nose. The most severe damage had come from a jagged, amber-colored bottle embedded in his throat. It appeared to have sliced through skin and muscle without impediment, driving itself deep.

Nick reminded himself to breathe.

He stood frozen over Börne's ruined body. The investigator lay motionless, eyes wide, mouth agape. He made no sound. No movement beyond a subtle twitch of his hand. As Nick watched in horror, it too came to a stop.

The conclusion he came to was a difficult one. Börne was gone. There was nothing he could do. His focus shifted, and while he was sure it was too late, he needed to get help. He needed to alert someone.

Most of all, he needed to get the fuck out of that room.

But the room had other plans. When he turned to go, his heart stopped. The door they'd entered through was closed.

Fear unleashed a frozen river, chilling his insides. Ice crystals flowed through his veins. Nick placed his hands on the slab of wood. He was certain they'd left the door open. He was the last one through, and he hadn't closed it. He was pretty sure Börne hadn't, either. Why would he? They had no reason to close it, and every reason in the world not to.

Nick ran his hands over the door. Like the outside, there was no visible handle on the inside, either. *How do you open a door without a handle?* He pressed the edges of the door, hoping to somehow pop it open. He slid his fingers over the seams in search of a latch or trigger and once again came up empty. The door to the secret room offered no sign of how to open it. Much like the room itself, the trick to opening it from the inside remained a well-kept secret.

Sweat streamed down Nick's face.

His already elevated heart rate pulsed faster.

The walls were closing in. The room's sparse amount of air seemed less willing to give itself up. Nick pounded the door with his fists. He kicked it, not once, but twice. He screamed for help. It was a fool's errand. There was no one in the theater to hear.

Or was there?

Nick fell silent. He glanced around the shadowy room before closing his eyes. He took in a deep breath, held it to calm his racing heart, then released it. It was a crazy thought. A terrifying notion. He tried to force it from his mind, tried to reject it.

He couldn't let the thought go.

Was there someone, something, in the room with him?

He opened his eyes and turned his back to the door. He surveyed the room, contemplated the situation with more focus. There was no denying the facts. Perfectly sturdy shelving units don't topple on their own. Doors don't just close. And it wasn't as if precedent hadn't already been set within the walls of The Chamberlain. Absurd as it might seem, that he wasn't alone in the room was the only explanation that made sense.

Nick used his already saturated bandage to wipe sweat from his eyes. He sucked in another deep breath. He couldn't believe what he was about to do, what he once would have considered ridiculous.

He had no choice.

"F-Floyd?"

His voice echoed off the stone walls. The sound of it within the quiet room caused the hair to stand on the back of his neck. He thought of Claudia and the first time she'd tried to summon The Chamberlain's previous owner.

Claudia.

His heart threatened to break at the thought of her. His eyes threatened to tear up. He shook himself free of the emotion and shoved the sorrow down a cavern somewhere deep. There would be time enough for heartache later.

"Floyd," he repeated. "Are you here?"

A green bottle slid from its crate near Börne's lifeless body and clanked onto the concrete floor. It rolled out from under the heap, its label counting off each revolution. The bottle didn't stop until it had made its way across the room to Nick's feet.

His blood ran cold.

His spine tingled.

His question had been answered.

THIRTY-SIX

Claudia opened her eyes.

A shallow sense of something wrong greeted her.

She sat up in bed, pulling the comforter up to her chest. Reaching for Börne, she found only a cool sheet. Her husband's side of the bed was empty. She checked the desk where he had been working before she'd drifted off to sleep. A streetlight outside the window spotlighted the chair. It, too, sat empty.

"Börne?"

A large mirror flanked the wall at the foot of the bed. In it, she could see the bathroom door. It stood open, revealing nothing but pitch inside.

"Liebling?"

Dread woke the butterflies in her stomach. A long time had passed since she'd last experienced that feeling. Not so long, however, that she would have forgotten. The last time she'd felt something was wrong, her intuition had been dead on.

Which didn't soothe the butterflies one bit.

Claudia cast off the comforter and swung her legs over the side of the bed. Her slippers awaited her at the foot, as did her robe. She sidestepped them both on her way to the bathroom.

"Börne?"

She didn't wait for an answer. Wasn't sure she expected one. She pushed the door open and reached for the light. The sudden brightness made her squint. She looked behind the door, pulled back the shower curtain. The bathroom, like the rest of the small hotel room, was empty. She returned the bathroom to darkness and walked out.

Where the hell could he be? Had he gone downstairs to the lobby? Outside? Börne was no stranger to late-night walks. They helped clear his head, helped him to think. Especially when the two of them were engrossed in a troublesome case. But he usually left a—

She went to the desk and turned on the tiny lamp. She found his laptop, a half-empty bag of vending machine pretzels, two pens, and a small notepad emblazoned with the hotel's name and logo. What she didn't find was a scrap of paper or scribbled-on napkin. No note of any kind. She lifted the laptop and felt the underneath. It was cool to the touch. He had, more than likely, been gone awhile. Setting the laptop down, she noticed the cord to his cell phone charger plugged into the nearby wall. The other end hung limp off the side of the desk.

Hope seeped into her heart. Börne had taken his cell phone, something he didn't always remember to do when his mind was consumed with work. She'd chided him about it on occasion, and he'd promised to try harder.

She grabbed her own cell off the nightstand and checked it for messages. The screen was blank. No texts. No calls. No notifications of any kind. Biting her lip, she brought up Börne's contact and hit the call button. As she waited for the call to go through, she pried at the small gap between her two front teeth with her thumbnail. She stared out the second-story window, where night was giving way to morning. Except for a white and black squad car slowly making its rounds, the street below appeared empty. The buildings across the way showed few lights in their windows. Angler Bay was still asleep.

A single ring came through the phone, then a voice.

It wasn't the voice she'd hoped to hear.

"I'm sorry. The person you are trying to reach is unavailable…"

"Shit."

Nick stared at the green bottle at his feet and ran his hand through his dampening hair. "Shit. Shit. Shit."

When he'd first considered calling out to The Chamberlain's previous owner, he'd failed to consider what he would do if he got an answer. And if a bottle rolling across the floor wasn't an answer, he'd hate to see what one might look like.

"Floyd," he started, making it up as he went. "I need to get out. I need to get help for my friend."

It was a lie. He was no doctor, but even he knew Börne was dead. He was gambling on the hope the spirit wouldn't be as observant. The *vengeful* spirit, he reminded himself, who may or may not be responsible for Börne being in that state in the first place.

He also wondered what the repercussions might be for trying to deceive a vengeful spirit.

Tread softly, ol' buddy.

Silence controlled the room. Nothing stirred. The only hint of movement came from the flashing red light on the camcorder, signaling it was still recording. Everything remained as still as when they had first discovered the secret room. How long had it been? Minutes? An hour? He had no idea. He only knew he didn't care to stay any longer.

After several minutes passed with no response to his plea, Nick refocused his efforts on finding a way out.

He ran his hands along the walls beside the door. There had to be a panel, a switch, something. There had to be a way out. In the days when the speakeasy was in use, they would have kept the door closed. Even with patrons inside. *Especially* if there were patrons inside. So there had to be a way of opening the door from inside the room, for safety reasons if nothing else. He ran his hands along the edges.

"Come on, dammit!"

When further inspections of the door and wall came up empty still, his panic escaped in the form of an angry outburst.

He punched the door. The hollow thud resonated in the room's thick air, but it did little to alleviate the situation. He'd achieved nothing and received only bruised knuckles for his effort. The pain didn't quell his rage. He kicked over a nearby wooden chair. He grabbed it and swung it through the air, smashing it against the door. The chair disintegrated in his hands, sending a barrage of splintered wood ricocheting across the room.

A giggle from somewhere in the dark.

Nick spun, dropping the chair's legs. "What the—?"

His heart climbed up his throat. Was he hearing things now? Was that… laughter? He couldn't be sure. It had been faint, brief, making little sense. He snorted. *What about this whole fucked up situation made sense?*

Sweat now soaked his hair, his shirt. He was dehydrated, could feel it. Light-headed. Dry-mouthed. Perhaps he was hallucinating, too. Perhaps…

Nick tried to push the phantom laughter further back in his troubled mind. At the least, he needed to stow it for processing later when his mind was more reliable. He chuckled at the thought. *A reliable mind.* When would he ever possess one of those again? The whole ordeal was reminiscent of opening night. The only difference was that this time it was real. Every horrifying detail. No matter how much he wished it to all be a drug-fueled hallucination.

For the first time since that night, he wished he had a stomach full of Xanax. It would be better than the alternative.

He leaned his back against the wall and slid down to the floor.

Frightened, anguished, and growing increasingly exhausted, he lowered his head. He cradled it in his hands, the weight of his circumstances too heavy to bear. The voice of reason insisted on making things worse, whispering, *Nobody will come to look for you.* And it wasn't lying. He had no one at home to miss him. No one to notice he was gone. Even when Claudia grew concerned over Börne's absence, a secret room in the bowels of the theater would be the last place anyone would know—or think—to look.

Bowels.

Nick chuckled at how appropriate his word choice was. Not only did it describe the location of the room, but he was also in some seriously deep shit.

THIRTY-SEVEN

Nori's alarm clock went off at 5:45.

It was the same time as every other day, only this morning its bleating irritated her more than usual. She'd gotten little to no sleep. She'd been unable to get the events at The Chamberlain out of her mind long enough to allow more than a few periodic minutes of restless slumber. She'd tried pulling the covers up over her head. Even barricaded it beneath her pillow in an attempt at stifling the mayor's screams. Nothing blocked them out. It was only once she turned on her police scanner and lost herself in the chatter that her mind became distracted enough for sleep to take over.

Then the damn alarm had gone off.

She gave up on the idea of sleep and pushed herself up in bed, resting her back against the headboard. The sun hadn't quite shown itself. Its first rays were only starting to infiltrate the darkness outside her bedroom windows. She reached for the water bottle on her nightstand, took a long drink, then returned the bottle and retrieved her cell phone.

Static cackled through the police scanner's tinny speaker.

She spent the next several minutes scrolling through emails. She thumbed passed one after another until a day-old email from her mother halted her progress. Nori tapped the screen. Her parents were confirming the flight itinerary for their visit next month. She sighed. It wasn't that she wasn't excited to see them. She was. It had been six months since their last visit. What she wasn't excited about were all the questions they would undoubtedly pack in the luggage they'd bring along. Why doesn't she ever visit? Why wasn't she married yet? Why does she hate them so much as to deny them becoming grandparents?

She rolled her eyes and sniggered. Not that her parents had ever phrased it that way. That's just how she took it.

As she closed the email, her thoughts turned to the new box of green acai tea sitting in her kitchen. An eager recommendation from Callie. With nothing on the news wires keeping her attention, Nori swung her legs over the side of the bed. A quick trip to the bathroom, then off to the day's first cup of tea. She tossed her cell onto the bed and greeted the morning.

The video camera beeped.

Nick raised his head. The recording device still sat on the box where he'd set it when the shelving had first collapsed. He'd forgotten it was still recording. From where he sat, he could see the battery symbol flashing on the screen. It was dying. He leaned over and retrieved the camera, clicked the button to stop recording, then set it on the floor beside him. Better to save the battery. For lighting, if nothing else.

Eyeing the last remaining light bulb, he hoped like hell it wouldn't come to that.

What he needed was his cell. Most likely, the reception would have been shit down there, but he could have used the flashlight app. He could see the phone resting in the console of his car where he typically left it. He wasn't one to take it everywhere he went, especially since he'd made a habit of dodging his accountant. He slid his hands into his pockets to be sure. He found nothing but his keys and wallet. Neither of which did him any good now. He would have cursed himself if he'd had the energy.

Börne.

He'd had his cell phone. He'd used it for the same reason Nick was saving the camcorder battery: to light the way.

He surveyed the mountain of rubble and the body caught halfway underneath. Hidden somewhere beneath the mass of wood, glass, and Börne was the man's cell phone.

Nick's stomach turned over on itself.

What he was considering would have ordinarily been unimaginable.

"What choice do I have?" he asked out loud. Besides the additional source of light, if there was any possibility of getting service in that underground room of stone and concrete, any possibility at all, he had to try. He just hoped the payoff would prove worth the gruesome endeavor. And that the accident hadn't killed Börne's cell phone along with him.

The rancid odor of death grew more stringent as Nick rose and approached the mass of debris.

Footing proved slippery, even treacherous the closer he stepped. By now, any bottles broken in the crash had emptied their contents. The floor was awash in varying shades of rust, brown, and red, swirled with more blood than he'd ever seen. There was also enough shattered glass scattered about to cut him from stem to stern if he should happen to slip and fall.

After turning away and taking a deep breath of the freshest air available, he knelt in the blood slick. A sloppy sucking sound rose from the floor. Fluids immediately soaked through the fabric of his jeans. The warm sensation on his knee wrenched his stomach, and he pleaded with its contents to stay put.

Börne's dead eyes gazed in interest as Nick reached in and began sorting through the muck.

Börne's hand was the first place he looked. Börne had been using the light from his cell to check the contents of bottles, so that was the most logical place to start. Hopefully, that would be as far as Nick would need to search.

A wooden crate pinned the man's arm to the floor. Nick reached under the shelving as far as he could but didn't come close to Börne's hand. He tried tugging Börne's shirt sleeve toward him, but the heavy structure wouldn't give up the arm.

Shit.

He let out a deep breath and ran through his options. He could try to move the shelving again but had no desire to crawl out of the muck just to have to crawl back in. He was already knee deep in it.

"Fuck it."

Nick kicked the crate. Then again. Soon, he was giving the crate hell with the toe of his shoe. Each blow splintered the wooden box further. Each blow sent Börne's arm splashing in the pooling sludge. The splashes made sickening, slurping sounds. He was potentially causing further damage to the man's arm. He cringed while forcing bile back down his throat. He considered stopping.

Did it matter at this point?

The next kick sent the crate collapsing in on itself. The shelving resting on top shifted but immediately settled onto other crates that took up the cause of supporting its weight. Nick reached in, wrenched out the ruined crate, and tossed it aside. Börne's arm, caught on the splintered wood, slid out with the crate.

Any hope of Börne still holding his cell phone plunged.

His hand was empty.

"Shit." With his head turned so as to breathe in as little death as possible, Nick reached back under the shelving. One by one, he cleared out broken bottle after broken bottle. He'd already pulled out half a dozen when he grabbed one larger and squishier than most. Turned out it wasn't a bottle at all.

He'd grabbed ahold of Börne's leg.

He yanked back his blood-covered hand in disgust. Another retch coiled his stomach. This time, he wasn't so confident in its contents staying down.

The only thing keeping his stomach from emptying itself was seeing Börne's cell phone lying face down inches away. The glow from the screen was turning the nearby muck into a makeshift lava lamp.

Nick's eyes widened.

It still worked!

THIRTY-EIGHT

It took a deep dive into the mountain of wet debris, finally vomiting, and more than a few scrapes of his arm to retrieve the phone. It was soaked and slick and difficult to hold. Liquor and blood dripped from its case, the sum of it running down his wrist. The screen was shattered, but the damage wasn't so extensive as to render the phone useless. The bright light shooting out the back kept hope alive.

Nick couldn't help but cackle while he raised the phone to the ceiling in a triumphant fist.

"Fuck you, Floyd! I don't need your help!"

It took only a few seconds for his independent pride to fade. There were no bars at the top of the phone's screen, no battery meter. In fact, there was nothing on the screen at all. Nothing except a thousand hairline fractures.

"Come on, baby…"

He tapped the screen—here, there, everywhere. He pressed all the buttons, trying to bring the phone to life. It failed to react like he wanted. In fact, it failed to react at all. Though the light continued to work, the screen remained blank. No matter what he tried, the phone refused to respond.

"Fuck!"

His frayed nerves got the better of him. He reacted before thinking.

He spun and sent the phone sailing against a nearby wall where it disintegrated on impact. He regretted his actions before the pieces even clattered to the floor. An array of swear words travelled from his mind to his mouth, this time directed at himself.

Nick leaned both hands on the grimy wall and hung his head between them.

Stupid!

He kicked the wall.

Stupid! Stupid! Stupid!

He cocked his foot back, ready to inflict more punishment on the wall, when—

A most welcome sound saved him the pain. Somewhere in the theater, a phone rang.

He popped his head up, tuned his ear and waited.

The phone rang again.

He stood straight, alert. *What the...* The only phone in the theater was the one in his office down the hall. But it was too far away, and there was no way he could hear it with the door—

His breath caught in his throat.

The door, once closed, now stood open.

Tiny fingers tickled the back of his neck as light from the storage room cut a sliver of yellow across the concrete floor. How? When? Why hadn't he heard the moaning of hinges like when the door had opened the first time? But then he realized he hadn't heard the hinges when the door had closed, either. A thought struck him. What if...

He didn't finish the question.

But it was too late. The thought had already taken root in his mind. What if the door had never closed? What if it had been open the entire time? The implications froze Nick to his core.

What if it was opening night all over again?

The phone in his office rang again, returning him to the present.

He wasted no time darting through the open doorway. He stumbled across the storage room—plowing over cardboard boxes and metal film canisters—and out into the hallway. The scent of buttered popcorn had never smelled so good.

The phone rang.

He didn't have to go far. The open door of his office stood a mere fifteen feet away. His breaths came rapid and shallow. His chest pounded. His nerves flared as he ran up the sloping hallway.

He tried to stop at the doorway and failed. The hallway's carpet may as well have been a sheet of ice the way his bloody shoes slipped and slid on it. He grabbed the doorframe on his way past, righted himself, and swung into the office he'd wondered if he'd ever see again. When he collapsed into his big black chair, it sailed backwards and crashed into the wall behind him. He spun the chair around, and with his chest heaving and lungs fighting for air, snatched the phone receiver.

"Hello!"

Silence. Nothing on the other end. Had the caller hung up?

"Hello!"

He was about to replace the receiver and start dialing 9-1-1 when a soft and fearful voice came from the other end.

"Nick?"

The sound of Claudia's voice split his heart in two. His eyes flooded with tears. He couldn't speak. He had only three words on his mind but couldn't bring himself to say them out loud.

I'm so sorry.

THIRTY-NINE

He'd never seen someone die. Had never seen a dead body, save the one belonging to a grandmother he'd hardly known. Nick could still see Nana Irene laying in her champagne-colored coffin, lips curled to the point of a grin, arms crossed over her abdomen like she was simply taking a cat nap. So calm, so tranquil, so at peace with her circumstances.

It was nothing like the corpse being rolled out of The Chamberlain on a stretcher.

A white sheet draped the body from head to toe. Blossoms of red bloomed in areas where blood caused the sheet to cling. The thick, black sole of a leather boot peeked out from under one side as a man and a woman with 'CORONER' stenciled in white across the backs of their dark blue windbreakers went about their day's work.

As the stretcher rolled through the lobby, Nick watched it over the shoulder of a detective intent on getting his statement 'while it was still fresh.' As if it would expire at some point. As if the sights and sounds of what happened in the secret room would someday fade from his memory. He scoffed at the notion. There was no chance of that happening. Just like there was no chance of him waking up and it all being a dream. A horrible, messed up dream.

Börne was dead.

That was as real as it got.

The detective lobbed question after question his way, only a few of which Nick had an answer for.

Did you see what happened?

No.

Was anyone else around at the time of the accident?

No.

What were you two doing in the theater so early in the morning, anyway?

What does it matter?

When the stretcher reached The Chamberlain's front door, Nori Park was there to hold it open as the coroners steered the stretcher through. With mouth agape, she watched as they carried it down the concrete steps to the awaiting white van. It wasn't until they lifted the stretcher up and into the back that she turned away and entered the lobby, hair damp, face drained of color.

She rushed over to Nick where he sat in a folding chair beside the concession stand.

"My God, Nick!" She knelt beside him and laid her hand on his knee. "What happened? Who…?"

He looked up at her with blank and distant eyes. The rims red. Tears recently present.

"What are you doing here?"

The lobby was a sea of commotion. Detectives, paramedics, and police officers shuffled about, communicating through shouts. To a passerby, The Chamberlain might have appeared the site of a major crime scene. Nick was oblivious to all of it.

"Police scanner," Nori said, wearing her concern like a mask. "When I heard there was an accident at the theater, well, I just…"

"Why's your hair wet?"

She scowled. "What? Why—"

"Your hair," he said, sounding distant. "It's wet."

She added a shoulder hitch to her scowl. "I'd just stepped out of the shower when I heard." She exchanged a quick look with the detective, then turned back. "Nick…"

His focus had already drifted. His mind somewhere else. Through the lobby's large plate glass window, a paramedic closed one door on the van, then the other. A moment later, the van pulled away, leaving an empty space on the street. A melee of emergency vehicles and a police barricade held gawkers at bay.

"Nick." Nori patted his knee, trying to bring him back around. "Nick, who was that? Who was on the stretcher?"

His gaze returned, but his focus lagged.

"I'm sorry." He searched her expression, certain she'd asked him a question but unsure what that question was. "What did you ask me?"

"Excuse me, Mr. Fallon."

A second detective approached. This one was tall, dark and imposing, his head shaved clean. A badge hung from a chain around his neck, and his sleeves were rolled up on his light blue button-down. A faint stain marred the breast pocket, looking to Nick like the result of dribbled coffee. He stared at the stain, unable to steer his eyes away from it as the detective's voice droned on. "About what happened to Mr. Forrester—"

Nori gasped, covered her mouth with both hands.

Nick tore his eyes away from the stain on the detective's shirt long enough to make eye contact with her.

"Börne." The word spilled from his mouth like broken teeth. "He's dead, Nori. Börne's dead. He was…" His features sagged, as if his plug had been pulled and all his air was leaking out.

Nori's reaction was instantaneous. Her eyes welled as she slogged her head back and forth. When she dropped her hands from her mouth, they revealed a quivering chin.

And for some reason, her reaction surprised Nick. He expected it to be more professional, less personal. She was a reporter, after all. But what did he know?

Nothing, that's what. He didn't know shit. Nor did he have answers for the detective, who stood over him tapping his ink pen against the underside of his chin. Somehow, not having the answers made him feel even worse. He owed Börne more than that. Way more. More of an explanation as to why he was being rolled out of The Chamberlain under a white sheet instead of walking out on his own two feet.

"Mr. Fallon? Did you hear me?"

He hadn't. Hell, he didn't even realize the questions were still coming. When he met the man's stare, the detective gave him a frown. Turning away, the man called out to one of the lingering paramedics. The black bag she carried was the size of a small suitcase, and Nick started a mental list of all the things that might be inside.

"Hey, Marie," the detective said as the paramedic approached. "Can you give Mr. Fallon here a once over for me. I don't think he's entirely with us."

TIM McWHORTER

Act Three

FORTY

It had been a week since tragedy at The Chamberlain had once again brought news vans to Angler Bay. A week since Mayor Blackwood left a letter of resignation on his desk before disappearing like his two sons. And a week since Nick shut the theater down for good.

In many areas of Angler Bay, things were returning to normal. The town was savoring what remained of its summer, the news crews had packed up and left, and framed photos of the Deputy Mayor's family now sat on the desk where Blackwood's once had.

Yet, The Chamberlain remained shuttered.

Nick was in the market to sell and stood to lose his ass. Not that he couldn't unload the property. The realtor who'd brokered his own purchase of the theater assured him even murder houses sell, sometimes before the new paint has even dried. The problem was that even if the right buyer happened along, they wouldn't have to open their wallet very wide. Haunted buildings were a buyer's market by nature. There simply wasn't much interest or competition among buyers. Haunted buildings were the equivalent of used cars on the lot with salvaged titles: they still ran fine but were considered damaged goods. Make an offer somewhere in the ballpark of reasonable and it's yours.

Yet, as Nick sat at his kitchen table surrounded by what amounted to a lifetime supply of Raisinets, Sno-Caps, and bags of unpopped popcorn, his theater wasn't the loss he mourned most.

The secret room had been investigated, wrapped in a bow of yellow police tape, and ceremoniously forgotten by everyone. Everyone, it seemed, but Nick. He couldn't forget if he tried. And he did try. The images were still too vivid, the sounds too clamorous, the guilt too damn oppressive. Restful slumber had become a forgotten luxury.

Hence, the half-empty bottle of bourbon sitting among everything else on the table. It was his third bottle of the week. Dulling the senses seemed the perfect antidote for what ailed him. It paired perfectly with the "pissed at the world" song list he played too loud. He was sure his neighbors despised him by now, wished he'd leave. He gave no shits. Why should they be any different from everyone else in town?

With his laptop open in front of him, the beginning of PJ Harvey's "Long Snake Moan" blistered forth. The scratchy guitar chords. The steady, pulse-pounding drums. The visceral lyrics so painfully delivered. It was the perfect song to drown out the sound of Börne's gut-wrenching death. Which was the whole point. Sure, he could have turned the volume off on the video, but that somehow felt wrong. Like a slight to Börne's tragedy. His thought process made little sense, but what did anymore? The images meant more than the sound, anyway.

Nick opened a box of Raisinets and hit play on the video.

Twenty. That's how many times he'd watched the footage over the past week. At least that many. After handing it over to the police, he'd requested a copy for himself. It was difficult to watch. The angle was off. The room was poorly lit. At the time of the accident, his back had been to Börne, the camera down at his side. Which meant everything the camera recorded was upside down. The footage of that fateful moment was only partially caught in the frame. The fact the camera had caught anything at all could only be chalked up to luck.

As if he anything about that morning could be considered

lucky.

Nick sipped from his glass as his speakers fell silent in anticipation of the next song. When it started with the wail of guitar feedback, he didn't recognize it. It must have been one of those "because you listen to…" selections the streaming service would drop in whether you wanted them to or not. As the drums kicked in and searing vocals started talking about caution tape and security gates, he found himself bobbing his head up and down.

"Who the hell is this?" he asked the empty kitchen. He pulled up the streaming window and checked the song.

BROKEN BRICKS by The White Stripes

"Hmmm," he said, collapsing the window. "Might have to add this one to the playlist." He took another sip of bourbon, leaned back, and watched more upside-down footage on his laptop.

And then he saw it.

He had always seen it, really. It was right there in front of him. If it had been Harvey's Long Snake, it would have bitten him. It had just taken The White Stripes in his ear for it to click.

He tapped his laptop's mute key and silenced Jack White's shouting. He leaned in toward the screen. "Holy shit."

It was so obvious.

"Why are all the walls concrete except one?"

Nori pulled her cell from her ear and checked the time. Nearly midnight. On a Wednesday. Hadn't Nick spent the day at The Chamberlain clearing out his belongings? Shouldn't he be exhausted, both physically and emotionally? Yet, he sounded not only wide awake, but energized.

She couldn't say the same for herself. "I'm sorry?" she asked, rubbing fresh sleep from her eyes. She'd been up nearly twenty-four hours straight working on a story and had only recently crawled into bed.

"The secret room," Nick continued. "All the walls down there are concrete block except one. The wall where the shelving was. It's brick. Why is that?"

She gave it only a few seconds' thought, because, well, she wasn't a building contractor. How was she supposed to know?

"Nick, my friend, do you know what time it is?"

"I do."

"And do you know how long I've been up?"

"I do not. But—"

She closed her eyes and laid her head back. It didn't surprise her there was a 'but.' He'd probably watched the video a hundred times by now. And if she knew his mental state—and she liked to think she was getting to know him pretty well—a bottle of bourbon most likely sat within reach.

She worried about him. Nick could be obsessive. Nobody blamed him for Börne's death. Not the police. Not Claudia. That didn't stop him from shouldering more than his share of guilt.

The reporter in her had taken it upon herself to question the investigators. There was speculation the sudden change in humidity could have weakened the old shelving unit, the secret room having been sealed off for decades. Another theory was the shifting of weight from Börne shuffling around the bottles and crates was the cause of the shelving's topple. Perhaps he'd incidentally triggered the collapse himself.

Neither explanation suited Nick. And to be honest, she wasn't sold, either. How heavy was a bottle of gin, anyway? But they were biased. Nick, of all people, expected answers. More than anyone, save maybe Claudia. But when it came to answers, or anything resembling proof, there was a glaring lack of it. All anyone seemed willing to offer was speculation. Nobody wanted to put their neck on the line to contradict what appeared to be, by anyone's standard, nothing more than a freak and tragic accident.

Nori sat up in bed, put her cell on speaker, and reached for the bottle of water she kept on her nightstand.

"Okay, Nick," she said lifting the bottle to her lips. "The walls. Let's hear it."

She listened while he explained how he came to question the brick wall in The Chamberlain's secret room. How the change in building materials pointed to the wall having been constructed long after the rest of the room. Why, or for what purpose, he couldn't offer an opinion. Nor could she when pressed. What a brick wall—regardless of how out of place it might seem—had to do with the accident, she was equally unsure. It was just a wall. Walls didn't kill people. Accidentally or otherwise.

"I'm heading over there," he said, his words and breaths both coming in short bursts.

It sounded like he was in the process of either getting dressed or putting on shoes. She exhaled deeply. She needed sleep, was so tired she could hardly think straight. She also wasn't about to let Nick go down into that room alone. And by the sounds of it, he wasn't in the market for excuses as to why they shouldn't.

She sighed. "Meet you there in thirty," she said, and tapped the screen to end the call.

FORTY-ONE

Hunched under The Chamberlain's darkened marquee, Nick fumbled with his keys. He wished he hadn't turned off the exterior lights when he'd left that afternoon, but he'd had no reason to leave them on. He couldn't afford the added electricity any more than he could afford the lease. Or the insurance. Or any other expense the theater brought with it. Besides, for all he'd known, he wouldn't be returning to The Chamberlain until it was sold. And who knew when that might be?

Yet here he was.

His furlough from the theater had lasted all of four hours.

The first thing he did after locking the door behind them was flip on the lights. Not just one or two. *All* the lobby's lights. He could blame it on habit, but there was more to it than that, if he were honest. Ducking behind the concession stand, he brought the thermostat to life as well. Deep inside the theater, the furnace rumbled to life for the first time since Spring.

"Should only take a few minutes to get the chill out of the air," he said, rubbing his hands together.

Nori nodded and worked her hands up and down her arms.

It wasn't only cold inside The Chamberlain. It felt lifeless, void of a soul. Like its personality had been stripped away, leaving only an empty shell to speak of the grandeur it once possessed. Framed movie posters no longer lined the walls but lay stacked in his spare bedroom. He'd donated the fake palm trees with their gold, ornate pots, to the Angler Bay public library. Even the concession counter and its glass display case had been stripped of everything but dust.

In a matter of days, the historic Chamberlain Theater had been reduced to nothing more than a sterile, blank slate. A stark reminder his list of failed business ventures had yet another entrant.

"Is…" Nori started, turning to look toward the hallway. "Are we sure it's even safe? I mean…"

She didn't have to explain herself. He knew why she was asking.

"Should be," he answered. "The room's empty. Door's been removed. We won't be down there long. Just wanna get a look at the wall. See it in person."

Nori wasn't wrong to be concerned though. With everything he'd seen over the last month, he would have thought the theater had nothing left with which to put him on edge. But things were different now. Someone had died. The ante had been raised.

Now he knew what Floyd Cropper and The Chamberlain were capable of.

"Wouldn't remember Claudia's prayer, would ya? I mean, just in case?"

She shook her head. "Didn't pay much attention really. When she was reciting it, I was thinking to myself how stupid I was for putting myself in a situation where I needed a prayer of protection."

He nodded, understanding all too well. Even now, as eager as he was to check out that wall, his feet were reluctant to take him there.

"Hey." She reached up and took his arm. "You okay?"

And for the first time since hearing the White Stripes song and noticing the difference in the walls, he considered it. Was he okay with it? Was he okay with venturing back down into the belly of the beast where a vengeful spirit caused the death of someone he'd invited down there? He wasn't. But it didn't matter. He owed it to Claudia, and to a greater degree, Börne, to do everything he could to find out what happened. He only wished he could channel some of Börne's courage.

He offered a slight smile and nodded. "I'm good. Let's go."

From the moment they'd hung it, the police tape had seemed unnecessary. Nick kept The Chamberlain's front doors locked at all times. Nobody but he came and went. No one else wanted to since most the townsfolk believed The Chamberlain to be cursed. On one occasion, he'd even witnessed an elderly couple cross the street, taking a wide berth around the property so as not to get too close to the theater on their Sunday stroll.

"Sorry."

He rushed over to the gaping hole and began ripping down the yellow strips. If he'd known Nori would be following him back here, he would have removed it earlier. It seemed, 'if he'd only known' was a regret he was becoming all too familiar with. One by one, the strips came away, and one by one, he fashioned them into a growing ball of yellow. When he was done, he looked around for somewhere to put it. Like everything else from the storage room, the trashcan now sat in his apartment. With nowhere to dispose of it, he tossed the ball of tape into a corner. A parting gift for the next owner.

Nori took in the barren storage room from the doorway.

"I love what you've done with the place."

He broke into a full-on chuckle. She joined him, seemingly relieved that her icebreaker had landed as intended. The empty room soon echoed with the sound of levity. It was the first time laughter had graced the room as far as he knew, and it was very much welcomed. What it wasn't, however, was destined to last. As they turned their gaze to the opening in the wall, their laughter died a slow death.

Nori sucked in a deep breath and let it out. "So that's it, huh?"

He nodded, knowing what she was thinking: while they'd been talking in his office that evening, the theater's best kept secret had been ten feet away.

He stepped toward the empty doorway. "Come on."

Once inside the room, finding the pull string for the lights took only seconds. This time, he knew where to look. When he pulled it, the dreary room flooded with a brilliant white. The original yellow bulb, along with its two burnt out siblings, had been replaced with new LED bulbs during the accident investigation. The room was much brighter now. Would things have gone differently that morning had there been this much light to see by? He doubted it. The lack of proper illumination hadn't been a contributing factor. Still, with so many unanswered questions, nothing was off the table when it came to 'what ifs.'

At least all morbid reminders of the accident had been cleared away. The wooden shelves and shattered crates were long gone. Shards of glass no longer littered the floor. The cleaning crew he'd hired had mopped up the copious amount of blood, along with the many gallons of decades-old liquor. What remained was a clean spot in the middle of the otherwise grimy and dust-covered floor. It stood out like a bruised thumb caught in a car door. In its own way, it spoke almost as much to Börne's violent end as the blood and debris would have.

Almost.

It was still better.

Nori stared at the floor. He could see her mind directing a film on how the accident might have played out. She would likely get the details wrong, but the ending would be the same. He scrambled for a plan to draw her attention away from the floor. The best he could come up with was to move things along.

"This is it," he said, approaching the wall. He raised a hand to it but stopped short of touching it outright. He hovered his hand an inch from the brick, trying to feel any sort of energy coming off the wall. It was stupid, he knew. He wasn't Claudia. He didn't share her insights.

He moved in and placed his hand on the wall. The bricks were cool to the touch, the mortar between them, rough and sloppy. He traced his finger along the vertical and horizontal lines.

Behind him, Nori inspected one of the concrete walls, then another. Approaching the brick wall, she said, "It's the only wall without a trace of ash or soot on it."

It dawned on him now why the space had seemed oddly shaped. *The brick wall.* It appeared to cut off one of the room's pre-existing corners at a strange angle. He ran his hand over the brick. "I'd say someone, at some point, sealed off part of this room."

"Why?"

"Million-dollar question."

"What's on the other side of it?"

"Even better question."

Her eyes locked onto his. "So, the secret room…"

He nodded. "Is hiding a secret of its own."

She started to say something more but stopped. "Do you hear that?" She craned her neck. "Is that…"

"It is." He gestured toward the wall that separated them from the auditorium. "It's happened before."

Though the concrete muffled the sounds, soft music could be heard playing through the auditorium speakers. Calliope music. The low drone of a narrator's voice told an audience to sit back and enjoy the ride.

"I've come into work a couple times," Nick continued, "and the movie's already playing. Always the same one. The matinee for the kids."

Nori turned to him. "Thought you shut the theater down?"

"I did."

She tugged on her earlobe. "And the control room?"

"Disassembled."

"Then how—"

He shook his head, bewildered that the film could still be playing since he'd unplugged all the equipment. Bewildered, but somehow not surprised.

"Because, somehow, the energy isn't coming from inside the auditorium. Or even the control room. That was Börne theory, and I think he was right. The source of everything we've seen and experienced at The Chamberlain originates from right here."

He rested his hand on the brick wall. "Behind here."

"But…" Shaking her head, Nori backed away from the wall. "I'm sorry," she said, her voice taking on a slight tremble. "I just… I can't…" She turned and made her way through the open doorway.

The fear he saw in her eyes sent a chill rippling through Nick. Partly because he wanted to check on her, and partly because he didn't want to be in there alone, he, too, hurried from the room.

He caught up with her as she made her way up the hallway toward the lobby.

"Hey," he said, taking her arm. "You okay?"

She nodded and wiped at her cheek. "I'm fine. It's… it's probably stupid. I just… Nick, that music? Playing by itself? While we stood on the very spot Börne… It was just too much."

"I know," he said. "I know."

When they reached the end of the hallway and spilled into the lobby's harsh light, he let go of her arm. "I'm gonna check the control room real quick," he said. "Wait for me."

She grabbed his hand before it could drop away. "Be careful," she said.

He held her gaze for several seconds, then nodded and turned away.

At the control room's red door, he didn't hesitate. If he had, he may have talked himself out of going in. He thrust the door inward and entered. There was no one in the room to surprise. No one to catch red-handed. The tiny room was as empty as he'd left it that afternoon.

Yet, he could see through the small window to the auditorium that the film still played on the screen. Its music flowed through the speakers.

"How the fuck?"

He knelt and scanned beneath the projection console with the light from his cell. He'd expected to find things just how he'd left them: the plug pulled from the outlet and the cord snaking lifeless on the floor. That's not how he found things now, however, and he gasped. The cord had been plugged back into the outlet. By whom, he didn't know. Yet, somehow, he once again wasn't surprised.

"You're not gonna believe this," he said, returning to the lobby and finding Nori perched atop the concession counter. And yet, even as he said it, he knew she would believe it. Nothing about the theater crossed the line into disbelief anymore. "Damn thing was plugged back in. After I'd unplugged it this afternoon."

Her jaw dropped, but she recovered quickly with a shake of her head. "I believe it."

Nick chuckled. "Knew you would."

"Which makes up my mind even more." She folded her arms across her chest.

"What do you mean?"

"We need to get Claudia back in here," she said. "Before we go any further."

On the surface, Nick was offended. But deep down, he knew she was right. Claudia was better equipped to deal with anything they might encounter moving forward.

"Okay," he said, putting a hand on Nori's knee. "But do we even know if she'd step foot in here again?"

"She will."

"And how can you be sure?"

"Because I called her on my way over here," Nori said. "She

was up. Seems none of us are getting much sleep."

Claudia tossed her cell phone onto the bed and returned to her happy place. Photos of Börne surrounded her, spread out across the bed. The feeling she got lying next to images of him was the only peace she'd known the past week. They were all she had left.

Sure, she had hundreds of hours of footage they'd filmed from investigations, but except for a brief appearance here or there, the videos contained more footage of her and the locations than Börne. And then there was the horrifying video of that fateful morning. For obvious reasons, watching that one didn't fill her with the same peace as the others.

She still watched it, though. For different reasons.

Among the photos spread out on the bed, a few were of Börne alone, but most were of the two of them. There were the photos from their wedding, their many ski trips in Mittenwald, and Oktoberfests in Munich. There were photos commemorating their arrival in Boston where they'd spent their first day in America on a duck boat tour soaking up their new country's history. Since then, it had been mostly work with little play. There were only a few photos of them taken in the past ten years.

Perhaps their distant past was all she had left.

With a deep breath and long, drawn out exhale, she began gathering the photos and placing them back in the old shoebox.

"I'll see you again real soon, *meine Liebe*." Bringing it to her lips, she kissed the wedding photo of Börne kissing her on the forehead. If she had to choose, she'd claim that one as her favorite. "I've got work to do."

After placing the lid on the shoebox, she carried it to the closet she and Börne had shared in their tiny house. It took rising onto her toes to slide the box back into the open slot on the top shelf. With the photos returned to their proper place, her focus shifted. Pushing aside the ornate gowns she wore for work, she pulled out their black, soft-sided suitcase.

Nostalgia can be a wonderful place to visit, but you can't live there.

"Time to finish what we started."

FORTY-TWO

Lightning cracked the night sky. A low rumble followed. Icy rain found its way inside Nick's collar, running down his neck and inside his shirt as he fumbled with his keys for the second time in as many nights. This time, he'd left The Chamberlain's marquee lights on, electric bill be damned. And even though it had helped him unlock the door in record time, the damage had already been done. Rainwater soaked through to his unmentionables.

Thankfully, he'd left a modest collection of cleaning supplies in one of the cabinets behind the concession counter. He ducked behind the counter where a stack of white rags awaited him. He grabbed one off the top and shook it from its folded state. He brought it to his face.

A whoosh entered the front door.

A gust of wind coursed through the lobby.

For the first time in over a week, Claudia Forrester stood inside The Chamberlain Theater. The torrential rain had flattened her fiery red mane. Streaks of black trailed from her eyes. A stream of water sloped down her nose before plummeting onto her waterlogged black trench coat.

An equally miserable-looking Nori Park entered behind her.

Nick grabbed two rags from the stack and rushed them over. "Sorry. Best I've got."

They both thanked him and proceeded to rid themselves of the evening's weather.

As Claudia worked the rag through her damp hair, Nick found it difficult to look at her for fear of making eye contact. He had, after all, been the last person to see her husband alive. Not only was he the reason she was a widow, but that guilt had kept him from making the trip north for the funeral. Which made the burden of his guilt that much heavier. It was a vicious cycle.

"Nice to see you, Nick." She smiled weakly and began glancing around the lobby.

He looked to Nori, raised his eyebrows.

"Yeah, um, Claudia. Good seeing you." He looked again to Nori and shrugged. Her soft smile and encouraging nod eased his anxiety by a bit.

"Can't say I like what you've done with the place," Claudia said. "But I get it. And I'm sorry."

It was the first time he'd heard her speak since the day after Börne died. The day she'd packed up what remained of F.A.U.S.T. and followed his body home to Chicago. Her voice was timid now, softened by loss and sadness.

"Claudia, I'm… I'm so sorry. I can't—"

Claudia raised her hand. "It wasn't your fault, Nick. Truly. Börne was always… hazardous to his health. Fearless. Didn't always make the best choices for his own well-being. It was a side of him that both inspired and scared the hell out of me. I've watched it, you know. The footage you shot that night. Several times."

Her eyes were on him, but as far as he could tell, she was looking *through* him more than at him.

"I kept trying to see something," she continued. "Anything that might explain what happened."

The thought of a grieving Claudia sitting alone in her empty home watching that footage on repeat ground his heart to nothing. A cigarette butt under a boot heel.

Outside, thunder stole silence from the night.

He cleared his throat.

"It simply tips over," he said, recalling the video. "The shelving unit. It doesn't appear to be pushed or shoved or anything. It just… topples."

Claudia nodded her head. And for the first time since the conversation started, her and Nick's eyes met. "Even using Börne's sophisticated software to enhance the video," she said, "I couldn't find anything that might have caused it to move. No shadows, no sudden glitches in the footage. Nothing earthly, at least."

Earthly.

Nick understood what she meant. There were two worlds to consider. Even for him, it was too late in the game to question the existence of the paranormal.

As Claudia's eyes started to glaze with moisture, she reached the damp towel out to Nick. When he took it, she excused herself and turned for the ladies' room. A moment later, she disappeared through its swinging door.

Nick approached Nori, who also handed him a damp towel.

"Did you see that?" he said, nodding toward the restroom door. "Looked like she was starting to cry."

Nori took a moment before answering.

"I think it's just being here," she said. "Remember, she never came inside that day. The police kept her out. This is the first time she's stepped foot in here since Börne…" Her voice trailed off. She didn't have to finish the sentence. He knew where she was going with it.

He blew hot air into his hands. "So, are we sure this is even a good idea? Her being here? Maybe we should have done this ourselves."

Nori eyed him for a few seconds, then looked to the restroom door. When she turned back, her wheels were turning. He knew her well enough at this point to know that didn't always mean good things for him.

"Do you want to tell her?" Her eyebrows arched as she tilted her forehead toward him. "Do you want to be the one to tell Claudia she shouldn't look any further into why her husband might be dead right now?"

Put that way, of course he didn't.

Claudia emerged from the restroom, hair tied back, eyes dry, face free of smear.

"Don't even think about it," she said, rejoining the group. "I'm absolutely seeing this through. Don't ask me to walk away now. I didn't spend all day driving here to turn back."

Nori and Nick exchanged a look. Had their voices travelled that far? Or was telepathy another sense the spiritual Mrs. Forrester possessed?

"Okay," he said.

"Okay," Claudia repeated, then peered over at the mouth of the hallway. "So, are you gonna show me this room, or what?"

He nodded and said, "But we should say the prayer first. Just to be safe. We didn't say it that morning. And… well, we should say it now."

Claudia reached out her hands.

As the three of them clasped one another's hand, they closed their eyes. A moment later, the prayer of protection had been said and everyone dropped their hands.

"And the pendants?" he asked, pulling his own necklace from his pocket and slipping it over his head. "Everyone have theirs?"

Claudia reached into the front of her blouse and produced the black tourmaline hanging by a leather cord around her neck. "Always."

Nori pulled her pendant from the collar of her blouse as well.

Then Nick caught a grin from Nori. She looked to be doing her best to hide it, but the grin wasn't having it.

He lost his train of thought. "What?"

Nori disposed of the evidence, and with a straight face, said, "Nothing. Never mind."

He held her gaze for a few seconds more before letting it go. "So," he said, taking the first step towards the hallway. "Shall we?"

Claudia turned to Nori, smiled briefly, shelved it, then followed.

A moment later, Nori did the same.

Standing in the middle of the empty storage room, Nick cast a sidelong glance Claudia's way as she stared at the doorway to the secret room. He couldn't imagine what it must be like for her. She was about to enter the room where her husband had taken his last breath. And a grisly last breath it had been. He was wary of entering again himself. Each time he did, he felt he was playing a dangerous game of Russian Roulette.

Awkward silence reigned. He wanted to give Claudia time, wanted her to go at her own pace. At the same time, he could feel himself growing anxious. The nest of hornets in his stomach were growing increasingly agitated.

"Anyone else notice how quiet it is in here?" Nori asked. Still damp and shivering, she shoved her hands into her jean's pockets. "I mean, it's coming down in buckets outside, and we can't hear a thing."

Nick nodded. A movie theater, by nature, is designed for optimal acoustics. That included a decent amount of soundproofing. Not to mention the fact The Chamberlain was old. Buildings built back then were more solid, more structurally sound. Which made the theater not only the perfect place for a speakeasy, but for any other activities deemed necessary to hide from the outside world.

"Well," Claudia shrugged, "we could stand here all night, but that wall's not going to investigate itself."

They'd delayed long enough.

Nick took the lead and disappeared through the darkened doorway. A shiver rattled his shoulders as he entered the adjoining room. Though he was already damp, the chill in the air was unmistakable.

He turned on the lights and wasted no time making his way to the wall where the shelving unit had once stood. He'd hoped to move Claudia swiftly past the gleaming spot on the floor. It had caught Nori's attention the night before. He hoped it wouldn't catch Claudia's.

Possibly with the same intent, Nori appeared beside him.

Claudia soon followed.

Nick stepped to the side, allowing her full access. While she ran her hands along the wall's rough façade, he inventoried the barren room. It didn't take long. What he needed was some kind of tool. A big, heavy one. He cursed himself. It seemed he'd come as woefully unprepared as the night before. He'd been in a rush, nervous about seeing Claudia, unsure what her wishes would be, how she would want to proceed. Now, having laid eyes on the wall a second time in as many days, there was really only one course of action: they needed to bust through it. After all, it was brick. There were no secret doors to uncover this time.

Only problem was, he had nothing at his disposal worthy of creating a hole in a brick wall.

"What you need is a sledgehammer."

Nick chuckled at Nori's ability to read his mind. "What *I* need?"

"Your theater." She grinned. "Your wall."

He couldn't argue her point. It was his theater, and a sledgehammer was indeed what he needed. "Wouldn't have one in your pocket, would ya?"

"Sorry," she said with a shake of her head. "Left mine at home."

"Same." Claudia hugged herself and rubbed her arms. "What

about you, Nick?"

He chuckled. "Do I look like a guy who owns a sledgehammer?"

"So," Claudia said, "where would someone find one this time of night?"

Nick and Nori exchanged a look.

"City council still debating each other on how to pay for the sand dune restoration?" he asked.

Nori shook her head. "It's been worked out. Project's almost done."

"Almost, huh?"

She nodded.

Nick smiled. "Then I guess I know where we can get a sledgehammer."

"Good," Claudia said. Her expression grew serious as she turned and placed both hands on the wall. "Because there's definitely something behind here, and we need to get to it."

FORTY-THREE

Thirty minutes later, Nick was in possession of a well-used twelve-pound sledgehammer, and the construction company rebuilding the retaining wall along the beach possessed one less. Leaving a trailer full of expensive tools unattended at night seemed like a poor business practice, even in a town the size of Angler Bay. If there was any question before, Nick had proved it so. But then, wasn't that what insurance was for? Now if there was only a policy covering the loss of revenue due to vengeful spirits.

"Here goes nothing." He wiped his hands on his jeans and approached the wall. When he lifted the hammer, the lights flickered. They didn't go out. He stood frozen, the sledgehammer poised over his shoulder, and exchanged a look with Claudia.

"New bulbs, right?" she asked.

He nodded.

She returned the nod. "He's here," she said, and Nick thought she was referring to Floyd. Then she smiled and said, "Börne is with us." A tear ran from her eye and down her cheek.

A chill ran down Nick's spine.

The first strike rang out like a church bell. The impact of the forged steel hammerhead against the brick reverberated throughout the room. The other walls shook, freeing themselves of years of dust and ash and soot, and the floor vibrated beneath their feet. The echo of the blow pinged around the room, taking several seconds for the clamor to die out. It all spoke to a much greater strength than Nick possessed.

"Wow," Nori said. "Now there's an argument for having the right tool for the job if I ever saw one."

Nick glanced around the room, wide-eyed and chilled. "Right tool or not, no way that was all me."

A chunk of brick the size of a shot glass lay at the base of the wall. A substantial fracture now zigzagged a good eighteen inches down through the mortared seams, nearly reaching the floor. One blow, and he couldn't be happier with the immediate results. If someone had enlisted the brick wall to keep a secret, its tenure was about to end.

The second strike of the hammer chipped more brick, cracked more mortar. Once again, the ground and walls shook out of proportion with Nick's strength. The rumble took a good ten seconds to fade out. What filled the space in its wake was a sound all-too familiar.

"Um, Nick," Claudia muttered. "What is that?"

"Children's matinee," he said. "Playing in the auditorium. It happens." The film had started from the beginning, the narrator welcoming everyone aboard the submarine. It would soon dive and show its passengers a world they had never seen before. The film, and their adventure, was just getting started.

"Interesting," Claudia said, face to the sky, eyes closed.

"Creepy is what it is," Nori said.

Claudia held her pose and slowly breathed in and out.

He could only imagine what was going through her mind. The spirit most likely responsible for the accident claiming her husband's life was making an appearance. And if Floyd hadn't caused the accident outright, he was at least somehow responsible. Bizarre as it might sound, no other theory made sense. Floyd Cropper was as much responsible for Börne's death as Nick.

With the muffled sounds of whimsical music playing in the background, Nick took another deep breath and swung the hammer a third time. The solid strike again rocked the room. He was making progress. The brick now displayed a deep crater. A ragged blemish on its uniform façade.

Tiring, Nick drew a couple of deep breaths and wiped sweat from his hands. "One more might do it," he said, and hefted the sledgehammer. After first drawing it back, he brought the hammer around with a swing that would make Babe Ruth proud. When the steel head connected with brick, there was no question steel won the battle.

And the devastating blow was felt by all three.

A hole opened, and a cannon blast of air, white ash, and the deafening screams of children erupted from it. The concussive burst of wind, like a freight train, knocked Nick, Claudia, and Nori off their feet. They hit the floor in a tumble as everyone scrambled to cover their ears.

Like the cries of tormented banshees, anguished wails rushed from the hole in the wall, threatening eardrums. Pain and sorrow filled the room. Bits of brick and ash swirled above like a tornado unleashed, peppering faces and arms, stinging their skin. All three light bulbs shattered, and darkness overcame the room.

As the tornado slowly lost strength, so did the cries. A moment later, they'd faded completely. Only soft music and a muffled narrator describing how coral reefs were formed disturbed the silence.

A light sprang up in the darkness. Nori shined her cell phone on Claudia first. Blanketed from head to toe in white and grey, the investigator used her hands to fluff ash from her hair, appearing otherwise unharmed. Nori turned her cell light on Nick next. Sitting dumbfounded on his backside, sledgehammer between his outstretched legs, he wore the same thin layer of snow-like ash.

The overwhelming reek of burnt wood and old smoke filled the air.

"Everyone okay?" Nick asked.

No one answered or said a word as they quietly climbed to their feet and began brushing themselves off. Eventually, it was Nori who broke the silence with the same question that ran through Nick's mind.

"What… the fuck… was that?"

As was his usual response, he looked to Claudia for the answer. She had retrieved her cell phone and was using its light to inspect a small mound of ash in her hand. She swirled a pinky through it, then brought it to her nose.

"What's the saying," she said, dropping the mound of ash and brushing her hand on her slacks, "I'm no rocket scientist, but I'd say there was a fire on the other side of this wall at one time."

"Yeah, but, those screams?" Nori asked. "What does your Spidey sense tell you about those?"

After taking a moment to think it over, Claudia answered with a shake of her head, equating to no answer at all.

"Outstanding," Nick muttered, his ears still ringing. "Just great."

After retrieving his own cell phone, he trained its faint glow on the hole in the wall. Within a matter of seconds, the light from Nori and Claudia's cell phones joined the party. The crater surrounding the hole was large, but the hole itself was roughly the size of a fist.

Even with three lights trained on it, he could see nothing but pitch black through the opening, which one would think would be a good thing, but somehow wasn't. His heart rate was going, in Börne's words, apeshit. He expected something to emerge from the hole at any moment. Rats. Spiders. A hand. A scene from the movie *Jaws* flashed in his mind: Ben Gardner's severed head appearing at the hole in his sunken boat's hull. Even though Nick quickly struck the image from his mind, its residue lingered.

When Nori cleared her throat beside him, he almost pissed himself.

"So, who wants to take one for the team?" She turned her light away from the hole long enough to question Nick and Claudia with it.

"What does that mean?" Claudia asked. "Take one for the team?"

"She's asking," Nick chimed, "who wants to be the first to go look in the hole. Because anything we find through there was meant to stay hidden. So, it can't be anything good."

"I think it's safe to say," Nori added, "that at some point in time, something far worse than simple drinking and gambling took place down here."

In The Chamberlain's bowels, he thought.

"Well, then," Claudia said, "let's keep chipping away. No one's seeing much through that little hole."

The sledgehammer made a sound like fingernails on a chalkboard as Nick drug it across the ash-covered floor toward the wall. Two blows later and the hole had doubled in size. It was now roughly the size of a basketball, large enough for someone to poke his or her head through, though nobody rushed forward to do so.

After a few more swings, the hole had once again grown. First doubling, then tripling. The weight of the sledgehammer had also grown. His shoulders screamed for mercy. His back muscles waved the white flag. Despite the chill in the room, beads of sweat ran down both sides of his face. He didn't envy those who made their living swinging sledgehammers all day. He dropped it to the floor and shook the sting from his hands.

Then he stepped back from the wall.

The three stared at the opening.

The opening stared back. Its gaping maw beckoning, awaiting the bravest among them.

Nick shook from a sudden chill.

As his imagination paged through possibilities of what might await them on the other side of the wall, each one more diabolical than the previous, he struggled to maintain his courage. Were Nori and Claudia as nervous as him? Did any of them have the nerve to be the first to climb through the opening?

"So," Claudia said before echoing Börne's own words, "rock, paper, scissors?"

FORTY-FOUR

"God, it smells."

Standing several pitch-black feet behind her, Nick knew to what Claudia referred. The acrid stench of rot, stale smoke, and charred wood oozed from the opening like a sewage leak. When he thought the smell couldn't get any worse, the thick, nauseating odor grew even more overpowering. Within seconds, it had infiltrated the entire room.

He gagged and pulled the collar of his shirt up over his nose.

"Damn," Nori said, waving her hand in front of her face. "Smells like something crawled in there, caught on fire, and died." Her eyes widened and she grimaced the second the words left her mouth. She turned to Nick and mouthed the word 'sorry.'

Claudia pulled back from the hole. If she'd heard Nori's comment, she showed no indication of it. "Should've checked that trailer for some portable lighting, too."

Nick looked skyward, imagining the rain still falling outside. "Wanna go back out there?"

"Not really." Claudia turned her cell phone back to the hole. "Not excited about going in there with nothing but these, either."

"Guys," Nori interrupted, her eyes darting around the darkness. "You hear that?"

The music had stopped, having been replaced with a new sound altogether.

After a moment, Nick nodded. "Feel it, too."

The air didn't just hum, it buzzed. Static energy more indicative of an electric substation filled the space around them. The hair on his arms and neck tingled as the energy grew. It was as if someone were turning up a dial. What had started out as nothing more than a low, barely perceptible murmur only seconds earlier, had quickly intensified into something more tangible.

In the dark, Claudia's silhouette nodded toward the opening in the brick wall. "The answers we seek lie in there."

Nick swallowed hard. "About Börne's accident?"

"About everything," she said. "All the activity you've been experiencing here at the theater. This is where the energy is the strongest." She shined her light on his chest, while illuminating his face. "I sense a vengeance was born behind this wall."

Once Nick's initial shock faded, he furrowed his brow. "Wait, a second," he said. "Floyd. He, you know... out on the front steps. About as far from this room as you could get."

Claudia swung her light back to the opening. "I'm not so sure our spirits have anything to do with Floyd anymore."

A chill ran through Nick from top to bottom. His stomach churned hot lava rocks. "Yeah, but—"

Before he could finish his question, Claudia ducked through the opening and disappeared into the darkness.

"Well, alright then." He took a deep breath of stale air, then let it out and scrunched his nose. He looked to Nori and gestured with his hand. "Ladies first, I guess."

Nori snickered, placed a hand on his chest. "How very chivalrous—"

A gasp came from the other side of the wall. It was Claudia's, and it was abrupt.

"Shit." Without hesitating further, Nick ducked through the opening.

Beyond the wall, the buzzing was stronger. The energy, more palpable. With no light from the storage room doorway to penetrate the space, the darkness inside proved even more cavernous.

Oppressively so.

"Watch your step." Claudia instructed. "There's… I don't even know what you'd call it."

Once through the opening, Nori slowly scanned the floor with her cell phone, then sucked in a sharp intake of air. "I'm not a cop," she said, "but I'd call it evidence."

FORTY-FIVE

They huddled around their trio of cell phone lights like homeless around a barrel fire. Scattered in and out of their beams were items not normally found in the basement of a theater. Or a speakeasy for that matter. Everything they'd stumbled upon was burnt, destroyed, and horrifically out of place.

Nick couldn't believe his eyes.

Balled up just inside the wall, was the remnant of a light blue shirt. It looked to be a child's shirt by the size of it. But with the layer of grey ash covering it, and the fact most of the shirt was burnt away, it was difficult to tell for sure. A stacked, but equally scorched pile of clothing sat beside it. A pair of chipped dinner plates with matching mugs sat beside the pile. More than one blanket lay strewn about. A toy building set and many miniature cars, all metal like the ones Nick himself had played with as a kid, lay scattered about. Spines and partial covers from numerous books littered the floor. Most of their pages were missing, and he assumed they accounted for much of the ash covering everything. Where ash hadn't settled, black soot coated the surfaces.

One after another, long-hidden objects revealed themselves at the behest of cell phone flashlights.

Nick hung inside the opening, a swirling cloud of disturbed ash engulfing his shoes. He couldn't yet bring himself to venture further. Nor was there much room to do so. He turned back to the wall itself, drawing his finger across the stone. It came away clean.

He tried again in a different spot with the same results. The wall was free of ash, soot, or any other tell-tale signs a fire leaves in its wake.

Static electricity hummed at full strength.

"Guess we know which came first," he said, shouting over the buzzing. "The fire or this wall."

Claudia appeared beside him. "Interesting."

"Why?" Nori asked.

"What do you mean?" Nick said. "Why is it interesting?"

"No, I mean. So there's a fire, right? And a bunch of shit down here that probably shouldn't be." She scanned her cell phone back over the burnt debris. "For whatever reason. But why seal this area off instead of just getting rid of… whatever all this is?"

"I don't know," Nick said. "Maybe there's more. Something down here that'll tell us…"

The sudden pained look on Claudia's shadowy face put a stop to his thought process. She had a hand to her temple. She squeezed her eyes shut. Given enough time, she looked as if she might faint.

"Hey," Nick said, putting a hand on her back. Her body trembled beneath his hand. "Are you okay? Is it the electricity?"

Claudia opened her heavy-lidded eyes, but they didn't focus on him.

"No. It's," she said, but stopped. Seconds later she continued. "What I'm feeling. It's… overwhelming. Like nothing I've ever felt. Stronger, like the buzzing. Like…" Her eyes shot open as she spun toward the far corner, taking the light from her cell phone with her.

Nick swung his cell around.

Nori's light made three.

The beams from all three cell phones converged on an array of blackened and burned blankets and pillows nestled on the floor in the corner. But it wasn't *that* they were nestled that caught Nick's attention, but how. They formed a distinct, and unmistakable lump.

Covering that lump were the charred ruins of what looked to have once been sleeping bags. The huddled lump underneath was the size of a human being. Maybe two, if small.

Nori gasped and clamped a hand over her mouth. A scan of her light up and over the lump brought a brief outburst of distress.

Nick swallowed hard, fighting back a rising anxiety.

Whispers began flowing from Claudia. "No, no, no, no, no…" She shook her head back and forth, eyes closed, mumbling through trembling lips. At some point her words changed from pleas to a softly recited prayer.

Nick looked to Nori. Wide eyes greeted him. She made no move, offered no words. Shock kept her from registering any more of a response.

He turned back to the pile of blankets and sleeping bags. Though an icy hand of dread gripped his soul, he had to follow through. There was no stopping now. They were too close to the answers they sought.

He stepped over what had likely been the remains of someone's last meal—soot and ash-covered plates, forks, and what appeared to be a smattering of chicken bones—on his way to the lump.

The closer he drew, the sharper the buzzing in his ears became. It was painful now, a mini electrical storm brewing in his head. Pressing against his temple offered no relief. Cupping his hand over his ear proved no better. The sensation of something trickling from his ear and down his cheek entered his conscience.

At the edge of the pile, he knelt and cast a glance behind him. Nori looked on with hands clasped over her ears. Claudia's eyes remained closed. Tears streamed from them. Her lips worked feverishly.

He turned back to the blankets and breathed deep. As he reached for the edge of the sleeping bag, the buzzing hit a crescendo. The floor vibrated, causing the forks to dance and rattle on the stacked plates. The walls shook. The ceiling rumbled. Light ash fell like soft snow.

He grabbed a fistful of nylon.

His heart threatened to rip free of his chest.

The room threatened to rip itself apart.

He couldn't stop now. His only path out of this was forward. One, he counted. Two. He tore away the sleeping bag.

An explosion of ash filled the air as The Chamberlain gave up its most heinous secret. All other excitement in the room ceased. The trembling stilled. The buzzing fell silent.

The crescendo of ash settled.

Nick stumbled backward, landing on his backside among the cups and plates and half-burned books. A tragic realization dropped his jaw like a sucker punch.

Nori screamed in despair.

And as Claudia opened her tearful eyes, a tender smile crept onto her face. "It's okay, little ones," she said, taking in the two tiny skeletons. "You're free now."

FORTY-SIX

For the second time in over a week, Nick leaned against the concession counter answering a detective's questions as a body made its way through The Chamberlain's lobby on a stretcher. It was two times too many. What made this time worse, was the additional body bag following close behind the first. It would be a few days before positive identifications could be made. Dental records would be required due to the advanced state of decomposition. The consensus, however, was that the identities of the two small skeletons were already known.

The Blackwood brothers, Stephen and Mitchel, hadn't been lost at sea after all. They'd been here, under the town's nose the entire time. Entombed in Floyd Cropper's Chamberlain Theater.

"I just don't get it." Nick leaned forward, elbows resting on his knees, and massaged his temples once the detective had taken her leave.

"It actually explains so much," Claudia said, sipping from a cup of coffee. "The two sets of hands coming through the screen. The times you'd come in and find the movie playing. The *kids'* movie."

"And why they didn't lash out when the students were here," Nori added.

Claudia nodded in agreement. "It must have thrilled them having other kids to watch the movie with. Why would they want to scare them away?"

The three fell silent, reflecting. Despite the discovery, Nick still had more questions than answers. Or, perhaps because of it. What happened in that secret room? Why were the boys down there in the first place? Had Floyd kidnapped them? Had he been hiding them from their abusive father after they ran away? Is that why they'd reacted so violently toward the mayor? These questions would never be answered. And he'd have to be content with that knowledge. There was one question, however, that continued to niggle at the back of his mind.

"The smell of smoke in the auditorium," he said. "What do you guys make of that?"

Nori nodded. "How it would come and go. Not always there, but sometimes really strong."

"Now that's a question I can answer." Claudia grinned and winked at the two of them. "When the smell was the strongest? That's when the boys' spirits were the closest."

EPILOGUE

It was determined over the following week that the two young brothers had died of smoke inhalation. The fire had probably been a small one, limited by the lack of oxygen in the room. Small, but deadly enough. It was speculated that Floyd Cropper had entombed the bodies where they lay—in essence, burying them—instead of risking discovery by disposing of them outside The Chamberlain.

What couldn't be determined, and never would be, was the motive. Why was the old man hiding the brothers away in the first place?

Regardless, Floyd's good standing among some in the community, at least that of his memory, sank faster than a storm ravaged ship with a breached hull. People couldn't distance themselves from past associations with him fast enough. Others stood by their claims that Floyd was a good man. All over town, debates took place over whether or not a crime had been committed. Was he a saint for helping them escape their abusive father? Or was he a sinner who'd never had kids of his own and couldn't resist the temptation of two young boys out on their own at night? The debates typically went something like…

"If he'd only had children of his own."
"That's no damn excuse!"
"What if he was trying to help those boys?"
"Doesn't matter. Hope he's enjoying his time in hell."

It seemed there were only two things the townsfolk of Angler Bay could agree on: the entire ordeal was a horrible tragedy; and The Chamberlain's doors should never reopen.

"If it were up to me," the scruffy cashier told Nick as he handed back his debit card, "I'd finish the job. Burn the whole damn place to the ground." The man, somewhere around sixty years of age, turned and spit on the floor behind the counter.

Nick had become all too familiar with the sentiment. He could only offer a nod as he stuffed his card back in his wallet and retrieved the two paper cups from the countertop. "Have a nice day."

And as he exited the diner and stepped out into the cool autumn morning, his thoughts turned to the fifteen-hour drive ahead of them.

"What did they have to do, roast the beans?" Nori asked as he handed her one of the cups through the passenger window. "I told Claudia we'd be in Chicago by nightfall."

Nick circled around and climbed up into the cab of the rental truck, which held most of their worldly possessions. At least everything they'd deemed necessary for a new start. She a big city reporter. He investing in F.A.U.S.T. His next business venture. Only this time he'd have a partner, and she knew what the hell she was doing.

"Guy was old school," he said. "Had no idea what a skinny chai latte was. Looked at me like I was from another planet."

"Geez," Nori said, taking a sip from her steaming cup, "things are gonna be so much different in the big city."

Nick considered the reality of her statement as he pulled onto a street that would put Angler Bay behind them. "That's the hope, at least."

About the Author

Tim McWhorter was born under a waning crescent moon, and while he has no idea what the significance is, he thinks it sounds like a horror writer thing to say. A graduate of Otterbein University, he is the author of several horror-thrillers and lives just outside of Columbus, OH, with his ever-supportive wife, Julie. He is currently hard at work on several projects and relies on interaction with readers for those much-needed breaks…

Email:
tm5to1@live.com

FB Author Page:
www.facebook.com/pages/Tim-Mcwhorter-author

Instagram:
https://www.instagram.com/tim_mcwhorter

More by Tim McWhorter

Shadows Remain
Bone White
Blackened
Let There Be Dark
The Winding Down Hours

More horror from Manta Press

Tearstone
David Day

Gone Where the Goblins Go
Matt Betts

The Mouth is a Coven
Liz Worth

Who Holds the Devil
Michael Dittman

Holburn
Tim Jeffreys